Other Novels by Rosemary Aubert
In the Ellis Portal Mystery Series

Free Reign
The Feast of Stephen
The Ferryman Will Be There

Leave Me By Dying

Leave Me By Dying

AN ELLIS PORTAL MYSTERY

Rosemary Aubert

BRIDGE WORKS PUBLISHING COMPANY
Bridgehampton, New York

Published by Bridge Works Publishing Company, Bridgehampton, New York, an imprint of The Rowman & Littlefield Publishing Group.

Distributed in the United States by National Book Network, Lanham, Maryland. For descriptions of this and other Bridge Works books, visit the National Book Network website at www.nbnbooks.com.

FIRST PAPERBACK EDITION 2004

The characters and events in this book are fictitious. Any similarity to actual persons, living or dead, is coincidental and not intended by the author.

Library of Congress Cataloging-in-Publication Data

Aubert, Rosemary.
    Leave me by dying : an Ellis Portal mystery / Rosemary Aubert.—1st ed.
      p. cm.
    ISBN 1-882593-73-1 (cloth : alk. paper)
    ISBN 1-882593-93-6 (pbk. : alk. paper)
    1 Portal, Ellis (Fictitious character)—Fiction. 2. Toronto
(Ont.)—Fiction. 3. Law students—Fiction. I. Title.

PR9199.3.A9L43 2003
811'.54–dc21

                          2003001905

10 9 8 7 6 5 4 3 2 1

♾ ™ The paper used in this publication meets the minimum requirements of American National Standard for Information Sciences—Permanence of Paper for Printed Library Materials, ANSI/NISO Z39.48–1992.
Manufactured in the United States of America.

This book is dedicated to my brother, Joseph Proe,

and to Susan, Katie, and Colden

I would like to offer thanks to the following for sharing their remarkable knowledge, often firsthand, of the modern history of Toronto:

Don Cullen
Maureen FitzGerald
Doug Newman
Doug Purdon
Fred Sheward
David Skene-Melvin
And the men of the Canadian Lesbian and Gay Archive

I would also like to thank Justice Eugene Ewaschuk for sharing his knowledge of the legal world of the city of Toronto during the 1960s, knowledge that greatly aided me in the research and conception of this story.

Leave Me By Dying

"I lift my lamp beside the golden door."

—EMMA LAZARUS, *THE NEW COLOSSUS*

Prologue

Magistrate B. Sheldrake Tuppin, who knew more about the administration of justice than any man I'd ever met, once told me, "You can give up the practice of law, but you'll be a lawyer until the day you die."

Which was, apparently, a view shared by the Fellowship of Barristers and Solicitors of Upper Canada. I studied the letter that had arrived by courier moments before. "You are invited," it informed me, "to regularize your situation before the bar."

My eyes strayed from the letter, with its rich seal printed in deep blue ink, to the window. I could see my son Jeffrey. Despite leaning toward a tripod on which was perched some sort of surveying tool, he was not, by profession, a surveyor, nor was he about to go on a wilderness adventure, which the khaki safari suit, hiking boots and Tilley Endurables hat might lead one to believe. Beside him with her hands on her hips stood a young woman dressed totally in black, also wearing substantial boots. She leaned forward and planted a kiss on Jeffrey's cheek.

These two were my partners in the restoration of a 1960s-era apartment building on the rim of a ravine in the valley of the Don River, which runs south through the city of Toronto and spills into Lake Ontario. Jeffrey was in charge of the outside. Tootie Beets was in charge of the inside, and I was in charge of Jeffrey and Tootie. An architect turned conservationist, a street girl turned building superintendent and a disgraced judge turned real estate investor. We were an unlikely but highly workable confederation of misfits. I returned my gaze to the letter.

"Payment to the Fellowship of outstanding arrears will qualify you for reentry training, which can culminate in readmission to the bar."

I tried to count the years since I'd been a practicing lawyer. A decade as a judge in the criminal courts. The better part of an additional decade living as a vagrant in the same ravine Jeffrey now surveyed, followed by a slow recovery that finally saw me physically and financially restored. My life in the law had followed a bumpy and circuitous path, a rise to greatness and a fall from grace. In general it could be said that the law had served me no better than I had served the law.

So why would I want to be a lawyer again?

Why had I wanted to become one in the first place, nearly forty years earlier . . . ?

Chapter 1

My brother Michele's gaze was riveted to the TV screen as the camera scanned the rows of senators and congressmen, then settled on the lined face of President Lyndon B. Johnson. "I am taking the step of addressing this unusual evening joint session of Congress in order to urge immediate passage of legislation to remove all illegal barriers to the voting rights of Negro Americans."

"Selma," Michele muttered under his breath. "Remind the people about Selma."

"I'm missing my program," our mother complained. "I waited all day and now you've got this on. Turn the channel."

"This is on every channel," Michele said, not taking his eyes from the screen. "And so it should be. The whole world is watching Selma."

"The whole world would rather be watching *I've Got a Secret*," my mother retorted. I tried to ignore the TV and the argument, too. I didn't have time for panel shows or addresses to Congress, either. In the kitchen, I grabbed a glass of milk, gulped it down and headed for the back door. "Angelo!" My mother was beside me before I could step out into the cold, wet March night in 1965. "You eat. You gotta eat before you go someplace." She shoved a plate of breaded cod toward me. She was capable of producing such food out of the air. I shook my head, smiled, brushed past her and out onto Clinton Street. Fat flakes of snow danced in the light from windows behind which other immigrant families played out their own mundane dramas. The snow hit the sidewalk as rain and I hit the college streetcar and rode it to Yonge Street, transferring to the subway. I exited at Queen and walked through the slick streets until I got to Lombard and the Toronto city morgue.

I had no idea why I'd been summoned here and felt considerable irritation at having my studies interrupted. Nevertheless, I checked my watch and hastened my steps, running past Maxie's Smoke Shop, Ideal Printing, Nu-Style Chesterfield. In the mist, the Gothic hulk of Fire Station Number Five rose in silhouette against the dull city lights, but the nearby building that housed the morgue was low, solid and perfectly rectangular, like a large burial casket. At the top of the stone steps that led to the thick wooden door, Gleason Everett Adams was pacing. His expensive fedora sat low on his handsome brow and his beige trench coat cinched his trim waist. I pulled my own shabby coat a little tighter around my ample body and negotiated the stairs.

Seeing me, Gleason stopped pacing and jerked his gold wristwatch up toward the light over the door.

"Sorry I'm late, Gleason."

He frowned, nodded. He glanced in the direction of a nearby street lamp, beneath which sat his new Jaguar, its wet, dark green finish as sleek as the rainy street. "If you have to take the subway," he said, "you have to take the subway. I got us an appointment for seven-thirty and it's now seven forty-five, but then, we're not as late as most of the people in here, are we?"

The grim joke had an awkwardness totally out of keeping with Gleason's usual glib repartee. I was about to ask him what was wrong when the door opened and a uniformed man, a guard of some sort, cigarette dangling from his mouth, stepped out, closing the door behind him. Despite our appointment, the guard seemed startled to see us. I shot Gleason a look, and he took the cue. "I have an appointment to see Chief Coroner Rosen at seven-thirty. We're from the Law Faculty at the University—law students—and we . . ."

The guard seemed flustered by Gleason's little speech. He took a series of sharp, rapid drags on his cigarette, tossed it down and ground it out with his shoe. He fumbled with a ring of keys as if determined to select the one most capable of keeping us out of the squat building. Without a word, he opened the door just enough to slip back in and pulled it behind him. We could hear him shoot the bolt.

Under ordinary circumstances, Gleason would have had plenty to say about this strange treatment, but at the exact moment the guard disappeared, a silent procession of three cars turned off Lombard Street and entered the wide metal gates on the west side of the morgue. One car was a yellow police cruiser, one was a long black limousine. The last car bore the insignia of the chief coroner's office.

Gleason flew down the steps and I followed. But by the time we reached the gates, the last of the three vehicles was disappearing into the darkness behind the morgue. Gleason rattled the high iron gate, but it had locked automatically. "Oh, forget it," he said to no one in particular.

"That didn't get us anywhere," I commented.

Gleason dropped his hands to his sides and turned to face me. "Thank you for that information, Ellis Portal," he said, sarcastically using my legal name. When away from my Italian neighborhood, I also got away from my Italian name, which was the same as my father's, Angelo Portalese. "Point out the obvious. Bill by the hour. You've got the makings of a fine solicitor."

"Shut up," I said defensively, but he ignored me, turned and gave the gate a final, futile shake. I followed as he stomped back up the stone stairs and raised his fist at the bolted door. If it had been his intention to knock, this proved unnecessary. Before he touched it, the door sprang open, the guard stepped out, and we were unceremoniously shown in.

"The chief says he don't want nobody on the steps," the guard explained.

I wondered how people were supposed to keep an appointment if they had to avoid being "on the steps," but I didn't ask. "Why *are* we here, Gleason?" I whispered, instead. If he heard me, he didn't show it. Silently we were led to a rather grand staircase carpeted in red that curved toward an upper floor. Immediately beneath the staircase and to our right was a door opened just wide enough to show a small anteroom with the same stiff formality as the "lounge" in a funeral parlor. I realized with discomfort that this was where the bereaved waited to identify the dead bodies of relatives and friends.

The mystery was beginning to make me nervous. Gleason fancied himself a trickster and was fond of practical jokes, but his demeanor was so uncharacteristically edgy, angry even, that I was afraid to demand an explanation for our being treated simultaneously as outcasts and guests in the home of the dead. As the guard rushed us up the stairs, I thought I heard a hushed word and observed a slight shift in the quality of the little anteroom's light, as though some unseen occupant who had been seated had suddenly stood up, changing the arrangement of shadows.

Gleason, as usual, was too impatient to look behind or to the side. His eyes were trained on the figure who awaited us on the second-floor landing, a tall, lean man in a white coat of the sort worn by doctors and lab technicians.

"This way," the man said to us with a nod. "I'm Dr. Slater, the night pathologist." He appeared to dismiss the guard, who passed us and made his way down the second-floor hallway, pausing, it seemed to me, to sneer at us before he disappeared. We followed the white coat and ended up outside another wooden door, this one bearing a brass plaque that read, "Levi M. Rosen, Chief Coroner." The name alone was enough to make me quail. Rosen was a controversial figure, an inquisitive, outspoken man whose disregard for the staid traditions of his office had wreaked havoc among his conservative colleagues.

I suppose Gleason assumed we'd be announced, since he'd said that we were expected. Instead, we were instructed to remain outside the closed door while Dr. Slater went into Dr. Rosen's office.

It wasn't hard to hear the rhythm of two voices coming from behind the door, though only a few words were comprehensible. Clearly, the easily inflamed Rosen was irritated. Clearly, the night pathologist was calming and conciliatory. The conversation paused for a moment. With jittery impatience, Gleason leaned closer to the door and put his ear to the wood. Reluctant at first, I eventually did the same. I distinctly heard five words. "As long as it's B." I had no idea what this meant and no opportunity to listen further. The door unexpectedly burst open, nearly knocking us off our feet. We sprang back and tried to act nonchalant.

The pathologist didn't seem to notice anything unusual in our behavior. He asked us to follow him and once again we did. We descended the carpeted stair and I hesitated a moment on the last step. From this angle I could see a raincoat folded on a red-upholstered chair in the formal parlor, but I saw no one, heard no voices. At the bottom of the stairs, we turned sharply right and paused before yet another wooden door guarded by our friend with the massive key ring. He selected a key, unlocked the door and led us into the netherworld.

There was no rich carpet here. Directly in front of us a floor-to-ceiling wire-mesh gate about twenty feet high separated us from a long, narrow hallway lit at intervals by dim bulbs in wire protectors. Absurdly I wondered whether the dead were so rambunctious that they threatened the light fixtures.

Our steps echoed on worn linoleum. Somewhere in the distance, something slammed. Metal on metal, a door or a drawer. A low constant hum like that of a refrigerator permeated the quiet.

Off the dim central hall to the right, the gray expanse of wall with its enamel sheen was broken by a single wide door, which was open. When we passed it and I glanced in, I saw row upon row of shiny metal doors each about two feet square, the width, I suddenly realized, of the shoulders of a man. A rush of cold air escaped the room. The air smelled like raw meat, metallic and gamey.

On the other side of the hall, to our left, were three more wide doors, all closed. I could see painted on them, in large black letters, A, B and C. Beyond the doors, at the end of the hall and facing us as we walked, loomed a final door, this one of corrugated metal on pulleys. I understood immediately that beyond this door lay the loading dock where corpses were brought in day and night.

In front of this door stood two men. It was hard to see them clearly, but they seemed to be studying our approach. One had the characteristic slouch of a teenager who has suddenly attained unaccustomed height. He was wearing the same uniform as the key-bearing guard, though the jacket was too wide in the shoulders and the trousers too short. The other man wore a suit. When Gleason saw this man, he seemed to start, taking a step forward as if to greet him. But the pathologist put out his hand and stopped my friend from moving. The two figures at the end of the hall shifted, disappeared into the shadows.

Of course, I expected our guide to show us into room B, but that is not what happened. He walked past B and pushed open the door marked C. Gleason was walking slightly ahead of me and I could see him open his mouth as if to comment on the error, but the words stuck in his throat as he stopped in the doorway, silently gaping at the sight before us. I gave him a little push to get him to cross the threshold.

It was a large room, maybe forty feet long and twenty feet wide, brightly lit and, at first glance, a repository of brilliant white: a white tile floor with drains, like a shower. White walls along which ranged long rows of glass-fronted white cabinets. White enamel tables. White racks lining one wall. And all along the sides of the room, empty gurneys covered in white sheets.

Because of all this whiteness, the red sweater on the cadaver in the middle of the room was like a splash of blood on snow.

With the emotionless precision of a man who is used to such things, the pathologist strode to the examination table and stood beside the corpse. Stumbling a little, Gleason followed and again I followed him. I was so curious I had almost forgotten that I had no idea what I was doing here. As I moved closer, I observed an oval rack that circled above the table, the way a shower curtain rod circles an old-fashioned bathtub. From the rack were suspended stainless-steel gadgets gleaming in the bright white light of the room: pressure gauges, forceps, tongs, various sizes and shapes of scissors, a saw. Lengths of rubber hose led from the table to steel cylinders beneath. Beside one of the cylinders sat a tape recorder, the two large circular reels still but waiting. The first tool Slater grabbed from above was a microphone. He attached the mike to a clip on his lapel and I marveled that the mike could move with him as he circled the body on the table.

Both Gleason and I stood several feet away from the table, but close enough to see that this had been no ordinary death. I knew enough about autopsies to realize that the pathologist would begin by describing the body. Even though I was looking directly at it, I felt curiosity about how the doctor would put this startling sight into words.

His toneless voice held as little apparent emotion as that of the room's low, persistent mechanical hum. "The subject," he said as he moved slowly toward the top of the table, "has a bag that appears to be brown burlap over its head. This bag is tightly cinched at the deceased's neck by means of a length of rope. One end of this rope is loosely grasped in the deceased's left hand." The pathologist paused, reached into the breast pocket of his lab coat and extracted a pair of tweezers with which he cautiously lifted the rope end, studied it, squeezed it gently, then replaced it. "The rope is a pliable, one-quarter-inch-diameter, gray-and-beige woven braid of the type used to decorate upholstered furniture."

Beneath the table, the reels of the tape recorder spun when the pathologist talked and stopped when he didn't. I was captivated by this advanced technology, but I forced my eyes back to the cadaver. Gleason's eyes never seemed to leave the body. He looked thoroughly shocked, his face pale, his eyes sunken. Shock was not an emotion I usually associated with him. His habitual demeanor was contemptuous and insouciant, as if he were convinced he knew more than everybody else but was indifferent to their ignorance.

From somewhere I didn't see, the pathologist procured a measuring tape and extended it from the top of the bag to the foot of the corpse. "The subject is a slender, tall female, seventy and two-thirds inches long," he intoned.

My eyes followed the line of the tape and back again. The clothes of the corpse were simple, but old and cheap. On her feet, she wore low-heeled pumps of scuffed black leather. One of her dark beige stockings sported a wide run that extended from the arch of her foot to the hem of her plain, gray-wool skirt. Beneath the rent in the stocking, the skin of her leg shone pale and hairless. Her blouse, with its Peter Pan collar and row of pearl buttons down the front, had seen enough washings to render it a slightly less than respectable shade of yellow. The light wool cardigan was pilled and unraveled at the edges of the sleeves. I wished that I could see her face, for her body filled me with a sense of the vulnerability of the living and the dead. I was curious from a human, as well as from a legal, perspective. A young woman so abruptly removed from life and we were not permitted to see her face.

"The subject's clothing is not in disarray," the pathologist observed. "Her ears and fingers are devoid of jewelry. On her right wrist she wears a Timex watch." He leaned closer to the table. "The crystal is cracked but intact. The hands are stopped at five minutes after twelve."

I had as yet no idea of the significance of anything I saw, but already I knew every minute detail had to be recorded, analyzed, reported. I'd been a law student since the middle of the previous September. How many hours had I spent in *Criminal Law and Procedure* listening to the professors' tales of cases won or lost on the strength of a single small detail convincingly remembered?

"A cursory examination of the clothed cadaver exhibits no bruising or discoloration of the skin—" The pathologist suddenly stopped as if he realized he'd made an error or had noticed something he'd failed to see before. He bent close to the neck of the body, his face near where the edge of the burlap met the discolored nylon of the dead woman's blouse. For an eerie instant, it looked as though he were kissing the corpse. I stepped back. Gleason sucked in his breath. But Dr. Slater seemed to have forgotten that we were in the room. After a moment's further observation, he stood upright and pulled a pair of rubber gloves out of a pouch suspended on the overhead rail. He tugged them on, then with his right hand, reached for the throat of the deceased. "Gentlemen," he finally said, "observe . . ."

Gleason and I moved closer. For the first time I noticed the dead body emitted a peculiar odor and I fought the urge to gag. I could detect a hint of the meat smell I'd earlier noticed in the room of drawers, each of which, I now realized, must hold a body. I could smell stale perspiration mixed with some sort of deodorant. I could smell Yardley's English Lavender. And I could detect an indefinable musky scent that was vaguely familiar, though I had no idea why.

I expected—feared—to see some unusual bruise or laceration, so I was disappointed to discover that all the pathologist wanted us to look at was a thin gold chain around the neck of the dead woman. With fingers made awkward by the thick yellow gloves, he reached for the chain, but it eluded his grasp. In the first show of emotion he'd allowed himself, he angrily yanked off the glove and grabbed the narrow thread of gold with his bare hand.

But the chain did not yield to his tug. He paused, then fumbled with the tiny pearl buttons of the yellowed blouse and unfastened the top few. Gleason and I leaned farther forward. All of us were surprised to see that the chain was attached to a small cloth packet about one and one-half inches square and that this mysterious item was pinned to the strap of the slip the woman wore over her brassiere.

Wordlessly, the pathologist located a pair of long-nose scissors on the overhead rack and snipped off the corner to free the little packet. Using his tweezers, he held it up. As we studied it, I expected him to set the tape reels spinning with his description of the object, but he said nothing, just laid the small bundle in a glass dish on a nearby white enamel table. Gleason's eyes followed the movements of the pathologist's hand. His interest was clearly evident. So was his disappointment that his curiosity as to its contents was not about to be immediately satisfied.

Again donning the yellow rubber gloves, Slater announced, "I am now about to remove the clothing of the deceased." He took the largest of the scissors that hung over his head and lifted the wool fabric of the gray skirt. He slipped the bottom blade between the deceased's legs. I suppressed a gasp at this violation. I had never seen clothing cut away from a body, and the process seemed an obscene invasion of the privacy of the dead.

But just as steel touched cloth, the phone rang. The brash sound of it echoing in the white room seemed to startle the pathologist. He jumped and the scissors flew out of his hand and landed with a sharp crack on the tile at Gleason's feet. Gleason realized how close he'd come to being stabbed and he laughed. Nothing delighted Gleason more than an opportunity to cheat fate.

The phone sat on a counter near the door, and its black bulk stood in contrast to both the white surface it rested on and the yellow-gloved hand that held the receiver. It disgusted me that the pathologist would be so careless as to touch the corpse with a bare hand, then touch the telephone with a gloved hand, but I said nothing lest Gleason call me an "old lady," his favorite insult for me among the many in his considerable collection.

After a short, hushed conversation, the pathologist hung up and signaled to us to approach the door. "Gentlemen," he said, "I've been asked to attend upstairs. I can't leave you alone with the deceased, but I'll return shortly to proceed with the autopsy. My instructions are to ask you to wait outside the building until I return."

"Yeah, great," Gleason said. "I can use the air."

The pathologist ushered us back out into the hallway, locked the door of the lab, then gave the door handle a strong shake to ensure that it was secure. We followed his white back down the dimly lit hall until we passed through the wire-mesh gate and the wooden door in front of it.

"What's this all about, Gleason? What are you up to?" I was genuinely curious.

"Nothing good, old lady, what else? Let's get out of here. I need a cig."

We stepped out into the night. It seemed to have become warmer in the short time since I'd left the house on Clinton Street. There was no possibility of snow now. The street lamps on Lombard created hazy circles of light in the mist-filled air. Across the shiny black pavement, the red neon sign announcing "Auto-Rite Collision—auto-body repairs" flashed on and off. Next door to it, the Liquor Control Board of Ontario liquor store was closed up tight, though the cheerful sound of slightly inebriated voices was faintly audible from the door of the Scottish Club, conveniently located in the same building.

Gleason pulled out a slim silver case and lit up. He lounged against the morgue's stone door frame and let the smoke from his cigarette mingle with the mist. "Somebody sure did a job on that one," he remarked. I waited for the irreverent comment that I was sure would follow, but my friend was strangely reticent. Perhaps the sight of the body had shaken him. Not something I would have expected, given that he was always unflappable. "But I suppose even a case like this one wouldn't be good enough for *you*," he finally added.

I didn't take the bait. I was sick of arguing with him about the law school projects we had regrettably been thrust into. Both of us had four-year pre-law degrees, which, though prestigious, had put us behind the two-year students now taking the same first-year law classes. Because of this, Gleason and I had been offered the opportunity to accelerate by participating in a special summer program. We could work independently or as a two-man team, but to qualify, we needed a strong proposal. And our time was extremely limited. The more senior students had already secured their assignments. Competition for the few remaining slots was stiff.

I didn't want to work with Gleason. I assumed he would use the contacts of his influential father to find him an assignment in banking or real estate law. I, on the other hand, was far more interested in my own project: to get Magistrate Sheldrake Tuppin to take me on as his judicial intern. Everyone, including my academic mentor, Professor Kavin, told me I was crazy. It was unprecedented for a first-year student to serve as *anyone's* intern, let alone Tuppin's, who always refused to take on an intern. Nevertheless, I was convinced that I could change the magistrate's mind. I'd been scouring the law library, the archives, even the daily papers for a case unusual enough to get Tuppin interested in me. Gleason's escapade was interrupting me in this task. An uncomfortable thought hit me. Was this gruesome cadaver part of *his* project? Was this visit to the morgue Gleason's way of roping me into helping him?

I pushed that thought aside for the moment. "What could have happened to the woman?" I asked. "She didn't have a mark on her. Do you suppose somebody ambushed her and tossed that bag over her head before she could even turn around?"

Gleason shrugged. "Speculation is a poor substitute for knowledge, Portal," he retorted in one of those law school clichés that hook themselves into a lawyer's language and remain there for the duration. "Who knows what happened? Who needs to ask? When Dr. Death comes back downstairs, he'll figure it all out, talk it into that machine of his and give us all we need for our project. You can write it down and hand it in."

"Maybe you work that way, Adams. I don't." Here was Gleason patronizing me as usual and making me get angry, which was exactly what he intended. We'd known each other for a long time, long enough for him to realize that if he baited me until I lost my temper, he could then manipulate me through my guilt over having relinquished control of myself.

"Everything's simple," he said, studying the glowing red end of his cigarette, "as long as you can get someone else to do it for you."

I wanted to punch him. Instead, I left him silently smoking and took a short stroll down the street. The grimness of the evening seemed appropriate to the fate of the dead. Even the stolid, civically responsible Victorian mass of the firehouse seemed to be mourning. It took me a few minutes to walk there and turn back. When I returned to the morgue, Gleason was lighting up a second cigarette. "Do you think he forgot that we're out here?" I asked.

"Let's find out," Gleason replied. He turned the handle of the main door. It sprang open without resistance. I expected a guard to jump out to stop us, but there was no one on the other side of the door. Even the wire-mesh gate was unlocked and unattended. I walked close behind Gleason as he made his way down the corridor, the smoke from his cigarette masking all other smells.

Almost at once we could see that the door to laboratory C was ajar, because a narrow band of light spilled out into the hall and faintly illuminated the closed door to the room opposite where the dead lay in their tidy rows of drawers.

Gleason tossed down his cigarette and ground it out on the linoleum floor. Then he gave the lab door a strong push. It flew open and the bright white light assaulted my dark-adapted eyes. I heard Gleason utter, "Damn it to hell." When my vision adjusted itself, I saw why.

The room was empty. The corpse was gone. The examination table with its complex rigging had disappeared. There were no hoses, no cylinders, no reel-to-reel voice-activated tape recorder. The small enamel table had vanished, along with the glass dish that had been atop it. The floor was as clean as if someone had washed all contaminants down the drain in the middle of the room.

That look of shock passed across Gleason's face again, but his fair, handsome features immediately hardened. "Oh, well," he said, "there goes our little homicide project, or so it seems."

I didn't answer. I just wanted to get out of there. I didn't wait for Gleason. I left the lab almost at a run.

He didn't catch up to me until I was on the sidewalk not far from where he had parked the Jag. "Slow down, old lady, slow down." He leapt ahead of me and stood in my way. "Take it easy. The bogeyman isn't going to get you. Don't be so concerned about what happened here. It's probably just a typical night at the morgue."

He didn't believe his own words and I knew it. I pushed past him, heading for the subway. My fear had turned to rage, but I couldn't say why. The image of the dead woman, her cheap clothes, her torn stocking, her sad and untimely end flashed through my mind with a vividness that had the uncanny effect of making me wonder if this seemed so real because it was just a dream.

Gleason caught up to me again. "Relax, Portal," he said. "I know this isn't the sort of case you want to deal with, but look at it from my point of view. Rosen's high profile. We *did* get in tonight. That means strings were pulled. Somebody up there likes us."

I stopped and stared at him. I really didn't want to hear about his fine family's sterling connections. My family had connections of its own, so to speak. Gleason was smiling now as if nothing we'd seen could touch him for long. In that moment, I hated him for his arrogance and callousness. If he sensed my hatred, it didn't bother him. His smile widened. "Come back to the car," he said. "I'll give you a ride home to Eye-talian town."

I gave up and got in. Before he started the car, Gleason studied me for a moment. "Who do you think that dead broad *was*, Portal?"

"Some unfortunate, Adams. Someone unused to privilege. Someone with no rich relatives. Someone, I suspect, whose death is being used by Rosen in some political way. What else would explain what happened tonight?"

"Obviously it's a murder case. Our murder case."

"What?" I said, feeling my anger rise again.

"Murder explains it all. Homicide. And we've got a clue."

"For heaven's sake, Gleason, grow up! This isn't *Perry Mason*."

"Look!"

Reluctantly, I watched as he opened his hand.

In the light from the street lamp outside the car, I could see the little cloth packet from the dead woman's chain in his palm.

Chapter 2

"I didn't steal it. I borrowed it for us to look at while we were waiting."

"Even *that's* tampering with evidence," I said. "How *could* you? Do you know what will happen to us if it becomes known that we stole evidence in a homicide investigation? We'll get thrown out of school!"

"Good," Gleason said with a maddening smile. "I don't dig it anymore. I've never been more bored in my whole life."

"Well," I replied with indignation, "I'd appreciate it if in your quest to alleviate your boredom, you would count me out. I don't want to have anything to do with stealing evidence."

"I meant to return it when we got back into the lab. How did I know the body was going to disappear like that?"

I turned to look at him. Profiled against the lights of the city night, his perfect face with the aristocratic high cheekbones was almost stern, his jaw clenched. "Gleason," I said, "I want you to tell me what we were doing in there. I want you to explain why Rosen let us see that body, then whisked it away. That's the only thing that could have happened. He's the only one with the authority to stop an autopsy that was already in progress."

"It's not an autopsy until skin has been cut," Gleason answered.

"That's a meaningless technicality and you know it."

He steered the Jag around a sharp corner. The tires slid sideways slightly on the wet pavement and I flinched. Of course Gleason saw the gesture out of the corner of his eye. Of course he laughed. "What's the matter, old lady? Don't you have the stomach for using a homicide as your law project?"

"Look, Gleason, I've got my own project. And I can't waste any more time. Besides, there's no way I want to deal with tainted evidence. I—"

"This would be a great project," he interrupted, some of his earlier intensity returning. "I don't want to waste time, either."

"This is criminal law, Gleason," I answered. "Dirty stuff. The bottom of the heap. Can you imagine what it would be like day after day working on messes like this? Women like her are *not* your kind of people."

"Don't you patronize me," Gleason retorted. I was amazed at his vehemence. "Just because you look at being a lawyer as a method of clawing your way out of the ghetto doesn't mean I have to worry about such ambition. I can be any kind of lawyer I damn well please. And I don't need you or anybody else to tell me what law project I will or will not take on."

"Fine, Gleason, fine," I said with annoyance. "But that's just my point."

When we reached Clinton Street, he braked so viciously in front of my house that I lurched forward and nearly smashed my head into the windshield. Such behavior saved me from feeling obliged to invite him in. Which I really didn't want to do, anyway. "I'll see you in class tomorrow, Gleason, by which time I'm sure you will have figured out how to return what you took. Otherwise, you're going to end up being disbarred before you're even admitted."

"Don't worry so much!" he called after me as I slammed the door of the Jag and headed up the driveway to our kitchen door.

My mother grew up in an Italian village with fewer homes than on our side of Clinton Street. She never saw a toilet, a banana or an object made of plastic until she was a teenager. But in the two and a half decades she'd lived in Canada, she'd become the match of any Canadian woman on the block. Like them, she had a television-watching regime as strict as the first-year law curriculum. No doubt her routine had been disrupted by the appearance of the American president, but she was now back on schedule, watching *I Love Lucy*. She got up to give me the supper she'd saved and to tell me the good news she'd received while I was out.

"Wash your hands, Angelo, then sit down and say grace."

I did what she commanded while she bustled around the small kitchen, talking nonstop as she opened the oven and took out the various dishes she'd set aside for me. We always ate far too much during Lent because to my mother, fasting meant that meals could be mammoth as long as they contained no meat.

She put before me a thick slice of homemade pizza crusty with browned mozzarella, parmesan and romano cheeses, from beneath which oozed bright, spicy tomatoes she'd canned herself. "I'm going to be the Blessed Virgin Mary in the Passion play at Mount Carmel. Me! Imagine that, Angelo! They don't pick Bruzzese, but they did this year!" Despite her modern ways, like most Italians my mother was hypersensitive to imagined slights about the region of Italy she'd left behind. "I get to wear a costume and . . ."

Despite my best intentions, I found I wasn't listening to her excited chatter. I kept thinking about the morgue. Why had Gleason been so nervous? Surely not because he was concerned about his law project. He didn't care about minor infractions, perhaps because he knew his father would bail him out of any real difficulties he got into—even failing at school. Still, it must have taken a lot of trouble to get an appointment after hours. And what had overruled the protests of the reluctant guard, who clearly had wanted us out? A person who enjoys a mystery would have welcomed the challenge of solving tonight's puzzle, but I couldn't allow myself to be distracted. I was studying to become a lawyer, not a police officer or a coroner.

I had no illusions about my disadvantages—or my advantages, either. Since the age of ten I had never been other than the top student in my class. But except for my uncle Salvatore, I had no relatives rich enough to fund a chair at the university, as Gleason had. From the first moment I'd sat in Sheldrake Tuppin's courtroom in the opening weeks of law school, I'd made up my mind that I would be his intern, that I would learn to balance just as he did the requirements of the law with the needs of ordinary people. But I understood from the start that Tuppin was no grassroots demagogue. He wore hand-tailored suits. He ate lunch every day either at the Windsor Club or in the Barristers' Dining Room. He was a wily, wise, sophisticated man whose family was as blue-blooded as Gleason's. There had been, I was sure, many times long ago when Tuppin's father, like Gleason's, had the connections—or the gift—that would ease his son's way. Gleason could afford to drop into the morgue a month before an assignment was due and decide on the spot that it might be cool to do homicide for a project. I did not have that luxury. I did have, it bothered me to realize, more curiosity about the pathetic victim than was comfortable. I could still see her in my mind's eye. I thought about the pathologist's hand poised over the shabby skirt. He had hesitated for a fraction of a second. As though he couldn't bear to cut. Or, I suddenly thought, as though he were *waiting* for that phone to ring.

"What's a four-letter word for guitar?"

I looked up from my supper, which now included a generous portion of the breaded fish I'd seen earlier, plus a heap of pasta in a creamy white-cheese sauce. My sixteen-year-old sister, Arletta, had joined me at the table. She held a torn-out piece of the *Toronto Daily World* up to her pert face. Before I could answer, she was joined by my brother, Michele, a first-year sociology student at the university. His hair, I noticed, was getting ridiculously long. Dark ringlets covered the top of his ears and brushed the collar of his shirt at the neck. "Folk," he said to Arletta. "F-O-L-K."

Today, Arletta's hair was piled in a cluster atop her head. She had the same dark curls as my brother, and me, too, if I'd not kept my hair meticulously cut. She calculated, wrinkled her nose, shook her head and said to Michele, "Can't be."

"B-A-S-S," I offered.

Arletta stared at the crossword again. "Yeah," she said. "Right on."

"What are you wasting your time for? I thought you hated crosswords," Michele said.

My mother laughed and put a dish of salad in front of me. Lettuce, plum tomatoes, black olives, artichoke hearts—all drizzled with olive oil and sprinkled with dried basil from her summer garden. "Arletta wants to see the Fab Four," she said, giggling.

"Yeah," Arletta concurred. "If I can get all the answers to this crossword right and I mail it in to the *World*, I get a chance to win two tickets to the Return of the Beatles concert in August. People are already lining up for tickets. Some of them stay out all night but—"

"August! That's five months away," I said.

"Yeah. Five months to pray that I win. I wish!" Arletta crossed the fingers of both hands, stuck out her pointed little chin and rolled her eyes toward the ceiling.

"You study. You forget silly contests." This from my father, who sat in a corner of the warm room sullenly studying his *Corriere Canadese*. We ignored him and went on with our conversation as my mother showed me a plate of sliced roasted red and green peppers glistening in olive oil and mixed with slivers of garlic and celery. I shook my head and she took the plate away.

"I need to talk to you about something really important," Michele said intently, sitting beside me and elbowing away an empty dish. "We have to go someplace when you finish eating."

"I'm done," I said, "but I'm not going anywhere. It's already after nine and I have to work on my project. I've already wasted the whole evening."

"You're wasting your time anyway, burying yourself in books. The action's not in books, man. It's in the street. How do you expect to impress anybody with stuff you read in books?"

"Leave me alone, Michele. By the time I meet Sheldrake Tuppin, I'll have read every word he ever wrote. Every judgment. Every—"

"Look, Angelo," Michele persisted, fixing me with his near-black, pleading eyes, "I met this guy in one of my field studies. He's got a problem and I want to help him with it, but I can't do it by myself. I need you."

I stirred sugar into the coffee my mother slid onto the table. "Michele," I said, "if you're going to study sociology, you're going to have to learn some objectivity. You can't help everybody whose sad case comes to your attention." The image of the dead woman at the morgue came unbidden to me, and as if to mock my own words, I felt a stab of pity, the dawning of a desire to right the unfairness of her grotesque fate. Nobody deserved to die so sadly, with a burlap bag wrapped around her head. But I followed my own advice and pushed the thought away.

Michele leaned closer to me, his body tense with emotion. Unlike me, he was wiry and lean. At that point in my life, differences were more important to me than similarities. I was forcing myself to learn to differentiate, to decide between one way and its opposite. To make distinctions. So when I thought about my brother, it was to think about how dissimilar we were. There came a time, many years later, when Michele was the only person in the world I could trust to save me from myself. Even then I did not see what I see now—the characteristics that made my brother and me the same: empathy, passion, determination, blood. He said softly, "I went down to Bleecker Street . . ."

"Greenwich Village, New *Yawk* City?" Arlette joked.

Michele didn't hear her. "I met a man there I have to do something for. He's got a serious legal problem. I told him my brother's in law and can help him out."

"Michele," I answered with annoyance, "that sounds like I'm a lawyer. "You can't go around telling people I'm a lawyer. I'm a law *student*."

"Man, Angelo, that's all the better! It means you're not going to be co-opted by the system. You're still free to do your own thing because the establishment hasn't got its hooks into you yet. You can still set things right."

It bothered me that a person of my brother's obvious intelligence could be so won over by catchphrases that meant nothing. "Forget it, Michele."

A look of sorrow crossed the strong features of his olive-toned face, but then he hardened his square jaw and stared at me defiantly, the way he used to when we were children and he had to defend himself against my superiority as the eldest. "You can pander to people like your law professors and that Judge Tuppin you're always on about, but you know in your heart that this is no time to ignore the underprivileged. Caring people must act."

I knew what was coming next. There had been an unseen presence in our house for days now. He seemed to stand beside Michele like a ghost, though he wasn't dead. Not yet, anyway. "Don't quote Martin Luther King to me, Michele. Just don't start." I stood up, made a pile of the empty dishes in front of me and carried them to the sink. Michele dogged my steps.

"Right this minute," he said to my back, "there are five hundred men and women with the God-given right to vote battling for that right against the troopers and sheriff's deputies in Alabama—"

"Michele, lay off. What do you know about Alabama? You've never been farther south than New Jersey!" I turned around to face him—he was the same height as me, putting us eye to eye. "Besides, it appears that a significant aspect of this Selma matter has escaped your attention. We're Canadian, Michele. We're not American. Not citizens of the good ol' U.S. of A. Have you got that, *man*?"

He sank back as if defeated, but only for a moment. "Didn't you ever hear of the Underground Railroad? Canadians have been helping American Negroes for over a hundred years. What difference does distance make? Yesterday at the capital in Ottawa five thousand people marched in support of what Dr. King is doing in Selma. That's the biggest demonstration in our history—*Canadian* history." He paused. "But it's nothing," he mused. "It's nothing compared to what's coming. Selma is one thing. And Vietnam is another."

"Oh, come on, Michele! Don't start on Vietnam. I haven't got time to listen to this. You do your school projects. I'll do mine. I'm busy."

My brother reached out and put his hand on my arm. "Please, Angelo. This guy just needs advice, that's all. Legal advice. Only an hour or two of your time. Besides, you're looking for a law project. Maybe Billy Johnson could be it."

"Michele, Sheldrake Tuppin was born, raised, educated and called to the bar and bench in Canada. Why would he be interested in the issues you're interested in?"

"Maybe he's not as limited as you are."

"What?"

"Don't get mad, just listen. If this judge guy is so great, won't he be into the latest issues? The whole world's changing, Angelo. People can't just think about their own bag anymore. What if you came up with something bigger than just us? Something . . . I don't know . . . international?" He hesitated. "I want to keep people happy. As many people as possible. Not because I particularly care about their happiness, but because I care about my own."

"What are you saying?"

"That's not me, it's your judge. It's a quote from B. Sheldrake Tuppin himself."

I glanced at the clock. "Michele," I said, "it's almost ten. And it's Monday. Where would we be going to meet somebody now?"

He smiled his broad, face-warming grin. "I knew you'd help, Angelo. I just knew it! We're going to Yorkville. Come on. Dad'll let us have the truck."

The thought of going anywhere in the old wreck my father used for hauling his bricklaying supplies to construction sites made me cringe, but it didn't seem to bother Arletta. "Yorkville!" she shrieked. "Let me come! I want to go, too!"

My father put down the *Corriere*, rose from his chair in the corner, walked over to the table and stood beside Arletta. For a short man he had a remarkable ability to give the effect of towering over other people. "*A letto,*" he commanded, "to bed."

My sister looked up at him and wrinkled her nose, but that was her only protest. She could manipulate my father and get him to thank her for it when she wanted to, but perhaps she'd calculated her chances of our taking her with us and decided to save my father's favor until the stakes were higher and the payoff better. She folded up her crossword and went to bed. Reluctantly, I headed to Yorkville with Michele.

If Toronto *had* had a Greenwich Village, Yorkville would have been it. We parked the truck three blocks away and walked to Cumberland Street, a narrow thoroughfare crowded for this late on a Monday night. Tall brick townhouses that must once have been the staid homes of prosperous Victorians were now brightly painted and divided into shops, galleries and cafés. Though the night was cold, below street level doors stood ajar, and from the establishments behind them spilled the sound of folk music. On the street young people hung out, all dressed in a studied Bohemian style. I couldn't imagine what sort of underprivileged person Michele expected to find here.

My brother led me along Cumberland Street, up Avenue Road, along Yorkville Avenue. We peeked into a dozen crowded, smoky clubs with odd names. The Purple Onion. The Devil's Den. The Penny Farthing. The Night Owl. Café El Patio. The Half Beat. The Green Door. Eventually we ended up climbing to a second-floor place called the Hawk's Nest. Despite the decor that seemed to have been lifted from the armory of a medieval castle, the place appealed to me. Although everybody there seemed to be closer to Arletta's age than to mine, they were neatly dressed, the girls extremely slim and sharp in fashionable little two-piece outfits with short boxy jackets and knee-length narrow skirts, the boys in jackets and ties. On the gleaming dance floor, a number of couples gyrated to one of the Beatles songs my sister listened to incessantly, "Eight Days a Week." I hated the whiny singing but was becoming captivated by the beat when Michele rudely pulled my sleeve. "Waste of time," he hissed. "Let's get out."

We went to the truck and got in. I was relieved to think he'd given up and that I was spared the trouble of helping his friend. But I was wrong. He pulled into a dark alley south of Yorkville, jerked open his door and signaled for me to come with him toward a dingy-looking, two-story warehouse tightly sandwiched between two taller buildings. The alley was lit by a single streetlight that cast its meager glow on a door with a window in it the size of a playing card. Michele knocked. There was a delay about long enough for someone to have looked out that little window and sized us up.

The door opened. Michele handed the man who stood there a couple of dollar bills. Ahead of us was a dim stairway. My brother went ahead. I could hear nothing at first. No music. No voices. Fear made my legs tremble as I started up the stairs behind Michele.

Of course, given Michele's consuming interest in Dr. King and the march in Selma, Alabama, I more or less assumed that the person we were looking to help must be a Negro. I had met very few Negroes in my life—Toronto had no Negro ghetto, of that I was sure—and the ones I had met were mostly religious, polite, well dressed.

Michele got to the top of the stairs and stopped. He was blocking my view, so I could see little except his back. Then I realized that someone had approached him. I heard a few whispered words of welcome. "Hi, Dave!" Michele answered, and Dave, whoever he was, said that as soon as somebody he called Marnie finished, Billy would read.

I didn't know what they were talking about. By the time I got to the top of the stairs, the slender, dark-haired man who must have been Dave was walking toward a stage, which was really nothing more than a spot of light shining on the only empty—or nearly empty—piece of floor in the place. The club was jammed and all eyes were on the skinny woman sitting in that patch of light. She seemed immobile. Her pale face, her catlike eyes, the curly fringe of her soft brown hair, even her lips seemed incapable of movement, though she was reading from a piece of paper. Her voice was more toneless than the sound that accompanied her, the soft, slow, sure beat of an Indian drum.

Both Dave and Michele seemed as fascinated by this woman as the rest of the audience was. As they stared, I checked out the scene. Unlike the crowd at the Hawk's Nest, there was nothing sharp about this gang. The men wore blue jeans and I was surprised to see some women in them too. Both genders sported sweaters and sweatshirts, one of which, I could make out, was emblazoned with a portrait of Beethoven. There wasn't a jacket in the place, except, of course, the one I was wearing. The girls had hair to their waists, hanging free. A couple of the men had beards and every man in the club had hair longer than my brother's.

It was hard to see much in the dimness, but what furniture I could see looked worn, shabby. The poet, for it was poetry this skinny woman was intoning, sat on a battered wooden stool, behind which was some sort of bedsheet pinned to the wall under a banner in labored lettering that read, "Send a poem of protest to the Pentagon." The sheet was covered with black scrawls in what looked like hundreds of hands.

Marnie finished her reading. A sturdy round of applause continued until Dave came into the spotlight and announced that after a short break, there would be a special treat for lovers of literature.

"What are we doing here, Michele?" I asked. But before he could answer, a man, a stranger, materialized out of the crowd and stood in the shadows beside us. "Billy," Michele said, extending his hand, "this is my brother, Angelo, uh, I mean, Ellis. Ellis Portal from law school."

At the exact moment Billy stepped forward, the house-lights came up. The place wasn't that much brighter with them on, but I could clearly see two things about Billy Johnson: he wasn't a Negro and he *was* a striking man, over six feet tall, slender but powerfully built, with shiny black hair that fell past his wide shoulders and brushed the colorful beadwork on the yoke of his fringed doeskin jacket. If he hadn't been a full-blooded Indian, the getup would have looked ridiculous. But he was and it didn't. I held out my hand and he grasped it strongly in long, cool fingers.

"Billy's Indian," Michele offered.

"No kidding?"

I smiled and Johnson smiled, too.

"Cree," Michele added. "He's also a draft dodger—or about to be."

I shot Michele a warning glance. I felt tricked. I could just imagine what Sheldrake Tuppin, whose great-grandfather had been an admiral in the British navy, would think about aiding and abetting cowards and traitors. As if Michele could read my mind, he said, "I know you're not into Vietnam, but this is more complicated than that, man. Way more."

"Michele, I can't . . ." I was about to tell him that I was leaving. That I had more important things to do than sit here on a rickety chair, assuming that I could actually get one, listening to some nonsense masquerading as literature. I was about to head for the subway and leave Michele to go home alone in the truck. I hated riding in that shameful heap of junk, anyway.

Only, before I could turn to go, the lights were suddenly doused again and I was stranded. I wouldn't have been able to find the door. I had no choice but to lean against the wall and listen to whatever came next.

To my surprise, Billy Johnson stepped into the circle of light. Pleased whispers rippled through the room. In a clear, deep voice, he took command of the crowd, told them how honored he was to follow somebody like Marnie, and began to read.

It wasn't until the spotlight fell on the planes of Billy's handsome face that I noticed an odd mark on his cheek. It was darker than his dusky skin, like a birthmark or a tattoo. I was too far away to see it clearly, but it looked like two moons, crescents facing each other half an inch apart.

He turned his head slightly and his cheek was swallowed by shadow. Distracted by this observation, I realized I'd not been paying attention to the introduction of his poem. The first words of it I heard were "If you love me, leave me a kiss in the white cup of morning."

I glanced at Michele to see whether the poem was making any sense to him. But I couldn't get him to look at me. He was staring at Billy with the same rapt attention he'd previously reserved exclusively for Martin Luther King, Jr.

Chapter 3

All night I dreamed alternately of Billy Johnson and the dead woman with the hidden head. At times she reared above me, erect and threatening. At other times she sat propped on the shaky stool in the limelight reading some incomprehensible poem. At one point I yanked the bag from her head and discovered she was Billy Johnson. But in the dream, I knew that was an error. As if my subconscious were compelled to correct the mistake, the same dream would start all over and proceed identically to the same ridiculous conclusion.

In the morning I left home as quickly as I could to get away from my brother, who was distraught because two civil rights marchers had been injured when mounted sheriff's deputies had charged the crowd of Selma demonstrators. Were I totally honest, I might have admitted to myself that I was also avoiding Michele's accusation that thus far my efforts to find a project compelling enough to capture the attention of Tuppin had failed. Despite the fascination I had for the power Tuppin wielded in his court, I had little interest in criminal law per se. Perhaps the violence and disorganization of the lower social orders were quaintly appealing to a spoiled brat like Gleason Adams or touchingly inspirational to a bleeding heart like my brother. To me, crime was desperate, frightening and avoidable. Which did not explain why I stopped in the law library before class to look for a book that might help me understand what I'd seen at the morgue the night before. Despite the bizarre spectacle the corpse had presented, six or seven months of law studies had already convinced me that nothing much is unique in this world. I was developing the lawyer's habit of seeking precedent. I was already used to hours of work before I even got to school. I had been doing that since ninth grade.

In the best modern way, the law library was sleek, cool and unadorned. Morning light from bare floor-to-ceiling windows competed with the banks of fluorescent fixtures stretching the fifty-foot width of the reading room. At plain teak tables, men in white shirts and dark ties were bent silently over their books, their crooked elbows shielding the volumes protectively.

I couldn't get much reading done in the hour that remained before my first class, but I did manage to find a few titles in the card catalogue that dealt with unusual methods of homicide. *Suspicious Death: A Compendium. By Whose Hand: Suicide or Murder? Assessing Evidence: A Guide for the Homicide Investigator.* I made a note of them for future reference, then walked over to Falconer Hall, adjacent to the library but clearly from another era. Its warmth embraced me the moment I entered its oak-paneled halls.

In the coffee room I searched for Gleason among the students gathered around the ornate silver coffee urn that was nearly as tall as the uniformed server who stood behind it. Everyone in the room wore a suit. Everyone was male except for one startlingly beautiful redhead. She winked when she saw me, and I made my way toward the little crowd that habitually surrounded her. "Have you seen Gleason Adams?" I asked her. She shook her head, sending the room's low light careering along the sleek line of her hair, drawn into a chignon.

"He was probably out playing last night, as usual," she replied, giving her head a small shake of disgust.

"I don't think so," I said, but I didn't tell her what I knew about his activities last night, about the morgue, about his unusual nervousness. Though it would have been totally out of keeping with Gleason's usual careless attitude, it was possible that he'd been too upset to come to class.

I myself had trouble concentrating in my classes: Criminal Law, Personal Property, Torts. Gleason had no such trouble, because he never did show. I gave up looking for him when he failed to appear in the student lounge for lunch. By then all my thoughts were centered on my impending meeting with Professor Myron Kavin, my assigned adviser.

If I missed the comforting clutter of law books in the library, it certainly wasn't a problem in Kavin's office, in the nether regions of Falconer. His room was a cell, no bigger than ten feet square. Worn Turkish carpets hid a cement floor. An iron-banded, wood-planked door creaked ominously whenever it opened. Shelves were stuffed with books, and more books covered the small lamp tables and a couple of scuffed leather armchairs. His desk and the chairs always had to be cleared before his students could sit and tutorials begin. This was a movie-set version of a law professor's lair. I had been there before and I knew the clichés ended with the decor. Myron Kavin was a modern man, a clever, hard-nosed realist.

"Good afternoon, Portal," he said, running his fingers through his sandy hair and rising from his chair to simultaneously usher me into the room and glance into the dim hallway in expectation of finding Gleason dawdling somewhere behind me. "Where's your disreputable associate?"

I smiled, moved a pile of books and took a seat. "Apparently lost in the labyrinth of the law," I responded.

Professor Kavin smiled back. "Has he let you in on the secret of his choice of projects?"

Secret? For a moment I wondered whether Kavin knew about the morgue, but I soon realized he was being ironic. As far as the professor knew, Gleason had no project. That, of course, was as far as I knew, too.

"What have *you* got for me, Portal?" He stacked several files and piled them atop a leaning hill of books on the corner of his desk, then waited expectantly for me to deposit the outline of my own nonexistent proposal in the space he'd made.

"I haven't finished the outline yet, Professor," I admitted. "I've completed my review of Tuppin's most significant cases, but . . ."

Kavin ran his fingers through his hair again. The gesture had no effect on the locks, which lay perfectly whatever he did to them. Nor did it have any effect on the professor's impatience, a trait for which he was famous. "It's the middle of March, Portal. You've known since January that you need a convincing proposal to present to the faculty. Tuppin is not going to be impressed by the fact that you've read a large number of books. What do you plan on saying to the magistrate, exactly?" He paused, searched for his pipe and tobacco beneath some journals, filled the polished wood bowl and tamped it down. He shook the pouch, put a few more shreds into the bowl, tamped it again and lit it with a few strong pulls of air against the flame of the wooden match. The smoke filled the little room and I fought the urge to cough. "Of course," Kavin continued, "if you and Adams *want* to be called to the bar a year later than everyone else, you certainly have the right to exercise that prerogative."

I shifted in my chair. "No, sir," I said.

He eyed me as if to say, "Well?"

My relationship with Kavin was not what anyone would call personal, but he and I had spent hours examining the intricacies of the law. He was my mentor, the doorkeeper, the person able to let me into the world I so longed to enter. I cleared my throat. In that moment I wanted to tell him what we had seen at the morgue, to explain to him that my desire to figure out what had happened was beginning to eclipse my desire to impress Magistrate Tuppin. Kavin would know whether homicide was the most likely explanation, I believed, and could tell me whether Chief Coroner Rosen's actions appeared in any way inappropriate. I opened my mouth to speak.

But then I thought of the little packet Gleason had stolen. I had no idea what was in it, but that was not the point. The item was evidence no matter what it contained. It was not only potential evidence of murder, it was certain evidence of our having stupidly put ourselves at risk. "I'm thinking of posing a central question about the law based on a thorough study of Tuppin's work," I offered.

Myron Kavin glared at me from behind the cloud of pipe smoke. His eyes were shrewd. He would have made an excellent judge because he saw everything, heard everything, analyzed everything, but never inadvertently let you know what he was thinking. "Portal," he said calmly, "you are a young man of exceptional talent. It mystifies me that you consistently fail to rise to the dictates of that talent. Tuppin wouldn't give a fig about a weak idea like yours. He's a warrior of the court. He's a man who spends every waking moment in the eternal battle between the law and the men the law seeks to control. Tuppin is not about books, he's about the drunk in the gutter. He's about the drug addict stoned in the street. He's about the thief who charms your mother while he's emptying her purse."

Kavin shook his head. "If you're really a book-and-paper man, criminal law is not for you. Compared to the orderly progression of the work of commercial lawyers or estate lawyers or of civil litigants, the work of the criminal lawyer is a daily descent into chaos and desperation. I thought you understood that. I thought you said you'd already asked yourself why a man would deliberately choose such a life." He paused for a moment. "Pose *that* question to Tuppin and he just might persuade himself to grant you a few moments' audience."

"Would Tuppin be interested in homicide?" I dared to ask.

Kavin's pipe suddenly required his undivided attention. "Repeat yourself, Portal," he finally said. "I don't believe I heard you."

"Nothing, sir," I mumbled. "I was just thinking out loud."

"Listen, Portal, you've still got a choice here," he said, biting down on the stem of the pipe and speaking through partially closed lips. "Either write a logical and articulate proposal outlining exactly what you intend to accomplish with Tuppin or drop the idea of meeting with him. Act strongly while you can still choose, otherwise your indecision will make the choice for you."

I had to smile. His advice sounded like the platitudes my mother dished out. *Make up your mind or it will make up itself.*

Kavin removed his pipe from his mouth and studied its shiny bowl. "Tuppin likes to surprise people, Portal," he said. "Don't let him surprise *you*."

Before I could ask the professor what he meant by that cryptic remark, our time was up. It was part of Kavin's job, as he saw it, to teach law students that lawyers never talk for free. Once your time with Kavin was up, it was up. I left his office confused and a little afraid.

WHY DID I GO in search of Gleason when I considered myself lucky to have him off my back? Maybe I feared he planned to blackmail me into helping him on his project. Considering the trouble I was having with my own, the thought made me laugh.

There were, I soon discovered, two families named Adams in the little enclave of Whitney Square, part of the upscale neighborhood of Rosedale. I had to make apologies to the people at number twenty-six before I found the right address.

Flakes of snow clung to the collar of my coat. I brushed them off, but more took their place as I shifted from foot to foot waiting several excruciating minutes for someone to respond to the cascading notes of the door chime.

I was not yet a person who knew how to measure land, but had I been asked, I probably would have guessed that

Whitney Square, which was really a kind of rounded tri-angle bordered by three city blocks, was an acre, an acre of land in the heart of an old, rich section of the city, an acre worth the same amount of money as a thousand acres to the north or the west or the east. At the center of this triangle was a park spread beneath two dozen stately oaks whose bare branches sketched a calligraphy of black strokes against grass that had yet to turn green. A wooden bench circled the base of one of the oaks, its dark green paint scaled by months of freezing weather. Soon a private gardener, or perhaps one of the minders of the city parks, would sand and repaint it, prepare it for anyone who wanted to sit here and dream of what it would be like to live in this part of town.

I glanced at the buildings on the square. The gray stone church with its strong, boxy Protestant tower, the stately red-brick Georgians, the stolid Victorian family mansions held little interest for me. I was captivated only by Glea-son's house, which sat at the southernmost corner of Whit-ney Square, nearest the bridge that led out of these hal-lowed precincts and back toward the streets of the poor.

It was a rambling sort of house to find in the heart of the city. I remembered my mother showing me houses like it when I was a boy and teaching me that every chim-ney meant a fireplace. I counted three in front and more in back, though I couldn't see much beyond the steeply sloping slate roof. In the front, Tudor-style timbers crossed in a high peak. On the ground floor, a carved stone arch beside an intricately leaded window an-nounced the main entrance. It was far more elaborate than the entrance to the house of God across the street.

The door opened suddenly, startling me from my mus-ings. I was even more startled to find Gleason himself standing there, instead of the maid or butler I'd expected. He was dressed in a suit that made his blue eyes look gray. For a moment he stared as if he'd never seen me before. He looked so solemn, so serious, so much more like a concerned man than a student. Embarrassed, I realized I'd obviously come at a bad time. Clearly I'd interrupted Gleason while he was engaged in some important matter. The fact that I'd never known him to consider *anything* important momentarily escaped my recall.

"I'm sorry, Gleason," I blurted. "I shouldn't have come here. I'll go. I'll see you at school."

I turned to leave, but he caught my arm with an urgency as unusual as everything else about his manner on this cold afternoon. "Hey, no. Come in," he said. "I'll take it like a man. You came here to bawl me out because I missed classes, right? And my tutorial with Kavin. I'm such a drag! What did old Smokestack have to say, anyway?"

"Not much, Gleason. Because *I* had nothing to say. You should have been there. You're better at snow jobs than I am. Maybe you could have told Kavin why a person from Rosedale is so interested in the death of some poor female rooming-house tenant. Maybe you could have made up some story about what we saw last night, make it sound like a case."

"It *is* a case," Gleason responded, ushering me into a small sitting room with the kind of old furniture that probably cost more than every item in my parents' house put together. "Wait here a minute, will you?" he asked me, then disappeared. A moment later I heard voices from another room—the stern tone of a man with the cultured accent, vaguely British, of the well educated and wealthy, interspersed with Gleason's more youthful tones and those of a third speaker, a woman who sounded distressed.

I strained to make out what they were saying, but failing, I amused myself by studying the room's fine furniture and accessories. On a table near me in a glass case sat a hinged enamel object shaped like an orange, encrusted with gold and set with what looked like diamonds, topaz and some deep yellow stone I'd never seen before.

"Portal, it *is* a case," Gleason repeated from the doorway. I wasn't sure whether he was referring to the woman in the morgue or berating me for showing impolite interest in the belongings of his family. He saw my confusion and laughed, but he quickly returned to his former seriousness. Again I wondered whether he had found our experience at the morgue as disturbing as I had found it. I had to ask him what he thought it all meant, to try to get him to explain not only how he had arranged our presence there, but more importantly, why. Anyone else would have responded to a straightforward question. That was the worst way to get information out of Gleason Adams.

He sat, legs spread, elbows on his knees, hands clasped before him. "I've been thinking about that dead woman all day," he volunteered. "I knew I wouldn't be able to concentrate on classes or Kavin today, so I skipped." He looked up as if startled by an idea. "You didn't tell Kavin about the morgue, did you?"

"Almost," I answered. "But what would I have said? I don't even know what we were doing down there. Did we go to Lombard Street to assess the legal implications of an unexplained death? Did you expect that you could build a proposal around something as vague as that?"

"Don't be so arrogant, Portal," Gleason said, springing up and nervously grasping the back of the chair—it looked like Chippendale—he'd vacated. "Unlike you, I may not have top marks, a stunning academic record, im-

44

peccable work habits and the ability to brown-nose Kavin, not to mention Tuppin, but I've got better than nothing. I've got a disappearing human body. Now you see it. Now you don't. *And . . .*" He drew out the word as he reached into the pocket of his jacket, "I've got *this!*" Like a magician holding up a coin he'd just pulled from behind someone's ear, Gleason held the little cloth packet between his fingers.

"I told you I don't want anything to do with that. You said you'd give it back!" I shouted indignantly.

"Keep your voice down," Gleason warned, making me feel loud and crude. I shrank back, humiliated. "If you came here to lecture me, you're wasting your time." He came close to the chair in which I sat and held the packet near my cheek. "I found this, Portal. It's my evidence now. And I've got a topnotch project, as far as I'm concerned. People don't just disappear. Not even dead people. I don't know about you, but I have every intention of finding out who that person was, why the coroner didn't want us to see her body, but the pathologist did. Somebody is trying to hide something."

"Oh, that's brilliant, Gleason! A brilliant conclusion. A dead woman with a bag over her head and you conclude someone is trying to hide something. Do you have any other startling observations?"

"Don't be a wise guy, Ellis. Something odorous this way comes. That fact alone is worthy of investigation."

"What were you doing at the morgue, anyway? Tell me, Adams."

He turned and walked a little distance away. I couldn't see his face, of course, but the set of his shoulders indicated his usual relaxed posture. "I was doing research, what else?"

"Why did you call me?"

"Because you're my friend."

He said it as though it were an answer on a pop quiz. I didn't have the heart to say he was wrong. Or the folly to admit he was right. "A friend would advise you to drop the matter, Gleason. The pathologist made a mistake showing us that body. I think the coroner might have wanted to spare us law students a bit of embarrassment. I got some books out of the law library at lunchtime. The most likely explanation for what we saw is—"

"Suicide? Some kind of perverted auto-eroticism?"

I glanced at him in surprise. I didn't know Gleason knew about the more bizarre manifestations of human desperation. Why should he? As far as I knew he'd had all he needed or wanted from the day he was born. He certainly didn't bother taking books out of the library to read the gruesome facts of other people's pathetic lives.

"Portal," he said, "that's the point, don't you see? No matter what caused that death, something exceedingly strange happened to the body."

"Forget it! You can't frame a law proposal on what we saw—which was next to nothing. We didn't even get to the point at which the clothes came off. And the evidence you have in your possession was illegally obtained. It's stolen!"

Gleason rarely showed anger, but when he did, it was as unpredictable and wild as his other mercurial traits. "You're a self-righteous prig!" he spat at me. "You've got a lot of pride for the grandson of a Dago monkeyman!"

No. No. I am not the grandson of an Italian street musician. But yes, I am Italian and passionate anger is no stranger to me. But I was beyond anger now. I'd had enough of this spoiled, ignorant brat. I yanked my coat from the back of the chair. The spindly furniture teetered but remained upright. I didn't bother to put my coat on as I made for the door of the room.

But Gleason was in the doorway blocking my exit before I could get there. "Aren't you forgetting something, Portal?" Once again he held up the little packet. "You were in that lab, too."

"So what? Get out of my way."

"I need your help, Ellis. I have to do this law project and I can't handle it alone."

"Why don't you do what you always do? Snow your way out of a problem. Or call Daddy and get him to donate a new building." I tried to push past him, but he wouldn't budge.

"Help me, old lady, or I'll have to tell Kavin how hard I worked to convince you to give back what you stole."

"Save your threats, Gleason," I said through clenched teeth. "For all I know, there isn't even anything in that pouch."

He grinned at me. He thrust the tips of two fingers into the gap made by the pathologist when he'd snipped the packet off the deceased. He pulled. The tiny cloth bag split and two items flew out, clinking onto the marble floor. Instinctively, both Gleason and I dove for the objects. He managed to retrieve one, then looked around for the other, but this time I blocked him. Behind the base of a stone urn, I saw the glint of metal. I stretched out my fingers and grabbed what looked like a wedding band. Holding it in my palm, I observed that it *was* a ring, half a gold circle welded to half a silver circle. In the glow of afternoon light through the sheer silk curtains at the window, I could see the ring bore an inscription. I read it out loud: "'If you love me . . .'" I glanced at Gleason. I'd already forgotten that I was angry with him. "That's all it says, Gleason. 'If you love me . . .'"

He looked inside the ring he held. It was also half gold, half silver. "'Leave me by dying,'" he read, then looked up. "'If you love me, leave me by dying.'" He slipped the ring on his finger. It fit. Strangely, at that moment, I had to admire Gleason. There was no way I'd put on my finger the ring of someone I had just observed cold and stiff in the morgue, not if I could help it.

"They look like wedding rings, don't they?" Gleason said softly.

"But why would a woman wear her rings pinned to her like that?" I asked.

"So nobody would steal them," Gleason speculated, rather ironically, I thought. "Or to keep them secret from somebody. Or from everybody."

I handed Gleason my ring. "Put this one on," I said. He didn't ask why, he just did it. The second ring fit him, too. "Wow," he said, "big fingers."

"Big feet, too," I said, remembering the run in the dead woman's stocking, the scuffed black pumps.

"Ellis," Gleason asked, again seeming so serious that I wondered what he'd really been up to that morning, "somebody made these rings out of other rings, don't you think?"

"It looks like it."

"We have to check this out. What else can it be but murder?"

"Gleason, we have to take these rings back. If not to the morgue, then to the police." I glanced around. It took me a minute to locate the phone—gray and matched to the decor of the room. Just about every phone I'd seen was black.

"No!" Gleason, agitated, jumped up and moved between me and the phone.

For a moment I stood motionless beside the stone urn. I experienced the intense desire to push him away, to go home and forget about him and the dead woman. Why was I bothering, anyway?

"Look, Ellis, you and I have been in classes together all year. I'm just asking for a little help, that's all. This school stuff is easier for you than for me. I'm not the student you are. Kavin's really into getting me kicked out. But if this is a homicide and we can work together to solve it, we'll have a joint project that we can present to Kavin."

He was nuts. I couldn't imagine that Kavin would ever accept such a vague and inappropriate project. Playing detective would just about finish Gleason off entirely as a law student and it wouldn't do much for me, either.

"Justice, Portal," Gleason whispered. "Truth . . ."

"What?"

His uncharacteristic intensity was alarming. "I need to know, Ellis. What does that inscription mean? Who made new rings out of old ones and why? Why did that woman have them pinned to her underwear instead of being on her finger and her husband's?" He paused. "And most of all, Ellis, who killed her and why?"

"An even more pressing inquiry, Adams, is how would you get anywhere on a case if your only clue was evidence you were withholding from the police?"

He turned from me and held his hands out, studying the two rings the way a wealthy woman might contemplate her jewels. He made me stand there watching this display until he finally said, "Portal, let's just do it. Forget about that Tuppin character. He's a drag. You'll be bored following him around. We've got something here that nobody else in the program has got."

"Yeah, stolen evidence."

"*We* do not have stolen evidence," he said. "What *we* have is an overlooked exhibit that *we* rescued when others failed to observe it."

"Stop saying *we*."

Gleason laughed, then made a face of mock displeasure. I didn't bother to comment on his childishness. I had begun to see a solution, not to the mystery of the dead woman, but to Gleason's predicament. "Maybe you can go back to that pathologist. You can say that you realized the packet had been left behind when he was called out of the lab, that you retrieved it, but that when you attempted to give it back, we were so quickly thrown—I mean, seen—out of the morgue that you didn't have time."

Gleason appeared to give my suggestion serious consideration. "That's cool, Portal. Truly excellent."

I didn't like it when Gleason agreed with me so readily. It usually meant that he had already discovered a way to act in exactly the opposite manner than I had proposed. "And while we're at it," he said, "we can question the pathologist a bit. We can find how the body was brought in, who the relatives are, that sort of thing. And we can see if he'll tell us why we were allowed to see the body for only a short time."

Those were exactly the sort of questions I was sure the pathologist would not answer. Like many workers for the solicitor general and the attorney general of Ontario, he would have taken a sworn oath not to reveal anything he had learned in the course of his duties.

"I don't think so. I . . . ."

"If we could get back in to see the pathologist, we could watch and listen carefully to get some clue, some idea as to whether the pathologist thought the woman's death was a murder. Maybe we can find someone who actually saw the woman and her husband wearing the rings."

No, no, I couldn't allow myself to be enticed into this. The best thing was simply for Gleason to give back the rings and choose some other way to placate Kavin. I told him to forget about getting me involved.

But the image of the dead woman and the puzzle of the rings were not so easily put out of my mind.

Chapter 4

The man lay in a dark pool of blood at the bottom of the stairs. From the wound on his head, the blood had spread to soak his hair, his clothes, the carpet beneath his arms—they had clearly been held out in some futile gesture of self-protection. Blood had splattered the open door at the foot of the stairs, staining it with a spray of drops that radiated from the victim's head like the halos in my mother's prayer book. Halfway down the stairs, a thin, five- or six-inch line of blood marked the wall. The awkwardly twisted body with its grotesque, smashed head seemed to clearly indicate a merciless crime, but it was not.

I read on. The man had been descending the staircase slowly. Halfway down, a broken stair rail bracket had snagged his hand and cut it. Distracted, the man lost his footing and plunged down the remaining stairs. At the bottom, his head, backed by the full weight of his body, had hit the knob of the door. That knob had made a hole in his skull the size and shape of a fist.

My nose buried in *Suspicious Death Scientifically Explained*, I didn't see Professor Kavin as he slipped into the library out of the drizzling rain and brushed the moisture from his collar and sleeves. "Got a minute, Portal?" he whispered.

"Sir?"

"I saw Adams this morning," Kavin confided, leading me toward a settee in the students' lounge, an open area at the front of the library. "He said that if I asked you, you'd be able to give me the details on something the two of you worked up yesterday."

I experienced an instant flash of anger, but I hid my reaction from Kavin. If Gleason thought he could manipulate me into helping him by telling Kavin about the body at the morgue, he was dead wrong, so to speak.

"Professor," I improvised, "the other night, I learned of a man my brother, a sociologist, thinks might have an interesting case. I met the man briefly but haven't spoken to him at length. My brother tells me that though Canadian, the man appears to be in danger of being drafted into the United States Army. He's an Indian, native. If you think Magistrate Tuppin would take an interest, I could examine all the arising legal questions concerning his status as a Cree, his citizenship in Canada and his eligibility to be conscripted into the service of a foreign military force." Buoyed by the sound of my own voice, I rushed on. "I can draft a proposal showing the kind of interviews that would be necessary to conduct with the man and his associates. I can do some preliminary research into relevant statutes and case law, as well as work up a few queries that could be addressed to citizenship officials. I can show that, depending on the findings, counsel can either suggest that the man surrender himself to American authorities or else assist him in possibly instigating civil litigation against the United States government."

Kavin stared at me. Several students were smoking in the lounge and he glanced toward them as though sorry he didn't have his pipe. He never liked to deliver an opinion without a cloud of smoke obscuring his face, giving him the advantage of inscrutability. Finally he returned his gaze to me. "I'm at sea here, Portal. This doesn't sound like the sort of thing Adams was suggesting at all."

"Uh, perhaps not, sir."

"Portal," he said, "you realize I am *not* recommending that you work with Adams. I'm much more impressed with this idea of yours. Magistrate Tuppin doesn't often have the opportunity to consider international law. When you think about it, you are really dealing with three nations on a case like this. I don't think you are going to find much on the man's rights as an Indian." He stared into space for a moment, as if mentally running through some book on the subject. "You can spend a few hours here in the library looking at treaty law for a start," he finally said. "Then you're going to have to see what we've got in the way of U.S. federal statutes." He nodded, smiled the discreet little crescent that indicated his pleasure. "Work it up. I'll present it as part of your proposal to intern for Tuppin when the project approval committee next meets."

I thought about Gleason, his unexplained urgency, his apparent desperation over the brilliance of his proposed project. Would Kavin's enthusiasm for my idea wipe out his interest in Gleason's proposal, which Gleason would now have to convince Kavin about himself? If that was the case, then so be it. I wasn't Gleason's babysitter, was I?

"Are you done with your classes for the day?" Kavin asked, glancing at his watch. It was five o'clock and I wasn't looking forward to another pile of dry, breaded fish and stiff, warmed-over pizza. I wondered what Kavin had in mind. Maybe he wanted to buy me supper, a big fat hamburger. It wouldn't have been the first time.

"Yes, sir," I answered hopefully.

"How about a little walk down University Avenue?" he said. "We can take a look at the progress they're making on the new courthouse and maybe drop in on a friend of mine at City Hall."

I agreed eagerly with Kavin's suggestion. Together we exited the library and, ignoring the light drizzle, sauntered down the curved drive that circled between the two Law Faculty buildings—Falconer Hall and Flavelle House. Both were gracious old mansions, especially Flavelle House, an Edwardian masterpiece of wood, stone, iron and glass built by the baronet, Lord Minto, in 1902 and willed to the university on his death. Kavin and I turned onto University Avenue, a broad boulevard that led south toward downtown and, at the bottom of the city, Lake Ontario. Ahead of us, the dark pink Victorian monolith of Queen's Park, the provincial parliament building, loomed in the mist. It was surrounded on all sides by a park not unlike the manicured swath of Whitney Square, except that this park was fifty times as large as the one in front of Gleason's house. As we crossed it, my stomach began to roll with anticipation. Had I already guessed where we were headed?

Traffic on both sides of the elegant expanse of University Avenue was brisk, speeding both north and south toward the arterials leading out of the downtown core and toward the bungalows and waiting wives of the suburbs.

"Wisdom begins in the street," the professor said, rather gratuitously, I thought. At the intersection of College Street, Kavin and I negotiated the crossover to the east side of University, happily dodging a cloud of white-capped nurses outside Toronto General Hospital. I followed them with my eyes as they fluttered down the street.

Kavin also studied the scene before us, the crowded sidewalks, the rushing cars. "There are those who think the law is an abstraction, a set of ideas, principles and rules," he said. "Such thinkers are convinced that human nature, indeed nature itself, is constantly in need of the application of reason, that we live on the brink of chaos, separated from it only by the narrow barricade of logic."

Being rather of that opinion myself, I said nothing. But I did think about my brother's nearly uncontrollable fury over the actions of the sheriffs of Alabama—and, of course, about Gleason's possession of stolen evidence. Principles and abstractions drove Michele. He thought about little else. As for Gleason, I didn't know *what* he thought about.

"Tuppin, however, is not such a thinker."

"Sir?"

"Magistrate Tuppin is of the 'Dirty Hands' school." Kavin smiled, waiting for my inevitable comment. Everyone knew Tuppin to be an impeccable man—even, his enemies sometimes charged, a bit of a dandy.

"I can't imagine the magistrate having any part of his anatomy less than perfectly sanitary at any time, but I do take your meaning, sir," I answered.

"If you want to impress Tuppin," Kavin said, "come down from your ivory tower, Portal."

I wasn't sure where this was leading, but I didn't really care. Walking down University Avenue on a spring afternoon in the exclusive company of a distinguished law scholar, discussing the legal leanings of an eminent colleague . . . The scene filled me with a heady sense of excitement. This was my world now, and it was only going to get better.

Of course, this walk with my professor through the streets of the city was not unusual. Kavin and I had done it before. There was even a winding lane on the university campus called Philosophers' Walk. Kavin had once told me the meaning of the word *peripatetic*—literally, "walking around"—a name given to Greek teachers of antiquity whose students followed them through the streets of Athens as they wandered about dispensing tidbits of knowledge. Today, however, Kavin was not wandering. He walked with purpose. I was beginning to suspect what his purpose was, and the thought filled me with happy hopefulness. We proceeded single file now along sidewalks that had, in the past few minutes, become jammed with dinner-hour shoppers, most of whom were talking in the high-pitched, staccato cadences of Chinese. Our pace slowed as we moved through open barrels of spiky-branched brown lichee nuts, tables of curled sheets of dried fish, baskets of squirming blue-legged crabs. In window after steaming window, glistening red barbecued meat, ducks with bills intact, racks of lean pork ribs, bulbous tentacled sea creatures hung from sharp iron hooks. Peeking in one window, I saw a huge cauldron of soup— with a chicken's foot in it! If Kavin was going to offer me something to eat here, I was going to have to decline. I had never eaten Chinese food in my life. Nobody in my family had. Which perhaps equaled the number of people in Chinatown who had eaten ravioli, lasagna or linguine.

Kavin stopped, not at one of the many restaurants advertising their fare on long strips of paper pasted to the walls visible through the open doors, but at some sort of pharmacy with shelf upon shelf of colorful jars and boxes and rows of herbs hanging from rope strung across the shop ceiling. He must have shopped here before, because he went straight for a waist-high bamboo basket filled with small packages wrapped in beige, brocade-like paper. Each of these was bound with a strip of white paper with black Chinese characters beneath a seal much like the gold seal I'd seen on a legal document.

Kavin grabbed a pile of these packages, five or six of them. When he gave the Chinese man at the counter a dollar, the man gave him a handful of change.

"What are they, Professor?"

He reached into the bag, took out one of his treasures and handed it to me. "Smell it," he said. I held the package to my nose. The exquisite scent of sandalwood mingled with the odor of the rain.

"Sometimes," Kavin commented, "a poor man can get more for a dime than a rich man gets for a dollar."

"Yes, sir," I said, deeply gratified that Kavin's example of the miracles of bargain-hunting involved Chinese soap and not Chinese soup.

We turned off Dundas at Elizabeth Street. I wondered whether Kavin would point out the virtues of another handy set of poor people, my own Italian relations and countless others like them, as well as their neighbors, eastern European Jews, who had populated these precincts before the Chinese, when the area had been called "the Ward."

"The Ward is gone now," the professor said as if reading my mind. "But something greater rises in its place."

It wasn't hard to see what he meant. At the end of Elizabeth, just a short block south of the teeming old shops of Chinatown, rose two curved concrete towers, one twenty stories high, the other nearly ten stories higher. This was

New City Hall, in the final stages of construction. At the rear there was not a single window in the stark, ribbed exterior of this gigantic cement parenthesis, but in front, the twin-curved structures were all glass and appeared to cup a large, clamlike concrete shape, low to the ground. I couldn't quite figure this building out, but had been assured that it was a highly efficient design capable of accommodating the government offices of the burgeoning metropolis, and I believed it.

Professor Kavin and I crossed the equipment-strewn plaza in front of the construction site and, my eye seeking color amid all the gray, I stopped to gaze up at the green copper roof of what would from now on always be called Old City Hall. It was a massive, four-story building in brownstone, its Victorian Romanesque solidity only somewhat alleviated by the soaring bell tower with its four-faced clock that began to toll the hour of five even as I stared at it.

"Who are we going to see?" I asked the professor. He didn't answer, just gestured at a wooden door on the west side of the building and held it open for me as I slipped in behind him.

Nobody knew the word "multitasking" in 1965, but everyone who worked in Old City Hall had the concept down pat, for in the two wings of this building, which covered a whole city block, all the functions of municipal government were carried out on the same premises as all the functions of a major downtown courthouse.

Which might explain why a string of shabby men, linked by handcuffs to a police officer, was snaking past the startled eyes of a young woman in full bridal regalia standing in front of a door marked "Wedding Waiting Room."

"Someone is confused," Kavin said. "The police cells and the Crown attorney's office are on the east side, not here on the west."

As if he'd heard the professor, the cop attached to his charges clicked across the black-and-white-tiled floor and opened a door leading to a central courtyard, a paved square walled on all sides by the building. Into this courtyard, day and night, passed the Black Marias, paneled trucks that rounded up prisoners from the city streets and dumped them into the ever-waiting police cells.

Every morning except Sunday, when judges and criminals alike were expected to be in church, the Magistrates' Courts of Old City Hall were in session. Magistrates had the power, with the consent of the accused, to sit on any nonjury trials except those in which the charge was murder, manslaughter, rape or treason. In the afternoons special courts of various sorts were held, but now, at five, most of the courts were down for the day. Though we didn't exactly have the huge building to ourselves, Professor Kavin and I met very few others as we climbed the marble stairs.

By now, I was fairly sure that Sheldrake Tuppin must have agreed to see me and that Kavin was leading me to him. A flash of alarm made me breathless as we ascended. I was by no means fully prepared for this meeting. What if Tuppin asked me the specifics of what I was working on? What *was* I working on? Neither my brother's potential draft dodger nor Gleason's fugitive corpse was going to help me out here. I searched my mind for some compelling legal issue from among the thousands of pages of cases I'd read. Nothing.

As if sensing my discomfort, Kavin turned and smiled. "You should eat less spaghetti, Portal. Climbing stairs would be easier if you were thin. And you should convince yourself that what a man thinks will always be more impressive than what he has or does."

With that useless advice, we continued our climb. Old City Hall had been built in the 1890s as a monument to municipal and judicial power in an age of imperial splendor. Though it wouldn't be for much longer, in 1965 Canada was still without a constitution of its own and its allegiance was to Queen Elizabeth II. The magistrates were the Queen's appointed minions, though few of them had ever seen her except on TV. And their prisoners were Her Majesty's prisoners. So it was fitting that glass, stained, etched, beveled and plain; marble, Italian and otherwise; wrought iron, swirled into wreaths and crisscrossed into grills; and wood, carved, dovetailed, molded and joined, should compose the materials of the old courthouse.

Past the Finance Department/Enforcement Branch and Arrears Office, the County Sheriff, the Grand Jury Witness Room, the High Court of Justice Assize Court, the chambers of Moore and MacRae, Timmins and Denton, Donley, McDonagh and Rogers, I followed Myron Kavin until, at the northwest corner of the building on the third floor, we reached a twelve-foot-high door that opened onto a corridor of nine similar doors. Each was of dark, red-hued wood, possibly northern maple, with the rich patina of years of use. Eight of the nine were graced by transoms and gold numerals—344 by the entrance of the corridor to 351 in the far end. The ninth door, the one without a transom, bore black numerals that said 221B.

Kavin was clearly delighted by my confused surprise. "His Worship is quite the Sherlock Holmes fanatic," he said. "But this isn't London or Baker Street or even a real room. This is nothing but a broom closet."

Door 351 sprang suddenly open with enough force to

bounce it against the wall. "Come in. Come in. Why are you dawdling out there like a couple of alley louts?" The voice was hoarse; perhaps a better description was gravelly. But there was an undercurrent to it, not merry or jolly but good-humored nonetheless.

"Good afternoon, Your Worship," Kavin said. He bowed his head a little and Tuppin received the honor, as though accustomed to the deference of lesser men. "You said you wouldn't mind if I brought my star student to meet you, sir, and I've taken you up on the offer."

Kavin's star student! I was flabbergasted to learn the professor held so high an opinion of me. I was also afraid I'd soon disabuse him of it. I remembered that Kavin once told me that silence is one of the barrister's tools. Perhaps I'd be wise to utilize it now. I smiled, but Tuppin didn't see. He was looking at my mentor. The old man's eyes were full of pleasure as he gazed on Kavin, who, I realized, must once have been *his* star student.

"Your Worship, Mr. Ellis Portal. Portal, His Worship Magistrate B. Sheldrake Tuppin."

He was lean and mean, was Sheldrake Tuppin, with a soldier's ramrod bearing and a boy's protruding ears. Some jokingly called him "the hanging magistrate," though it was never his job to sentence a man to execution. At a time when public inebriation was one of the most commonly encountered and thoroughly detested street crimes, he was undisputed lord of the vile No. 24 Court, the Liquor Court, the "drunk dock." He would throw a man in jail if he didn't like the smell of him.

But he called every drunk "Mr." He never kept an accused waiting, wallowing in fear. He was never rude, never haughty, never belligerent, never incomprehensible, even to men far less educated than he, which most men were. I already knew the only two things a lawyer had to know when appearing before Sheldrake Tuppin. The first was that you had nothing to fear if your client was not guilty. The second was that you had little to hope for if he was.

"Sir, it's an honor."

"Ah," Tuppin said, drawing a finger along the taut plane of his cheek, "Portal." His eyes raked me from head to toe. "I take it you're the young man who thinks I can't do this job without help."

"Sir?" I said in alarm.

"Aren't you the fellow determined to become my amanuensis, my sidekick, my intent-on-pleasing, hard-panting wee pup?"

Realizing I could answer neither yes nor no to this question, I glanced nervously around his chambers, which looked exactly as I'd imagined Holmes's 221B Baker Street. Scholarly, Victorian, male. I jumped when I saw a spot on the wall marked with a series of what looked like bullet holes made by a pistol of some sort, spelling out the initials ER—Elizabeth Regina, the Queen.

"Yes, Your Worship, I am." I gulped, and Tuppin made a sound I later learned was what, with him, passed for a laugh.

"Well, son," he said, opening an ornately carved wooden box and extracting three long cigars, "following me about is not going to teach you anything you didn't learn at your mother's knee." He handed one cigar to Kavin and one to me. I had no intention of smoking it. I slipped it into my pocket and kept it—for years, actually. The magistrate and the professor went through a complex cigar-lighting ritual. When they were both puffing away, Tuppin abruptly commanded me, "Go over to the window and tell me what you see out there."

There were many occasions in my early twenties on which I felt a distinct lack of respect from my elders and so-called betters. The time was coming, as my brother never tired of pointing out, when people over thirty would lose the automatic respect of those younger than themselves. But, close as it was, that time had not yet come. Like a dutiful boy, I walked over and looked out. On the street below I could see a few police officers outside the northern gate. I couldn't see the gate itself. Mostly there was nothing down there but people leaving work to go home, just as there'd been on University Avenue. "I see ordinary people, sir," I said hesitantly. Clearly anything Tuppin might ask would be a test. And anything I answered would contribute to a pass or a fail.

"What you see, young man, are plain, decent men and women. There are far more of them than there are criminals or litigants. Most of those people will see a lawyer only once or twice in their lives—when they buy their house and make their will. Sometimes I look out that window and realize that the day I walked into law school was the day I bid goodbye to those decent folk and their ordinary world."

Coming from a man who spent his days being respectful to drunks before tossing them in the slammer, this regret for mundane days gone by should have sounded somber, but I thought Tuppin's tone almost gleeful.

"Get back here and sit down, lad."

Once again, without protest, I did as I was told.

"You've heard stories about me, I suppose?" The magistrate studied the glowing end of his cigar as if he'd never observed such a phenomenon before. Highly unlikely. One of the stories I'd heard about Tuppin was that he had once smoked a cigar that cost a thousand dollars. I glanced at Kavin, who was grinning like a pet owner waiting to show off some marvelous trick.

"I have heard," I said, "that when you are in session on the first floor of this building and men are brought up from the cells in leg irons, you require the guards to carry the chains so they don't clank or drag on the floor and—"

"Why do you suppose I do that, Portal?"

I waited before I spoke. I'd not yet taken advocacy lessons, but I already knew that words framed by silence carry more weight. "In order to show respect to the court and to the accused by preventing sounds that could prejudice the presumption of innocence," I finally offered. Out of the corner of my eye, I saw Kavin nod reassuringly.

"Nonsense!" Tuppin shouted. "The fact is I'm hard of hearing. I can't have chains rattling about and feet dragging when I'm trying to hear what's being said in front of my bench. Besides, those lazy louts of guards do nothing but sit around all day. They need the exercise to keep them trim. Fat guards are useless."

I shrank back, wishing I could disappear into the pattern on the silk brocade of the chair's upholstery. I didn't have the nerve to glance at Kavin. I didn't want to witness his surprised displeasure. I kept my eyes downcast.

Which is why I was shocked to hear both Kavin and Tuppin begin to laugh.

"You're a bit of a scaredy-cat, aren't you, lad? You're going to have to learn to look up and argue, boy," Tuppin said. "The floor is not going to testify to a thing."

I smiled tentatively. Tuppin almost smiled back. "Magistrate Bigelow," Tuppin intoned, "a wiser man than I, once said, 'In the profession of law, the cardinal virtues of courtesy, consideration, dignity and patience are in importance of first magnitude.' You can't go wrong remembering that. You might also remember," he added, "that the smaller a man is, the heavier the responsibility of the law to guard his rights, whether he be a man in chains or the fellow who guards that man."

He took a strong pull on the cigar. In the seat beside me, Kavin was puffing away looking as if he were in heaven. I blinked my eyes. They were beginning to sting.

"On the whole, Portal, the profession of law is like any other. A money man is going to make money. A better man is going to make a name for himself. The best man is going to make a difference." His gaze met mine. His eyes were blue, hard and cold, but there were laugh lines at their corners. "How do you propose to make a difference, young man? More to the point, what do you think I could have to do with it?"

I fought the urge to fidget. As if I hadn't been reading about him for weeks, none of Sheldrake Tuppin's legal victories came to mind. He was waiting for an answer, but I couldn't think of one. All I *could* think of was my mother and father. How all my life they'd seemed to pin their future on my intelligence. Where was that intelligence now?

Into the embarrassing silence of the room came the melodious chimes of the City Hall clock marking the quarter hour. "Your Worship," I finally said, "I come from decent and law-abiding people not much different, I guess, from those people down in the street. But I know that not everyone has the privilege of living such a life." The image of the woman at the morgue came to mind. "I just want to use the law to help people who may not be aware that the law exists to serve us all."

"Noble sentiments glibly expressed, Mr. Portal. But

what do these notions have to do with me?"

With him? A man whose long line of educated ancestors stretched back for generations—men of business and the law, men born and raised in the New World? He could command respect not only from the lowly who were brought before him but also from the exalted who were his brothers on the bench. He had so much, read so much, wrote so much. What did my ideas, my feelings, my future have to do with him, indeed? Simply this: I believed I could become as good at law as he was and I wanted my chance.

"The worth of a man, Magistrate Tuppin," I said, "is not determined by where he has come from but by the place to which he has arrived. All I want is the opportunity to start my journey—to move toward where I deserve to be."

The hard blue eyes flashed. Anger at my impudence? Kavin drew an audible breath. Tuppin spoke. "You think you have the right to aspire to the bench, Mr. Portal? Is that why you wish to dog my steps? You think you can be that good? Well, young man, I have only two words for you. They are words you'd best be prepared to hear every day of your life. You think you're the best? Well, Ellis Portal, *prove it!*"

As we made our way out of the building, Kavin was silent. I wasn't sure what he had hoped to accomplish by springing the Tuppin meeting on me unannounced, nor did the professor reveal what he thought about my exchange with the old judge. Personally, I felt exhilarated. If Tuppin wanted me to prove my worth, clearly he thought I *had* worth. I hadn't the least idea what to do next, but I knew I could figure something out. The intimate tête-à-tête with the best-known magistrate in the city fuelled my ambition, made me more determined than ever to prove to Tuppin that I was his man.

Kavin and I headed back toward University Avenue and passed the Supreme Court of Ontario at Osgoode Hall. Just behind it, on Armoury Street, construction had stopped for the day on the site of the new county courthouse that would hear superior court cases, including murder. Murder. Nothing could be more important to the justice system than bringing a killer to justice. I felt I'd done fine on this first "test" with Tuppin because the door was still open. But I realized that now that Tuppin was aware of me, I was vulnerable to his displeasure. A wrong word from him could ruin me. If he thought I could work up a credible homicide case, he might be impressed. If, on the other hand, he ever found out that the evidence for that case was illegally obtained, he'd have me thrown out of law school.

"I'd get busy working up that international law matter if I were you, Portal," Kavin said when we parted company.

I GOT HOME TO find the house on Clinton Street empty except for my father. "Your uncle wants to see you," he said by way of greeting.

I didn't need to ask which uncle. Salvatore, my father's brother, the moneybags, was paying for my education and was becoming uncomfortably and increasingly interested in the outcome of his investment. "Yeah, yeah. I'll give him a call."

I went to the fridge. More out of habit than hunger. Kavin had indeed come through with a significant hamburger.

"Where is everybody?" I asked, but my father didn't answer. I noticed a glass of wine on the kitchen table in front of him. "Why are you drinking? Is something wrong?"

As was his habit, he spoke to me in Italian, but I was beginning to find it hard to understand him, as if I'd begun to forget his mother tongue, which was emphatically not my own. I had to strain to get what he was saying. "Today," he began, "Vince Caterina, my assistant, and I took off from the job early and went to Mass."

"Mass!" My father never went to church.

"We went as a remembrance for Giovanni Fusillo and the Mantellas and Carriglio and Allegrezza. You know who I mean?"

"Sure, Pa. The construction workers who died a few years ago digging the water-main tunnel up at Hogg's Hollow."

"Five years ago today." He took a sip of wine and stared at the golden liquid left in the glass. "Those men were down there with no hard hats, no flashlights, no equipment for oxygen. When the tunnel caved in, they were trapped, choked by smoke from burning cables and stuck in mud. There were no safety rules. None."

"I know, Pa," I said softly.

"Listen, son," he said, making eye contact with me, another thing he seldom did, "when you see Salvatore and he tells you how you're going to be as rich as he is being a lawyer with a lot of big clients, you tell him you're going to be the kind of lawyer who helps people like Giovanni Fusillo. Not rich people, but people like us. You tell Salvatore that, you hear?"

"Yeah, Pa," I said, convincing neither my father nor myself. "Sure I will."

Chapter 5

The x-ray showed more than a dozen wounds peppering the chest of what appeared to be an adult male. Against the fragile outline of his ribs, the dark shadows looked like moths caught in a cage. I studied the text, searching for the explanation of the photo, which I thought was of a man sprayed by machine gun fire. But, I soon discovered, this was not a gangster shot many times by a rival thug. It was instead a farmer hit once by the accidental discharge of his own shotgun. I closed my book and drifted off to sleep.

When I woke up, I saw that my brother's bed had not been slept in.

I hurried down to find him sitting at the kitchen table with his head half-hidden by a large bowl from which he drank *caffe latte* like a puppy lapping up its breakfast. Michele was wrapped in a dusty, damp-looking sleeping bag and my mother was buzzing around him like a helicopter, alternately berating him in loud, angry Italian and tousling his curly hair, which seemed to have bits of debris stuck to it. When he put down the bowl, I thought his lips looked blue. But otherwise, I couldn't see anything wrong with him.

"What's up?" I asked, grabbing the top slice from a pile of Italian-bread toast in the center of the table.

"Non capisco questo!" my mother screeched, "that's what's up. We come to Canada so your brother can sleep in the street like a dog. Eat this."

She plunked a bowl of mashed bread sweetened with honey and soaked with milk in front of Michele. He frowned and pushed it in front of me. I pushed it back.

"She's uptight because I stayed out all night."

Glancing at his rumpled, stained clothes, I couldn't pass up the chance to tease him. "Must have been some date. Are you sure she's the kind of girl you should be going with?"

"Yeah," Michele answered with a sneer, "I go for girls who sleep in the street and you go for girls whose fathers *own* the street!"

"Shut up!"

"You shut up!"

"Stop!" my mother yelled. "This is the holy season of Our Lord's sacred Passion. No loud voices in my house!"

Michele and I simultaneously burst out laughing. "Right on, Ma," Michele said.

"So what *is* up?" I asked, helping myself to a couple more pieces of the crusty toast, brown and crisp at the edges, soft, golden and dripping with butter in the center.

"A few of us skipped classes yesterday," Michele said, "and went down to University Avenue to demonstrate in front of the American Consulate. Show our solidarity with the Selma marchers. More and more people kept coming, and the pigs, the cops, I mean, were getting really uptight. Man, it was cool."

"You're not going to think it's so cool if you land in jail," my mother warned.

It wasn't a wise thing to say. At the very mention of jail, Michele's eyes lit up. I already harbored the legal professional's terror of having a criminal record. I was appalled at my brother's disregard for the likely consequences of arrest. He would surely become a hero among his friends if he were arrested, especially if it took place in front of the American Consulate, the most preferred site in the whole city to demonstrate for or against any cause.

"Anyway," Michele went on, "somebody thought it would be groovy to sleep there all night. So we did. Only, the pigs kept picking us up and dumping us farther and farther down the street, like in front of the Canada Life Insurance building." He shook his head. "It got pretty exhausting toward dawn. Plus it rained all night."

"Listen, Michele," I said, "maybe this isn't the best time, but I have to talk to you about Billy Johnson."

"He wasn't there. Selma's not his bag. He's more into Vietnam," Michele said. "Besides, he can't hang out near the consulate. Some Yank coming out of there might see him and turn him in." He cast me a hopeful glance. "Why do you need to talk to him? Are you going to help him? Is that what you're saying?"

"I may be in a position to suggest something," I told my brother. "But I need to know the details of his case. If you can arrange a meeting, I'll talk to him and see what I can do."

"Far out!" my brother exclaimed. He rose and reached across the table to give my shoulder a grateful squeeze. As he sat back down, he accidentally hit the table, causing it to jerk and tip his bowl of *latte*. A stream of brown liquid splashed up and landed on the sleeping bag he was wearing. He stared at the big wet spot, then rubbed it hard with his hand as if to massage it into the cloth. One more badge on the uniform of the resistance.

THE DAY TURNED OUT TO BE yet another on which there was no sign of Gleason in class. I didn't have a lot of time to waste looking for him or even thinking about him, I told myself. Yet I found it hard to ignore the fact that he had something on me. He could accuse me of stealing evidence, just as he had threatened to do. In reality, though, there were two more pressing reasons I needed to know where and how Gleason was. First, he held the only clues to the homicide, and second, more importantly, whether I admitted it or not, Gleason was my friend.

He didn't answer the phone and I ran out of dimes trying, so I decided to ambush him at his home again.

This time, a maid in a black dress with a white apron answered the chime. She let me step inside when I told her I was a friend of Gleason's from law school, but made me remain near the door while she went to announce me. She came back after a few minutes, took my coat and showed me into a sitting room, not the same one Gleason had ushered me into earlier, but a larger, more opulent one. Wallpapered in what looked like gray silk, it was dominated by an ornate, startlingly white fireplace and mantel, over which hung a life-size, three-quarter portrait of a young man whom I at first took to be Gleason. The subject of the portrait was as boyishly handsome, cheekbones and all, as Gleason, but, I soon noticed, looked taller and stronger, wirier.

On the mantel at the base of the portrait sat two black vases, each holding a bouquet of white lilacs and orchids, which sent a sharp, sweet scent into the cool air of the parlor. Threaded through each of the bouquets was a black satin ribbon that had been tied in a small bow in front, then left to trail down to brush against the stark white marble.

"There we have Gerard Alexander the Dead," came Gleason's voice behind me, surprising me so that I dropped my hat and had to suffer the indignity of picking the cheap thing off what was clearly an expensive Persian carpet.

At my look of confusion, Gleason smiled and said, "Sorry to keep you waiting." He gestured at a chair. "Sit down, Portal." He himself perched on the edge of a small couch upholstered in the same fabric as that on the walls.

I took a chair opposite him. He was dressed in a suit again. But not the same one. His attire struck me as appropriate for a house of mourning. "Gleason," I said, "I'm sorry I've been, uh, harassing you. I missed you at school and I thought I should come over here and check. I didn't know your brother had died. I . . ."

I didn't want to admit I'd forgotten whether he'd even told me he had a brother.

"Gerard died four years ago in a skiing accident in Switzerland," Gleason said. "He was caught in an avalanche and disappeared under a thousand tons of snow. They never found his body." He recited these facts with a chilling lack of emotion. I thought of Michele, grubby after a night working for the cause of justice for Negroes. If anything had happened to my brother, I'm not sure I could have borne my grief. "Three days ago," Gleason continued, "a ski patrol found what was left of Gerard at the base of a slope that had begun to thaw after an unusually warm winter. Ain't spring wonderful?"

His odd behavior at the morgue and in the days since seemed to make sense. Despite his cavalier attitude, he must have been profoundly disturbed by the grim discovery.

"Gleason," I said, looking at him, though he refused to make eye contact, "I'm so sorry."

He ignored me. "Now," he went on, "the parents have flown to Switzerland. Gone to get Gerard and haul him back. I offered to go with them, but they ordered me to stay home and work on my studies, such as they are, including my so-called law project." He laughed. "Sorry about telling Kavin you'd brief him," he said. "I presume he grilled you to find out what we're up to."

"It was careless to mention anything about that night at the morgue, Gleason," I admonished. "Kavin didn't ask any questions, but what would I have said if he had? You don't have a project here. You—"

"Not yet," Gleason interjected, springing up from his seat and reaching into his jacket pocket. With alarm but with no surprise, really, I saw he had not returned the rings. "But we have these. Don't you remember how in Criminology, old What's-His-Name told us that evidence is like a brick road? You lay the first brick, then you stand on that to get a view of where to lay the next brick."

"Look, Gleason, I know you're shocked about the finding of Gerard's body, but like I said, you've got to return those rings. Even if the death of the woman at the morgue was homicide, you're a law student, not a detective. Give back the evidence and forget about this. Let the police handle it."

"What police, exactly, Portal? Would that be the police who accompanied the body? Remember that cruiser? What was it doing there? Did it remain after the body was brought in? Was it the police who carted the body off before Slater could even start the autopsy?"

"Slater? Oh, the pathologist."

Have you seen anything about this in the paper, Portal?" Gleason asked.

"No."

"Doesn't that strike you as odd? A woman is found dead with a bag over her head, then her body disappears—" he paused "—but not before we saw it. And saw that in addition to what appeared to be her horrifically unusual manner of death, the woman was also harboring unusual secrets." Gleason began to pace, his leather shoes making no sound against the rich carpet. In fact, for a few moments there was no sound in the huge house at all except the stately ticking of a grandfather clock somewhere far off, like a heartbeat. "We can put this together, Ellis. We can build a case."

"For lawyers, a homicide case doesn't begin with a victim, Gleason," I reminded him. "That's police work. For us, a homicide case begins with something we clearly do not have here."

"What?"

"An accused," I answered.

"Exactly, Ellis. Exactly! That's what we're looking for. That's what we can find. *Have* to find."

I slumped back and the delicate chair in which I was seated creaked ominously. I felt defeated. Gleason was like a dog with a bone. With two stolen bones, actually. The easiest and maybe safest thing to do was to play along for now. I'd never known Gleason to be interested in anything for very long. In fact, the more unusual a problem was and the more passionately he embraced it at first, the more quickly and completely he forgot about it in the end. "So what are you suggesting, Gleason? What do you see as your next step?"

He sat down on the couch but leaned forward, eager to outline a plan he must have spent some time considering. I listened reluctantly at first, but soon found myself drawn in, if not by the logic of his reasoning, then by the intensity of his presentation.

"That dead woman," he said, "wasn't rich."

"No. Her clothes were inexpensive. And the only jewelry she wore was a cheap watch on her right wrist. Do you remember how the pathologist said the hands were stopped at five minutes past twelve—like in some murder mystery?"

"Forget the time on the watch," Gleason said, "it's too small a detail to help us at this stage and may just be a coincidence in any case. I think the woman must have realized she lived in a neighborhood where it wasn't safe to wear valuables. That would explain both the absence of jewelry on her body and the presence of jewelry secreted on her person."

I thought about that for a minute. "That's a narrow view of the evidence," I finally concluded.

"How so?" Gleason's voice had an edge of protest, as if he were unwilling to accept disagreement with his theory, whatever it was going to turn out to be. Too bad. I was already endangering my integrity as a future officer of the court by allowing myself to be in the presence of stolen evidence. I was not about to endanger my moral integrity— or my intellectual integrity, either—by keeping silent just because Gleason preferred me to.

"She may have been wearing jewelry when she died," I said. "If she was murdered, maybe the killer stole her jewelry. In fact, she may have been killed *for* her jewelry. Or she may have been killed because of the jewelry the murderer failed to find."

"That was a pretty complicated way to kill a person, and not possible without premeditation. The killer would have to have had the bag and the rope with him," Gleason speculated. "Could you see both ends of the rope that was around her neck?"

It pained me to do it, but I closed my eyes and forced myself to picture as much as I could remember about the corpse. In my mind's eye, I saw one end of the cord in the long, slender fingers of the deceased. Her nails were dark red. Or were they? I wondered. Was my memory now adding details to the scene? I also saw that one end of the rope was behind her back. And I saw something else that made my eyes fly open. The cord was just like the cord that lent a finishing touch to the silk upholstery of the couch on which Gleason sat.

No, Ellis, you fool, no, it isn't!

"What's wrong, Portal? You look pale. Almost like a white person," Gleason laughed.

"I am a white person, not that that's any guarantee of good manners, obviously," I shot back.

"Just a joke, only a joke," he protested. "You're always so sensitive, old lady. You better toughen up if you plan on being a lawyer." He studied my face and smiled. I had to smile back. There was something sweetly childlike about Gleason. It was hard to remain angry with him. "So, what did you remember just then?"

"I remembered that the cord or rope was more like this upholstery braid than the sort of rope you'd find in a basement or a garage. And I also remembered that one end was loosely in her left hand and the other end was behind her back. There's not much I can make of that. The hands relax when someone is choked, don't they?"

"The whole body relaxes," Gleason answered, wrinkling his nose at the implications of that.

"I wish we could have seen under that bag. If only they'd left us alone there."

"Now who's talking about tampering with evidence, Portal? Anyway, forget it. We have to go with the rings. It's all we've got." He bounced them in his hands like coins. The clinking sound made me cringe. My whole future was literally in the hands of this troubled and troubling companion. "Unless . . ."

"Unless what?" I asked in alarm.

"Unless we can get to that pathologist," Gleason answered. "I've thought about this a lot," he went on. "Maybe Slater was just doing his job. He seemed pretty cool before he disappeared. Remember, Portal, it's really two bodies that are unaccounted for, the dead one of the woman and the one still presumably alive."

"What are you getting at?"

"Let's take this prima facie. On the face of it, the pathologist is following normal procedure. He gets a phone call. He leaves the autopsy room. He goes upstairs and they tell him they know he's in the wrong lab and to get the body out of there pronto. He does. Next door he finishes the job. Learns the cause of death. Files his report. Case closed."

"No," I said after a minute's thought. "That makes no sense at all. Either he brought us into the wrong lab by accident, in which case he would have realized his error the minute he saw the corpse, or else he did it on purpose—and against the wishes of his boss. If that's what happened, why not just get rid of *us*?"

"Portal, that's what they tried to do."

"I'm not so sure. The pathologist didn't intend for us to be ejected. He said he'd be back. Only, as we know, that was the last we saw of him. Where does that leave us?" I asked.

"If they're on the level, it leaves us with a coroner's report that's public record, plus—" he raised his fist and jingled the rings again "—a nice souvenir of our friendly visit to the city morgue."

A thought struck me. "At what time did you know our meeting was on?"

"What?"

I cast my mind back to the evening in question. "When you called me, Gleason, you sounded rushed. You said you had a meeting at the morgue, an appointment to discuss your law project. What I want to know is when did you set up that meeting at the morgue?"

"I don't know," he answered offhandedly. "I guess it was the same day we went there. I read an article in the *Daily World* that morning. It said the attorney general and the chief coroner had had an argument. They'd almost come to blows at some luncheon they'd both attended. I thought that meant things at the morgue might get pretty interesting." Gleason's eyes were firmly fixed on the carpet, fully incapable, it seemed, of meeting mine. Since when had he ever followed news stories related to our field? This was the second time he'd mentioned the news.

"It's true, Portal," he went on. "Remember that discussion we had in Kavin's class? The A-G doesn't like that the chief coroner won't toe the political line. And he's not happy that the number of autopsies and inquiries has skyrocketed because the chief insists on paying attention to the questionable deaths of people previously ignored, like drunks who die in the street. Chief Coroner Rosen's got the notion that the public should be more involved in inquests."

I applauded Rosen's position, but I didn't see how it would further his cause to allow two green law students to view a possibly controversial and, I supposed, complicated autopsy. "I don't get it," I said. "If Rosen wanted observers who were representative of the public, why choose two innocuous law students? More to the point, why allow us in and then kick us out?"

Gleason continued to study the carpet with its muted colors and complex design, as if the pattern were some sort of code that might reveal the answers to our questions. "I don't know," he finally said. "It wasn't Rosen who let us in, it was Dr. Slater. Don't you think we ought to find that doctor and talk to him?" He opened his hand and stared at the rings that lay on his palm. "And we have to find out who made these rings. Because whoever made them is likely to know the people who wore them."

"Look, Gleason," I finally said, "I've told you before, I'm not into this. I'm not getting sucked into any sort of joint law project and I'm not taking the risk of getting into trouble over stolen evidence. You do what you want. I disavow any and all involvement."

"You're a coward, old lady. That's what you are, nothing but a lousy coward!" Gleason stood up and darted toward me. Startled by his sudden, uncharacteristic fury, I stepped sharply to the side. The back of my knee grazed a tiny table, and behind me I could hear some object teeter, then hit the carpet with a soft thud. I turned. A heavy ceramic jar lay on the floor. To my consternation, there was a huge chip visible at its base. How could I have chipped it when all it had hit was the rug? I bent down to pick it up.

"Don't touch that!" Gleason said.

I sprang back, expecting him to retrieve the object, but he left it. He came close to me, almost spitting in my face.

"You'll never be anything but the son of a construction worker, you know that, Portal? You want to be somebody's honest little legal lackey, some hero to the seamstresses and the pipefitters and the greengrocers? Fine. You do that. You love to follow successful people around like a pudgy puppy, but you don't have what it takes to be top dog yourself and you never will. If you don't take chances, if you're afraid of risk, if you're too much of a chicken to take the leap, you can count on getting absolutely nowhere as a lawyer. You can look forward to a fine life of writing wills for people who leave a pittance or getting them off drunk charges or signing their passport applications so they can go back where they came from!"

"Gleason, you'll always be a snob, and you're crazy, besides!" I backed away from him.

"You have to help me find out what happened to that woman," he persisted, as if he hadn't insulted me or heard a word of my protest. "If it's a murder and I solve it, I'm made."

He *was* delirious. He had to be. In the hierarchy of lawyers, it's hard to imagine a lower rung than that occupied by criminal counsel prosecuting—or worse, defending—the desperate killers of desperate people.

"Gleason," I said, moving toward him again, but avoiding touching him, "you may not realize it, but the discovery of your brother's body has affected you profoundly. I think you need some rest. Forget about your project. Maybe I can keep Kavin off your back. I'm working on something that you might be able to help me with."

He shook his head but didn't argue. He sat down and put his head in his hands. Despite the condescension he had just shown me—always shown me—there was something about Gleason that aroused my sympathy. I took the chair next to him. "Listen," I said, "if it'll make you feel better, I'll check around about the rings. And I'll see if that pathologist will talk to me. In the meantime you find a way to give the rings back. You've seen them. You don't need them. If worse comes to worst, you can write some note about how you accidentally found them in your possession and mail it with the rings back to the morgue."

Gleason didn't respond. I liked his silence even less than his hysteria. "Leave the matter with me for a day or two, okay?" I suggested. "But get rid of those rings now."

"Okay," he finally answered, but I had my doubts. Nonetheless, when he summoned the maid with my coat, he seemed composed, and I left Whitney Square, hopeful that either I'd handle whatever was bothering Gleason or that his grief over his brother would run its course.

As for my promise to him, I thought maybe I'd make a drawing of the rings and show it to a jeweler in our neighborhood. I also thought I'd look at obituaries in the paper, maybe even check out some funeral homes to see if arrangements had been made for anyone fitting the description of the dead woman.

It wasn't until later that I thought about the slimy pawnbrokers on Church Street and the shady embalmers known to my uncle Salvatore.

But before I delved into any of that, I needed to deal with something Gleason had said. If the autopsy of the dead woman had indeed been completed, he'd reminded me, there would be a coroner's report that was a matter of public record. I decided there was still time that afternoon to look it up.

It was ten to five when I turned onto Lombard Street, and a minute or two later I ran up the stone steps and pushed open the door of the morgue. I could tell by the distant clacking of a typewriter that I wasn't too late. I pushed open a second door, this a frosted-glass one with a gold-stenciled sign that read "Office," and stood before a waist-high counter. The only other person present was a small, pretty woman bashing away at a large black Remington. Perfect.

"I'm looking for a recent coroner's report," I explained. "For an autopsy that was performed last Monday—three days ago."

"Yes, sir." The young woman rose and came to the counter. I hadn't noticed, but there was a hinge in it and she lifted a section of counter, stepped out and pointed to a six-foot-high black filing cabinet near the door.

"The reports are always ready by the next afternoon," she told me proudly. "They're filed by date. There are carbon copies behind the original. The public is free to take those, but please don't take my original or I'll have to type the report all over again."

"I wouldn't dream of it," I told her with a grin. She gave me a sunny smile in return. This was a far cry from our dark and difficult reception at the morgue three nights before, and she was certainly more accessible than the shadowy figures that seemed to haunt the place at night.

The reports for the current week were in a middle drawer and right in front, too, so it didn't take me long to find the folder for the past Monday night. Each report in it was typed in clear dark letters on sturdy cream-colored paper with a narrow double red line on the left and the right to keep the tidy little typist from straying out into the wide margins. Behind each original, five onion-skin carbon copies were ranged in ascending order of blurriness.

My fingers raced through the pages. I was fairly sure the office would close at five and I didn't want the helpful clerk to have to stay late at work because of me.

I found three reports for that Monday. All the deceased had died of natural causes. All were male. I thumbed through the reports for the previous day and the one following, too. Then I sweet-talked the young woman into rechecking for me, in case I was looking in the wrong place. When she found nothing, I asked her if she wouldn't mind checking the file containing the notes from which she usually typed the reports.

In the end, concerning a female deceased, age about thirty, dead of strangulation, asphyxiation, or unknown causes, I found nothing. No autopsy results. No pathologist's notes. No coroner's report. No record at all.

Chapter 6

"The Russians walked in outer space today," my mother informed me, "but they won't let their people watch this show." She gestured at the TV occupying one corner of the room that served as our dining room on Sundays and holidays and was a multipurpose room the rest of the time. "They think if people see how good we live, they'll make big trouble." On the eleven-inch screen a housemaid named Hazel was staring indecisively at the contents of a large refrigerator. Maybe her refrigerator, like my mother's, was stocked with more food than an army needed.

"You see that?" my mother said. "Everybody in Russia is going to want a refrigerator as big as that one."

"If they don't have refrigerators, Ma," I asked her, "why do you believe they have TV sets?"

She shrugged. "Everybody around here is so smart."

"Why are you dressed like that?" I asked her. She wore a tidy housedress with a small collar, long sleeves and a narrow belt around her still-trim waist. But on her shoulders sat what looked like one of the blue cotton table-cloths she always took along on summer picnics, and on her head, a smaller tablecloth in white linen was arranged like a stiff veil. Beside her was a pile of linens from the closet in the hall: a stack of white pillowcases, a dish towel or two, a dresser scarf edged in lace. "And what's all this stuff? What are you doing?"

"It's for the Passion Play at church," she answered. Everybody has to make their own costume plus one of the . . . uh, the things people carry in the play. The . . ."

"The props?"

"Yeah. And mine is Veronica's veil. I have to make a Virgin Mary outfit and one Veronica's veil." She laughed at the way that sounded, but I was sure she took the task itself with the utmost seriousness.

I picked up one of the pillowcases and shook it free of folds. It still smelled of the fresh air in which it had hung to dry. Of course it was more closely woven than the burlap bag that had covered the head of the corpse, but it gave me an idea. I opened the case and made a move to put it over my head. I just wanted to see how hard it would be to breathe with the cloth covering my mouth.

But before I got the pillowslip past my eyes, I felt a sharp tug on the fabric and it was yanked away.

"What do you think you're doing?"

It was not my mother, as I'd at first thought, but my father who had put an abrupt end to my little experiment.

"Just something for school," I answered, but careful not to show my displeasure. I wasn't sure why he'd been acting so surly lately, but I didn't want to find out.

"Go in the kitchen and eat," my mother commanded. "I saved you a nice big bowl of pasta and beans."

"Thanks, Ma," I muttered, but I didn't go near the kitchen. I had taken the precaution of consuming a large steak-and-onion sub on my way home from the morgue.

There were three small bedrooms on the second floor of the house on Clinton Street. From one of the rooms came the annoying whine of a song about money and love. Arletta was conscientious about doing her homework every night, but she couldn't seem to handle silence in any significant way.

Nor could Michele. From his room, which was also my room, came the sound of the radio. My brother was listening to the news. I heard him whoop with glee when the announcer said, "Today Negro voters won the legal right to march the fifty miles from Selma to Montgomery, Alabama." I had no idea what that meant, since as far as I knew, the marchers had already been at it all week. But Michele seemed overjoyed and that meant I'd have to hear all about it if I went into the bedroom.

Of course my parents' room was off-limits. None of us ever went in there.

Which left me with the only place in the house where a person could get any privacy. I slipped down the hall and into the bathroom. I took off my shoes, and after arranging my books and papers within easy reach of the side of the bathtub, I climbed in and got to work on my studies. The indignity of this, plus the embarrassment of being a twenty-three-year-old man living off his uncle and his parents, didn't escape me. I had offered to work on construction with my father, but he had refused. My spending money I picked up by tutoring my mother's friends in English. Once I got the internship with Magistrate Tuppin, things would be different for sure, but for now I had no choice.

I cracked open another book from the Law Faculty library. I must admit that as my eye fell on the first disgusting photograph, I felt the tug of old injunctions I'd long ago consciously dismissed. It is a sin to have impure thoughts. It is a sin to provide "marital pleasures" for oneself. It is a sin to have guilty knowledge of sinful things. It is also a sin to look at dirty pictures behind closed doors. The person in the photo had suffered the fate that Michele and I, along with countless other Catholic boys, had been warned would happen if we engaged in hidden and forbidden acts of masturbation. The man in the picture had died *in flagrante delicto*, alone and on the path straight to hell.

The man's tongue protruded and so did his eyes. Even in black and white the icy pallor of the skin of the dead person was immediately obvious. Around the neck of this pathetic creature, who appeared to have died in the prime of life, was a metal collar attached by a long silver chain to the big toe of his right foot. The caption said that the man had died because he'd miscalculated the amount of pressure on the collar and had accidentally strangled himself instead of achieving the semiconscious state he was seeking for the purpose of increasing his erotic pleasure.

I felt flushed and sick, but I kept looking at pictures, hoping to find something that would help me understand what had happened to that woman at the morgue. But there were no women in this book. Could it really be that females never engaged in such shocking practices? I was mulling over that question when the inevitable happened—someone knocked on the bathroom door.

"I need to get in there!" my father yelled. Quickly I hid the book among some others and let him in. If he had been disturbed by my putting a pillowcase over my head, I could just imagine how he'd feel about the book I was studying.

While I was waiting in the hallway, Michele came to the door of our room. "Angelo," he said, "I talked to Billy Johnson. He's so happy you're going to help him. He keeps getting these ridiculous letters from the Selective Service." Michele shook his curly head. "I guess you'll have to figure out a way to show that Billy Johnson is an Indian and therefore not subject to the draft."

"I've been thinking about this, Michele," I said, "and I don't get it. Unless Billy Johnson is an American citizen, why would he worry about being drafted?"

Michele gave me a look I would one day know very well, the look of a client who has withheld some major fact and is now sheepishly about to disclose it. "He was born in Buffalo, New York, so maybe he does like have a problem."

"Maybe he, *like,* does," I answered in exasperation.

"Look, Angelo," Michele said. "I know you could do something different with your time. If you went to Bay Street and advised stockbrokers or went to one of the corporate firms with bankers and real estate developers for clients, you'd be as rich as Uncle Salvatore in a few years. But that's not the type of person you are. And that's not what you really want, is it? To get rich by helping the establishment stab poor people in the back?"

There was no arguing with Michele. At the moment, given the situation with Tuppin, I needed Billy Johnson more than he needed me. I longed to make use of the material I was reading in the gruesome books about homicide, but what could I do? To reveal my involvement there would be to risk everything. But the answer to Michele's question was yes. Yes, I wanted to be rich, rich enough to be able to choose the people whose cases I would work on. I wasn't really interested in international law. I was interested in life and death.

But I told Michele I'd meet with him and Billy on the weekend.

DURING THE NIGHT the weather changed. I was awakened by thunder and lightning shortly after 2 a.m. The wind was howling, and outside something was flapping hard against the side of the house. When I went downstairs to investigate, it was to find that we were in the middle of a blizzard. Snow blinded me as I forced my way out the kitchen door to secure the tarpaulin that had torn loose from my father's truck parked in the driveway. That stopped the flapping, but thoroughly chilled and wide awake, I despaired of getting back to sleep.

In the living room sat a stack of newspapers my brother had left. He bought American and Canadian papers because, as he said, reading several of each every day was the only way to watch history happen.

Idly, I thumbed through the papers. The American ones all had headlines about the Russian space walk, the dismaying escalation of the conflict in Vietnam and the events in Selma. For the first time I found myself wishing I were in Alabama. Just to be in the South. Just to finally get warm.

I shoved the U.S. papers aside and picked up the *Toronto Daily World.* On the front page was a warning that the deadline was rapidly approaching for the Beatles ticket contest Arletta had entered. I wished my little sister the best of luck, but I was far more interested in the headline that caught my eye: "What Is Going on at the Morgue?"

Two photographs accompanied the article. The first was of a stern-looking, middle-aged man whom I took to be the attorney general. The other picture was the Toronto chief coroner, the man whose voice Gleason and I had heard from behind his closed office door. I examined the photo. Rosen was a boyish-faced man about a decade older than I. He had a half smile, almost a smirk. But I liked the look of him, cocky and sure of himself, as if he weren't afraid of anybody, least of all the stuffed-shirt A-G.

I began to read. Outside, the wind sent up a wild, keening groan, but I soon forgot about it as I lost myself in the intricacies of the argument waged between the coroner, who was not a lawyer but a medical doctor, and the attorney general, who was one of the most powerful lawyers in the country. "Both men declined to be interviewed," the article read, "after being found engaged in a loud altercation on the steps of the Windsor Club this afternoon. Ironically, Dr. Rosen was the attorney general's guest at the exclusive club, a bastion of this city's elite."

The Windsor was Sheldrake Tuppin's club. Which meant, not surprisingly in those small circles, that the attorney general was Tuppin's friend. Did that make Tuppin Rosen's enemy?

"Chief Coroner Levi M. Rosen was heard to accuse Attorney General Allan Garrey of carelessness in the discharge of his duties. Garrey returned the volley, charging that Rosen has a wasteful attitude toward the public purse and a contemptuous disregard for the law. The continuing disagreement between the two men stems from Rosen's insistence on conducting full autopsies and, if necessary, coroner's inquests, in all cases of unattended death regardless of the previous living conditions of the deceased. Garrey insists that to spend taxpayers' dollars investigating the deaths of 'riffraff' is a shameful waste."

The article was full of examples of the sort of person whose death interested the maverick coroner: rooming-house inhabitants who failed to wake up in the morning, known drunks found dead in doorways, old people whose relatives had happened to step out just at the hour of their demise. Personally, I could not imagine a body more pathetic or of more concern to him than the one we'd seen. Remembering the three-car cavalcade that I speculated had accompanied the body that night, I recalled that a coroner's vehicle had been among the cars that had pulled in as Gleason and I watched. Had Rosen himself been in that vehicle? Did he have a personal interest? I wondered how difficult it would be to get to see Rosen. Had Gleason pulled some strings running to the coroner to get us into the morgue? I remembered Gleason's evasive reply when I'd put that question to him.

"The two men nearly came to blows," the article continued, "when Coroner Rosen charged that Mr. Garrey's policies have resulted in what Rosen called a 'cover-up' of deaths in 'questionable segments' of the city's population. When contacted later, neither man would elaborate on the meaning of this comment, but the attorney general stated that unless the coroner retracts, he faces being fired."

Could it have been the A-G himself who had ordered the disappearance of the body we so briefly saw? I assumed he had the power to make a report disappear from the files of the morgue. An unsettling thought occurred to me. Had there been any sort of written record of our visit to the morgue? I had as yet only a slender understanding of the structure of the law profession, but I had no doubt that if the A-G wanted to prevent two law students from ever becoming lawyers, he could find a way to do it.

Pushing this thought aside as one of those extreme ideas that come to one in the middle of the night, I decided to scan the obituaries. These were Thursday's papers, not too late for Monday's deaths to appear. Several columns of death notices chronicled the passing of ordinary people from ordinary causes. People whose contact with lawyers had probably extended no further than the boring, mundane transactions Gleason said I could look forward to. Gleason was wrong. I wanted as much from my legal future as he did. Someday, I promised myself, I would be a member of the Windsor. And I would not disgrace myself in public by conduct unbecoming a gentleman. I had a lot to learn, but on that windy night in my mother's parlor, I didn't know how much. Limited as my knowledge was in some areas, though, there were things I already well understood, and chief among them was the conviction that having power—or failing that, getting close to others who have power—was the most effective and fastest way of getting things done.

Despite myself, I was beginning to look forward to Sunday after Mass and my meeting with the most powerful man in our family. I hadn't yet figured out what Uncle Salvatore might do to assist me in getting the internship I so desperately wanted, but I knew that he could and would help me. All I had to do was ask.

Chapter 7

On Saturdays Michele, Arletta and I took turns helping my mother with the grocery shopping. I had performed this task since I was seven years old, and my exalted position as an adult and student of law did not relieve me of my obligation. "You live at home, you help," was my father's dictum.

My parents had come from Italy in 1928, and much had changed among the Italians of Toronto since. The son of an immigrant could go to the country's finest law school and a daughter go ape over the Beatles. But many of the little fruit markets and food stores along College Street were run by the same Italian families who had been there since before I was born. Most of these people were what my father called *termitani*. I never asked the exact meaning of the word, but I knew it was used to connote "Sicilian." These dark southern people were held in barely concealed contempt by the *muratori* of Friuli, the fair "wall-builders" of northern Italy like my father. My mother, being from farther south, held no such prejudice, but even though she frequented the *termitani* for small daily needs, she preferred to patronize the Jewish merchants of the Kensington market for the substantial load of groceries she purchased on a weekly basis. "Jews are the same as Italians," she often said. "They know what's what. First God, then family, plus eat right and stay loyal to your own. That's us and that's Jews, too."

This Saturday, the vernal equinox, we'd risen with the sun at six, happy to know that though the frigid weather was winter lingering, the increasing light was a sure sign of spring. The market was a short drive along College Street in the truck. My mother was uncharacteristically silent as we made our way through the narrow streets southwest of the corner of College and Spadina, found a place to park and wrestled with the cloth bags she had made specifically for this weekly exercise in the provision of necessities. We had a set itinerary with only a few minor seasonal variations. This Saturday, for instance, we headed first for the fish stalls on the south side of Baldwin Street rather than the meat market on the north side.

"Why are you so quiet today, Ma?" I asked as I helped her heave a piece of dried cod onto the scale that hung outside the stall.

She shook her head. "You and your brother and sister," she muttered. "I don't know . . ." She glanced at the scale, selected a second piece of fish, hoisted it atop the first, then nodded to the stall owner who had just seen her and come out to greet her. He wrapped the fish and she paid him. "*Grazie*, Hermie," she said.

"*Prego*, Mrs. Portalese," he answered.

"YOU DON'T KNOW WHAT?" I asked her as we crossed Kensington Avenue to the place that we always called the Jewish bakery. If there were Jewish breads and pastries for sale, I didn't know which ones they were. We had been shopping there for so long that bagels, challah, light and dark rye, kaisers, onion buns, and crusty white bread all seemed Canadian to me. My mother selected a dozen hot cross buns, three loaves of bread and a gigantic cheese bun. When she handed the ginger-haired girl behind the counter a two-dollar bill, the girl gave her a few coins in change.

"The bun is for Uncle Salvatore," she said as we re-crossed Kensington. "His wife is too stuck up to go to the Jewish bakery, but he loves these buns. So you'll take it to him tomorrow when you go, okay, Gelo?"

The thought of carrying a cheese bun to Uncle Salvatore's fine neighborhood would have been too embarrassing to contemplate had I not already done it a hundred times. Once, when I'd been about eleven, I'd tossed the bun in the garbage on the way there. Uncle Salvatore had never mentioned its absence. Neither had my mother. But I always suspected they knew what I'd done, and the guilt was enough to follow me for years. I had dutifully delivered the ridiculous gift without hesitation since.

In the cheese store across the street from the bakery, the wares were piled so high that my mother couldn't see the men behind the counter and they couldn't see her. Or so it seemed. "What'll it be, sweetie?" came a voice from behind a tower of Gouda.

"*Provolone*," my mother shouted. "Strong. Sliced. Not too thin."

"You want Italian or Canadian?" asked the voice behind the cheese.

"This you have to ask?" My mother's Jewish inflection was perfect. I heard delighted laughter from the invisible vendor.

"Time for a rest," she announced when we'd finished most of our shopping. Over steaming mugs at our favorite coffee shop, we sat in silence for a few minutes as was our habit. But unlike most Saturdays, my mother was clearly worried about something, and once again I tried to get her to talk. After a few futile questions on my part, she finally volunteered what was on her mind by asking a question of her own.

"That place over there that Michele is always talking about . . . ?"

"Selma? Selma, Alabama?"

"No, the other one."

I remembered the American newspapers. "Raid on North Vietnam: 130 U.S. Bombers Launch Third Aerial Offensive This Week." I reached across the small table and took my mother's work-roughened hands.

"Ma," I said softly, "that's got nothing to do with us. Michele can't be sent to Vietnam, if that's what you're worried about."

She shook her head. "Mrs. Catelli's nephew is going over there. He says he wants to fight the Communists." She hesitated, then she smiled. "After all, everybody should get to watch *Hazel.*"

I gave her hand a squeeze. "Michele is against the war in Vietnam. He's convinced young men are coming up here to get away from it. A Canadian can fight in the U.S. Army if he wants to, but Michele is trying to help people who want to resist the war."

I wasn't sure I'd put her mind at ease, but she seemed to relax. She sat back and sipped her coffee. "When you go to see Uncle Salvatore," she said, "don't tell him you have to put a pillowcase over your head for school."

I laughed. "No, Ma."

"Why did you do that, anyway?"

It hadn't occurred to me that my mother might be interested in the grim puzzle that I couldn't seem to get off my mind. I certainly wanted to spare her the disturbing image I now seemed to carry in my head night and day. But I often confided in her, so gently I began to reveal what was on my mind.

"Ma," I said, "the other night I had an appointment at the morgue. It was a fairly routine situation. Gleason Adams and I were supposed to observe an autopsy. You know what that is?"

She nodded. Her eyes were locked with mine and I knew she wanted me to continue. I struggled to speak slowly so that she could fully understand. "When we got there, there was a delay in letting us in, as if they'd forgotten the appointment or didn't want to honor it."

"You should have got family to set it up and not that school," she said.

"Yeah. Anyway, once they finally let us in, what we saw was . . . Well, I guess it was frightening. It was a body with a bag over its head. The bag was tied around the neck and—"

"The person was murdered? Like on *Perry Mason*?"

"I don't know. Maybe. That's what I'm trying to find out."

She looked alarmed—and confused. "I don't understand, Gelo. You can't try out killing yourself to see if it works in a project for law school! I'm not going to let you do that. No wonder your father gets so mad."

"The point is, Ma, I don't think just putting a loosely woven burlap bag over a person's head would do it. There's more to this. The woman may have died from the cord that tied the bag." I thought about her hand, which appeared to have been holding that piece of silky-looking rope.

"A person can choke themselves by tying something around their own neck?"

"Strangle," I answered. "The right word is 'strangle.' But I don't know the answer to your question. I'm trying to find out how a pathologist—that's a doctor who studies the cause of death—would know whether a person committed suicide or was murdered or perhaps met with an accident."

My mother considered this for a moment. "There is always somebody around who kills himself or even herself."

"What?"

"I don't like talking about stuff like this, son, but the Church says a person who kills theirself goes straight to hell. I don't understand why, because people who do that aren't right in the head. Sometimes they're real sick and they don't want to tell their family and be a burden. Sometimes they did a wrong thing and they're afraid of everybody finding out." She hesitated, drank her coffee, resumed in a low voice. "Shame is a bad thing to live with. And it only happens to people who are good underneath. If not, then why would the person care so much about doing something wrong?"

"You mean you think that if that woman in the morgue killed herself, it might be because she was ashamed of something she'd done?"

"Maybe."

I could think of only one shame that would be serious enough to cause a woman with no rings on her fingers to commit suicide. "I wish I could have seen the autopsy. Then I would have known whether she was pregnant."

My mother shuddered. "I know sometimes a nice girl goes around with people who aren't nice, but to kill yourself when you're expecting," she said with horror, "that would send you straight to hell."

THAT AFTERNOON I PLANNED to work on my Tuppin proposal. If Michele's friend Billy was an American citizen, there were whole new areas of law I needed to look into. Professor Kavin had told me, "Tuppin loves Americans but never admits it." I didn't know now what to do with that bit of information, but I planned to use it somehow.

However, after only an hour in the library, I gave up. Doodling in my notebook, I made a sketch of the two rings. It wasn't hard. I drew the two bands so that when the rings were right side up, they were mirror images of each other, gold and silver on the opposite sides. I showed how the inscription was engraved on each and then wrote it out separately. "If you love me, leave me by dying."

In all my long years of legal-case preparation to come, I followed a simple rule, one that I'd already figured out by the time I began my search for the maker of the rings: Begin with what is closest to you and use it as a step toward the next fact. I started with the Italian jewelers whom our family patronized. We were not rich people, but we had gold. Every Italian does.

"You're Angelo Portalese's boy, aren't you?" The first jeweler looked me over carefully.

I pretended to study a display case in which gold chain bracelets were lined up in increasing order of thickness. "Yes," I answered, waiting for the inevitable next question.

"Time's coming soon when you'll be looking for an engagement ring, eh?" This was accompanied by a knowing smile that sent me hurrying back out into the street. But it also made me think about the redhead at school and the ginger-haired bakery girl and even the pretty clerk at the morgue. I tried to remember whether I'd seen a ring on her hand when she'd lifted the section of counter to offer me assistance.

Thoughts of engagement rings led me to Durston's. This establishment, Toronto's answer to Tiffany, was a far cry from the local shop. Row upon row of gleaming glass cases harbored sparkling gems of the utmost clarity and depth of color: diamonds, rubies, emeralds, sapphires and lesser stones with names I did not know.

One case held nothing but wedding bands. I tried to get a good look at them without attracting the attention of a salesman, but of course, this proved impossible.

"Can I help you, sir?" The tall, lean man in a suit that looked nearly as costly as the ones Gleason wore bore a remarkable resemblance to David Niven.

"I'm looking for a particular style of band," I improvised.

The salesman made a sweeping gesture at the wares before us. "We have a large selection, as you see, sir," he said. "Would you care to look at one of these?"

As if thinking about what I'd like to be shown, I studied the rings in the case. Everything looked so new, not only because the rings were unworn, but also because of the style. Even the plainest band looked more modern than the rings Gleason and I were investigating.

"Do you ever do custom-made rings?" I asked.

I thought the man stiffened a little at the question, as though he was offended by the implication that the selection he offered might not be wide enough to suit my needs. Or perhaps it was my imagination. "We can arrange for you to speak to one of our jewelers directly, sir," he said, then added, "if you are sincere in your interest."

I took the hint. "Thanks," I said. "Thanks for your help. I'll keep looking."

A dead loss. I tried the jewelry departments at Eaton's, Simpson's and Hudson's Bay, but I saw nothing that gave me the least hint as to *how* a person would go about getting a ring made like the rings on the body at the morgue—or *why*.

Toward the end of the afternoon, I realized that it would soon be Saturday night. Arletta was not allowed to date, and she always spent Saturday night with her giggling girlfriends. As for Michele, he usually spent Saturday night in the company of long-haired women as intense as himself. What they did together I didn't ask. But it usually involved long conversations and the consumption of strong coffee and cheap red wine.

As for me, I sometimes had a date with one of the female students, though never with the elusive red-haired law student who was the only woman on campus—in the world, actually—I really wanted to date. On this night I had no date, and when I found myself walking toward Lombard Street, I toyed with the dumb idea of checking to see whether the clerk might work on Saturday and might be unmarried and might be free and might agree to go out with me.

I decided that was too many mights by the time I got to the corner of Lombard and Church. Instead of continuing on to the morgue, I made a sharp left and walked up the east side of Church, where, in the shadow of St. Mike's cathedral, the pawnbrokers' shops were lined up.

Musical instruments; typewriters; toy soldiers dusty but valiantly arranged in mock battles; books; trophies; insignia of forgotten schools and battalions, choruses and teams; hats; bats; binoculars; record players; objects made of iron, plastic, wood and lead, but most of all silver, gold and gems—jewelry. The teeming windows of the pawnshops on Church Street were cemeteries marked by the stones of lost hope, mistaken love, dashed expectations and, I was sure, narrow escapes.

The salesmen in these shops, I soon learned, were not as suave as David Niven, or nearly as curious as the Italian jeweler. They'd already heard every tale of woe. Their gruff manner as much as said, "Buy, sell or get out." It wasn't until the fourth or fifth shop that I found someone I wasn't afraid to approach with the type of question I'd asked at Durston's. "Do you ever see custom-made rings?"

"In this place what you don't see don't exist," the pawnbroker told me, leaning across a counter piled with black velvet trays of rings, one tray atop another. Against the velvet, the jewels sparkled in the low light of the shop, but once again I noticed how easy it was even for my untrained eye to tell the difference between these previously owned items and the brand-new gems in Durston's. "Are you buying or selling?"

"Neither," I ventured. "I'm just trying to find out where a person could get a certain kind of ring." I slipped the drawing out of my pocket.

"Let's have a look," the man said. I handed him the paper, a little embarrassed by my amateurish effort at drawing.

The pawnbroker didn't seem to mind my lack of artistic skill. He studied the picture so intently that I half expected him to subject it to scrutiny through the lens of the jeweler's loupe he wore on a frayed cord around his neck.

"You know," he said after a long pause, "a pawnbroker gets to see things that other people never see—same as a cop, I guess." He glanced up at me and for a moment I wondered if he thought I was a police officer. The thought flattered me. "But," he went on, "you get used to not asking too many questions, in case you find out something you don't want to know. You get a ring from a nice, good-looking lady and you learn the guy run off with some other dame on the morning of the wedding, that sort of thing."

"Do you think there's a story behind rings like these?" I asked him, trying to hide the desperate nature of my growing curiosity.

Again he studied my drawing and the cryptic quote at the bottom of it.

"Sure there's a story," he said, "and you don't gotta be a genius to figure it out. If this drawing is right, these rings were made of two old rings, one silver, one gold, but the inscription is new. See, you got it going across the place where the gold and silver are joined. Is that how it was on the real rings?"

"Exactly," I answered.

"One thing you always gotta remember about jewelry is that people get it in happy times and get rid of it in sad times. When did you get these rings?"

"I, uh . . . My friend got them," I sputtered. "But yes, you could definitely say they were gotten rid of in bad times."

Again he gave me a look, but I glanced away and he continued his analysis. "A ring's a circle because it's supposed to be eternal, but of course it never is. Sometimes people fool around with that eternity angle. They like to make rings that are circles of precious stones so much the same that you can't tell one from another. That means you can't tell where the circle starts and where it ends. Like I said. Eternity."

I was certainly conversant with the notion of eternity, having had hell mentioned to me on a daily basis for twenty-three years.

"So these rings that my friend has are meant to signify something eternal?" I asked.

The pawnbroker shook his head. He was a short, bald man, about forty, I thought. I wondered how long he'd been incarcerated here, speaking of eternity among the discards of other people's lives.

"Nah," he answered. "Here you got the opposite. You got two symbols of eternity cut in half, interrupted. These rings were made by somebody who wanted to wreck something that was meant to last forever. If the person who cut the rings was the same person who put them back together, then you got somebody—or two people—who wanted to wreck an old union to make a new one."

I looked at him in puzzlement. "What does that mean?" I asked.

He studied me in a way I didn't like, as if he were judging whether I was old enough or wise enough to understand what he was about to say.

"I've seen things like this a few times before," he began, glancing at the drawing, the trays of rings on the counter, the dusty shelves of the shop, but not at me. "I'd say a person who makes something like this wants to kiss the past goodbye."

I didn't quite understand the pawnbroker's meaning and knew better than to press. It was clear he'd told me all he was going to tell me. I was sure of that when he shoved the drawing back at me and said, "I'm busy right now, kid. Bring me one of them rings and I'll give you a hundred dollars. Bring me the two that match and I'll give you five hundred."

Chapter 8

Condominiums are being built in Toronto today with minaret-like balconies that face east to allow Muslims to kneel facing Mecca. In Nathan Phillips Square in front of City Hall, Muslims remove their shoes to pray. Hindus and Buddhists, Druids and Wiccans, Anglicans and Baptists regularly take to the streets for religious observances, sometimes in the dead of winter. Many people think the Italian Good Friday street procession is what started mass outdoor public worship in Toronto, and I am inclined to agree. Our family, friends and neighbors always went to modest Mount Carmel for Good Friday, and then maybe in a few weeks, we'd go again. But on an ordinary Sunday like the one in the spring of 1965, we ignored the politics of Italian churchgoing, refusing to settle on a parish to which we owed our loyalty. Instead, we decided to attend St. Michael's cathedral, where Catholics of all persuasions met in noncombative devotion.

By "we," I mean my mother, Arletta and I. Michele had declared himself to be against organized religion some years before. As for my father, a double *latte* and a chance to go over the soccer scores with his *compaesani* at the Cafe Diplomatico on the corner of Clinton and College were all the church he needed.

I couldn't concentrate on the prayers, which were beginning to be meaningless to me, or on the sermon, either. It was little more than a rant on the hot topic of the day: birth control. Arletta appeared to be listening raptly, but I wondered if her attention wasn't an effort to clue into the mystery of what she was so earnestly being warned to avoid. The only benefit I derived from Mass that morning was that it seemed to take forever, which meant that I had time to think about what to discuss with Uncle Salvatore. I kept awake during the sermon by planning how to ask my uncle about Chief Coroner Rosen or Attorney General Garrey. Since childhood, I'd been warned never to ask Uncle Salvatore a direct question about his acquaintances. In my earlier days I'd assumed that to be mere politeness, but by the time I was in law school, I had a different view of the matter.

KING GEORGES ROAD, Kings Garden, Kings Lynn Road, Kingsmill, Kingscourt. These were the streets I walked on and past to get to the Tudor-style, three-story mansion from which Uncle Salvatore reigned. "He lives in England now," my father had once jokingly said of his brother, but in a way, it was true. Though many of the finest residences in the city were built by Italians, including the workmen who were my father's equals and the contractors who were Uncle Salvatore's, my uncle chose to live in an enclave of old English wealth. The house crowned a treed embankment overlooking the Humber

River. Miles from the crowded grid of the city of Toronto, this curving road, called the Kingsway, graced the western suburb of Etobicoke.

Carrying the cheese bun, so securely wrapped by my mother that it could have stayed fresh until freed by a safecracker, I negotiated the flagstone steps that led to Uncle Salvatore's front door. Half his main floor was one vast room. Through the front windows, leaded glass set in gray, hand-hewn stone, I could see across the expanse and all the way to the set of windows at the rear of the house, beyond which was a blur of trees. In front of these rear windows now, a dark silhouette slowly paced. I adjusted my tie, swallowed, rang the bell.

Uncle Salvatore's wealth came from the import and export of Italian food. Crinkly cellophane packages of biscotti and pasta. Exotically shaped jars of peppers and artichoke hearts. Prosciutto ham and provolone cheeses, smoky, salty and smooth. Above all, it came from oil. Not the crude oil of rough places like Texas and Alberta, but the liquid gold of the sun-streaked olive grove.

"You can't tell what he does by looking at him," my mother always said, for my uncle was a slim man who dressed far more conservatively than the non-Italian businessmen who were his colleagues, his neighbors and his friends. His wife called herself "Fay" and told other matrons that it was short for "Faith." It wasn't. Her real name was Fietta. She came by her blond, fair-skinned looks honestly, though. Her people were from Trieste, a part of Europe that had been both Austria and Italy. Aunt Fay had a "past" in the person of another living husband. That she was divorced may have been of interest to her Protestant neighbors on the Kingsway, but it wasn't supposed to mean a thing to us, for as children we'd been instructed to act as if Aunt Fay, living in sin and causing Uncle Salvatore to live in sin, too, did not exist. However, as the years went by, we began to be punished for our rudeness toward her, which signified that time had somehow made her an acceptable part of our family. Unfair and illogical, I know, but not untypical of the Italians of those days.

It being the chronically resentful Irish maid's day off, Aunt Fay answered the door herself. I handed her the bag with the cheese bun, which she took between her finger and thumb like a gift of soiled laundry. "Your uncle Sammy is in the study, Angelo," she said. "He's waiting."

I glanced at my watch. I had phoned ahead to say when I expected to arrive. I was four minutes earlier than I said I'd be. Why was Uncle Salvatore "waiting"?

He didn't rise when I entered. Maybe he was tired from all that pacing. He sat in a high-backed leather chair beside a massive stone fireplace in which a low blaze flickered. His deep-set gray eyes followed me as I crossed the carpet and stopped twenty feet from where he sat.

"Sit down, Angelo," he said in a voice as cold as our winter weather. "Have some wine."

I moved closer and accepted a small crystal goblet of sweet muscatel. Afternoon light from the leaded windows behind Uncle Salvatore caught in the depths of the musky liquid and made it glow like an old topaz.

"How's school?"

I took a sip of wine. I took my time. Uncle Salvatore, for all his industry, was never in a hurry. Important men aren't. "Fine, sir. Thank you."

I could feel the cold eyes on me. "I hear you met with Sheldrake Tuppin the other day."

It had been a very long time since I had been surprised by anything my uncle knew about me.

"I hear that as soon as you turn in a proposal, things will get moving. So how's that proposal coming along?"

I shifted uncomfortably in my chair, and the burgundy leather groaned under my weight. "I work on it every day," I answered. It was one of those lies that you realize are almost true the second after you utter the words.

"And what exactly is this project?"

This was a question I'd been preparing to answer since I'd learned I'd been summoned to report to my uncle. "It's a matter of international law," I began strongly. "A potential challenge to policies of the United States government as those policies affect Canadian nationals."

Uncle Salvatore seemed to watch my lips as I spoke. I knew he always feared making a mistake in the correct use of the English language, a fear I didn't have myself, the only advantage I had over my uncle. I paused, but he said nothing. I took his silence as an invitation to continue. "I'm engaged in preliminary research to ascertain the rights of an individual whose citizenship is at present a matter of some controversy and—"

"There's no money in helping draft dodgers," Uncle Salvatore cut in. "And no lawyer—or judge either—is going to be interested in a client like that. You better come up with something more important than a bum who wants to get out of his duty to his country. And besides, you're a fool if you think a law student can take on the United States government."

Already that Sunday I had sat through a sermon I didn't want to hear, eaten a heavy lunch in a state of total anxiety, crossed town under the depressing gray skies of a winter that would not end, frozen my limbs walking through the meandering streets of this fake kingdom and been polite to Aunt Fay. But only now did a dangerous anger rise in me. I was not some obedient boy. I was not just another slab of comestible to be bought and sold by my rich uncle.

Not sure whether I was referring to the Billy Johnsons of this world or to myself, I vehemently declared, "The right of a man to control his own destiny is fundamental. A lawyer not dedicated to that principle is not the kind I want to be."

For the first time that day, Uncle Salvatore smiled. "You're right," he said. "You are going to control your own destiny."

Was he agreeing with me or threatening me? I didn't know which was scarier. I dared not say another word. When several long moments of frightening silence had passed, he stood and went to the window, staring out over the trees of the river valley behind the house. Soon they would burst out in the delicate green-lace foliage of full spring, but now they were nothing but bare twigs. As if the sight of them had given Uncle Salvatore back his voice, he turned to me and spoke.

"The most important thing a man can do, Angelo, is to invest. When we came to this country, we had nothing except what we carried in our own hands. But we invested our youth and our time and our hard work and pretty soon we had money to invest, too." His gaze met mine briefly, swung away to sweep across the huge room, then returned to mine. I blinked but did not look away. "The biggest thing a man can invest is his honor. When the war came, we were supposed to forget about Italy. We were supposed to fight for the English and the Americans. We did that, and even then, Italians were put in concentration camps here in Canada."

I fought the urge to shift in my seat again. I didn't want to hear about the internment of Canadian Italians. I didn't want to hear Uncle Salvatore say he'd invested in me. I wanted to go home.

"But we got over that," he said, moving away from the window, "and since the war, we're in a position in this country where nobody's ever going to lock us up again."

"Yes, Uncle."

"All I'm saying, Angelo, is I don't want you to forget what we're doing here." He leaned down and reached for the decanter beside his chair, walked over to where I sat and replenished the quarter inch of muscatel I'd drunk. I smelled the deep richness of the wine and also the astringent lime scent of Uncle Salvatore's aftershave.

"What exactly *are* we doing here, Uncle?" I asked. It was an impertinent question and I could see by the stiffening of his hand as he replaced the decanter that he had not expected further questioning from me. My mind raced. It occurred to me that my father had told me about my uncle's wanting to see me the minute I'd stepped in the door after the meeting with Tuppin. How could Uncle Salvatore have known so quickly where I'd been? Was this meeting with my uncle today, this warning, about Tuppin and the minuscule bit of work I'd thus far done on the Billy Johnson matter, or was it about the visit to the morgue, the stolen evidence? Had somebody tipped Uncle Salvatore off?

He sat, but he remained on the edge of his chair. "I want you to tell me, son. You tell me how the investment I'm making in you is going to pay off. I didn't send you to school so you could help strange people. I mean, strangers. I sent you to carry our family forward in the world and to preserve the honor of Italians in America."

Uncle Salvatore's sense of geography was different from mine if he thought Canada was part of America, though that would certainly explain his unwillingness to challenge the United States government. "Yes, sir." It is, I was learning, useful for a lawyer to appear to agree when there is no advantage to disagreeing.

As if changing the subject, Uncle Salvatore gestured toward the windows. "You like it here, Angelo?" I knew he meant more than the richly adorned study, more than the big house and the great view. He even meant more than the Kingsway. By "here," he meant the top of the heap.

"Yes," I said sincerely. "Yes, I do."

"A man who is smart and who works hard should have something to show for it."

I wondered what my father had to show for his years of bricklaying. Our own house needed tuck-pointing. The mortar was wearing away. The shoemaker's children go without shoes.

"What your father has to show for his hard work is *you*, Angelo," he said, reading my mind. He hesitated, as if an idea had just occurred to him. "Maybe you spend too much time studying. Maybe you and that brother of yours—did he get a haircut yet?"

"No."

"Anyway, maybe you and that brother of yours need a change. Maybe I should send you away."

"What?" I said in alarm.

Uncle Salvatore eyed me. "Away for a vacation," he explained. "How would you and Michele like to go down to the World's Fair over Easter?"

My first reaction to this offer was relief, a sense that Uncle Salvatore's interest in my studies—and my welfare—was as it had always been, that of a kindly benefactor. But I could not get over my feeling of unease at his apparent attempt to manipulate my law project. I also didn't want to interrupt my work, not now when I needed to talk to Billy Johnson again, despite my uncle's view of his case. Not now when Gleason Adams was acting so weird and had as yet offered no indication that he'd returned the pilfered rings.

Uncle Salvatore took my silence for consent. "Consider it arranged," he said. Then he appeared to reconsider. "Not for Easter," he declared. "Your mother will want you with her in church. The day *after* Easter. I'll get one of my secretaries to send a plane ticket to the house for both of you."

I nodded, smiled. A free trip to New York? Why fight it?

I can't say the rest of this visit was exactly fun, but at least Uncle Salvatore had said what he'd apparently summoned me to hear, so we could both relax. We drank the muscatel. We chatted. My uncle asked me about my friends and I told him a little about Gleason and the other law students I "ran" with, to use his term.

Then Uncle Salvatore began to tell me about *his* friends. At first he spoke of his neighbors on the Kingsway, their houses and servants, their horses and the summer cottages they kept on the wooded lakes in the district of Muskoka a hundred miles north of the city. He drew a verbal picture of a life of splendid leisure in which intelligent, influential people with exquisite manners took turns providing elegant entertainment for one another.

"On summer mornings," he said, "Fietta and I eat breakfast in our teak gazebo overlooking the lake. We own every lot on the shore. Nobody's going to ever be able to build there but me."

I wondered whether my uncle knew there was a sadness to this display, an undercurrent of loss and regret. He had no children to inherit his money, his land or his name. Aunt Fay had been perfectly capable of bearing children; she'd had two with her first husband. I sometimes speculated, when I became old enough to understand the complex morality of Catholics, that Uncle Salvatore and Aunt Fay had a platonic marriage in order to avoid the sinful consequences of divorce. My mother had told me to remember that I was like Uncle Salvatore's son, and that since he had no boy of his own, I should treat him with a son's respect.

So I listened. And before long, Uncle Salvatore's discourse shifted from the heights and settled down into the gang-riddled streets of the Toronto that existed before I was born. Now he became animated. He told tales of Italian cops he had known, the only "foreigners" allowed on the English-Canadian police force, and the crooks always one step ahead of them. Despite my ambitions, my fondness for Whitney Square, I found these tales more interesting than the stories about the Kingsway and Muskoka. And when Uncle Salvatore began to talk about his pals in the funeral business, I sat up.

"Business is always good for the undertaker," he said, "good in the funeral parlor and good in the basement." A hint of a smile curved his lips. "Who counts how many caskets go out of a funeral home? Or how many bodies are in each casket, for that matter." He hesitated and as if to caution me in some way, added, "Of course they're all legit now. You don't find any of the old boys pulling those tricks these days. Every Italian funeral is loaded with cops. You can count on it."

"Uncle Salvatore," I asked, "are the same people still in the funeral business?"

"What do you mean, Angelo?" I could see that my interest pleased him. I was also beginning to see a new avenue open in my investigation of the fate of the missing body. "Are the same families still undertakers, *nipote*? Of course they are."

"What are their names?"

He looked surprised. "I guess you're still too young to know the undertakers," he said after a pause. "Spardini, Bianco, Cataroli . . ." He rattled off six names. I wrote them down, along with their phone numbers, which Uncle Salvatore appeared to know by heart.

Again, my intense interest seemed to soften Uncle Salvatore. He rose, walked over to where I sat and put his hand on my shoulder. "Angelo," he said, "it's time for Aunt Fay and me to go to dinner. Our friends eat in the middle of the day on Sunday."

"Yes, sir." I made an attempt to rise, but he held me down in the chair. I wondered what next, until I looked into his eyes and realized the pressure of his hand was meant to be paternal.

"If there's anything I can do for you, Angelo, you just let me know. Anything."

His kindness was overwhelming. It called for a response and I found myself saying the first thing that came into my stupid head. "There is one thing, Uncle."

"And what's that?"

"Tickets. Beatles tickets. Could you get two tickets to the Beatles concert in August?"

Uncle Salvatore looked as if he had lost all hope for me. He took his hand from my shoulder.

Then I heard Aunt Fay's high voice. "Sammy," she called from just outside the door. "We have to go."

Uncle Salvatore laughed, a strong, genuine laugh. "Her, too," he said, nodding toward the voice in the hall. "She loves the Beatles, too. An old lady like her! I'll get the bunch of you all the Beatles tickets you want. You're my family, Angelo. Anything you want from me, you get."

Chapter 9

The days passed and still I had no word from Gleason. I wanted to tell him again he must be very careful. If the attorney general and the chief coroner were aware of our visit, we might be pawns in their feud. More realistically, I wanted to tell Gleason that my uncle was watching me. My only chance to work up a decent law project for Sheldrake Tuppin was to stick to my own work by writing a proposal about Billy Johnson.

I had to admit to myself, though, that what I really wanted to share with Gleason were the results of my "investigation." I wanted to tell him that the pawnbroker had said the rings were worth half a semester's tuition. And I also wanted Gleason to know that, just out of curiosity, I was planning to visit the people on Uncle Salvatore's undertaker list.

But when I called Gleason's home, nobody answered, not even the maid.

Nor had I seen Billy Johnson. I expected Michele to arrange for us to meet. He'd been annoyingly eager for this to happen before I'd decided to use Billy for my project, but now that I was depending on doing so, Michele was suddenly evasive.

"Don't bug me, man," Michele told me when I asked him to set up a meeting. "I'm really hung up on Selma right now. We're doing a sit-in at the American Consulate again tonight."

"Michele," I reminded him, "Easter's less than a month away. I've got to have this project completely finished by then. Especially since we'll be going to New York City right after."

Michele looked up from the protest sign he was lettering. "New York!" he said. "That is just far freaking out!" He shook his curly head. "Look, man," he said, "write out some questions—like what you need Billy to answer. I'll talk to the guy."

Michele was as good as his word. The very next day, he gave me a sheet of paper covered with the tidiest handwriting I'd ever seen. On it was Billy Johnson's own record of the history of his birth. He had been born near Buffalo, New York, during a short period in which his Cree mother had been staying with a Tuscarora Indian friend. At the law library, I researched the American federal statutes that affected Billy and found this clause:

The Immigration and Nationality Act . . . distinguishes between citizens at birth and those whose citizenship was acquired after birth. . . . The following shall be citizens of the United States at birth: . . . A Person born in the United States to a member of an Indian, Eskimo, Aleutian or other aboriginal tribe: Provided that the granting of citizenship under this subsection shall not in any manner impair or otherwise affect the right of such person to tribal or other property.

I studied the limiting clause. Did it mean that Billy's being a United States citizen could not prevent his owning tribal property? Or did it mean that if, under the rules of the tribes, Billy could not own property if he was a citizen of the U.S., then he could not claim such citizenship? Clearly the answer to this question, the interpretation of this section, decided his citizenship. It was an area I'd have to research further by coming up with some authority, that is, case law, to support the view I wished to take, which was that Billy was not subject to the draft because he was not a citizen of the United States. Would such a position prove untenable? That question would be, I decided, at the heart of my law project. I was pretty proud of myself. This was just the sort of legal reasoning a man like Magistrate Tuppin would appreciate. But I knew Tuppin's first question would be "What does your client think of this tactic?" Obviously, to see Billy Johnson in person was still a pressing necessity.

I handed the federal statutes back to the reference librarian. "Thank you, Mr. Portal," she said. She checked a mimeographed sheet taped to the wall beside her desk. "Your name is on the request list this morning, by the way. Check at desk three. I believe an interlibrary loan has come in for you."

I thanked her and went upstairs to the desk she'd mentioned. There waiting for me was a book far more interesting than the statutes. I buried my nose in *Auto-Erotic Suicide: Psychological, Pathological and Legal Implications*. Not only did I forget about Billy Johnson's citizenship problems, I forgot the time of Professor Kavin's tutorial.

"Well, Portal," Kavin declared when I finally arrived, five minutes before the tutorial was supposed to end. "Here's Adams early and you late. That's an unexpected and unwelcome turn of events."

I glanced over Kavin's shoulder. Gleason sat in the chair in front of the professor's desk, a Cheshire-cat grin directed my way.

I shot him an inquisitive glance.

"Didn't your father give you the message?" he asked. "I called you—three times, in fact. Once to remind you of today's tutorial."

My father had given me no messages. I frowned at Gleason. The deceitful little fiend. But on second thought, I decided I was glad to see him, relieved to be able to verify that he was indeed alive and in no trouble.

"Adams took your time slot, Portal. We're finished," Kavin said.

The professor nodded toward Gleason, who sprang out of the chair and grabbed the doorknob, pushing my hand from it. "I'll leave you two alone, then," he said with a leer. "But come by the house tomorrow, Portal. Don't forget. I'll fill you in."

Fill me in on what? What had he and Kavin been talking about? Had Gleason taken it upon himself to conduct some sort of investigation? Was that why he'd been absent from school? I glanced at the professor to see if I could read anything unusual in his demeanor. I couldn't.

"Adams claims the two of you are studying a homicide," Kavin said. "I'm puzzled as to how he expects to construct a criminal-law proposal at this late date and surprised to learn you're involved, but I'm going to give both of you the benefit of the doubt and assume that you've got your signals crossed and failed to communicate with each other before you came to me. I took you at your word regarding the international law project for Magistrate Tuppin. He may have chosen to spend the final years of his legal career in the trenches, but he has been a distinguished scholar of the law for far longer than he's been the drunk-court judge."

"Professor, I don't know what Adams has in mind. I am certainly working on the other matter, just as I said I would." An urge to beat up Gleason came over me.

"Sit down, Portal. I trust that you're on target with your own project. But I'm concerned about Adams. I have very little respect for him as a scholar of the law, but I do care about him as a student in this program." He looked around as though searching for his pipe. Finally, despite being unable to locate it in the mess on his desk, he resumed talking. "Sometimes I fear that young man is in danger of going off the deep end."

I reminded myself that everything is a test. Dealing with pressure was part, a big part, of surviving first-year law. I would no sooner "rat" on a fellow student than expect one to rat on me if I were having trouble juggling my studies and my personal life. Actually, come to think of it, I *was* having trouble and would keep having it, if Gleason didn't shape up.

What had he meant when he'd claimed to have spoken on the phone with my father three times? That was a lie as deep as the ocean. I had to believe that Gleason was still suffering from the grim discovery of his brother's remains in Switzerland. As far as I knew, he was all alone in his huge house and facing the return of his parents with the corpse. That, combined with what had happened in the morgue, would have been enough to make anybody lose his marbles. Wouldn't it?

But none of this was anything I intended to talk to Kavin about. "Look, sir," I said, taking the seat Gleason had vacated and finding the professor's pipe buried in the cushions, "I'll talk to Adams tonight. We kicked around a few ideas and he's been working on one while I've been working on another. We'll—"

"Don't confuse charity with obligation, Portal."

"Sir?"

"Adams is not the excellent student you are. You have to avoid jeopardizing your own project for the sake of assisting him with his."

"I realize that, sir," I replied. But I was confused. What *was* Gleason's project? How much had he told Kavin?

To fill the tutorial time—and to get off the subject of Gleason—I told Kavin about the U.S. statutes. He listened as I outlined the cases I planned to research. Once in a while he nodded, always a good sign with him.

"Stick to the international angle on this, Portal, and you've got something. Dig up the case law. The more cases you've got, the better your position is going to look. Be careful that the authorities, I mean the precedents, you choose are so close to what you've got with Billy Johnson that Tuppin can't get you off guard by particularizing differences. Unless, of course, they're truly inconsequential. You understand?"

"Of course, sir," I answered, though, to tell the truth, I wasn't sure.

He glanced at his watch. "Anything else, Portal?"

I surprised myself by asking Kavin a question that seemed to pop out of my mouth of its own volition. "Professor," I said, "can a person have a decent practice defending people charged with homicide? I mean, can a man make a respectable living at it?"

"Perry Mason seems to manage," Kavin said with a smile.

I smiled back. "Seriously, sir?"

Kavin bit down on the stem of his cold pipe and stared into space for long moments before he finally lit the damn thing and said, "Homicide is a neutral act. By definition, it is simply the killing of a human being. It can be purely accidental. The term implies no moral content whatsoever. Homicide is nonculpable or culpable. Culpable—that is, blamable—homicide is murder. Whether it is suitable or unsuitable to defend a man accused of murder depends, in my view, not on the moral strength of the lawyer or the accused, but on the strength of the case. This, I warn you, Portal, is not the common view. I'm sure the Crown feels any accused killer must be brought to justice no matter how slender the evidence against him. And I'm equally sure that defense counsel feels a man should be rigorously defended regardless of the strength of the damning facts in his disfavor. For myself, despite my many years in this profession, or perhaps because of them, I feel a door must be left open, an opportunity, if you will, for the entrance of natural justice. It is unfair for a lawyer to prosecute those against whom the evidence is slight, and unwise to defend those against whom the evidence is overwhelming."

It was a nicely put, if unconventional, theory. But Kavin had missed my point, or so I thought.

"As for making a living out of it, true, murder is the crowning offence of criminal law." He glanced up at me from behind the thin haze of tobacco smoke that surrounded his head like a mini-volcano. "Portal," he said, "you had the highest entrance exam scores in a generation of law school applicants. You should be looking forward to making law, not to saving reprobates from its clutches. You might have one or two good first-degree murder cases in a decade. Most of your time will be spent pulling desperate people out of fires started by their own foolishness. Those whom you save will love you at first, but they'll soon come to associate you with the bad times and want to have as little to do with you as possible. Those whom you fail to save will consider you a fraud. And both groups of clients will most likely reach these opinions before they've paid your final bill."

Unexpectedly, Kavin laughed. "Nothing deters the determined, though, does it, Portal?"

"Sir?"

"You might take up a criminal practice and indeed become another Perry Mason. You have a rare combination of qualities, Portal. You can think on your feet. You're a fast, effective researcher. You aren't afraid to take on tasks that may put you under considerable pressure. You also seem to be a compassionate man. What other kind would stay friends with Gleason Adams?"

I squirmed, uncomfortable in the glare of so much praise.

"Of course," Kavin added, "I must also say I've noted hints of the requisite hubris."

"Pardon?"

"Pride, Portal. Arrogance. A man who distinguishes himself by robbing the state of its opportunity to pin murder on a man usually has fairly high notions of his own worth. Take our friend, Mr. Knightsbridge, for example."

"Pardon?"

Kavin smiled. "Knightsbridge is the top criminal lawyer in this town. It's been said that Counselor Knightsbridge and the Queen found themselves in the same room together. When the time came to leave, an argument ensued as to who would back away from the presence of whom. It's said that that is how Elizabeth Regina learned to walk backwards in high heels!"

I HAD WRITTEN down all six of the funeral directors Uncle Salvatore had mentioned and found their addresses, but I didn't want to visit any of them before I called and I didn't want to call them from the house, fearing to alarm my mother or enrage my father. From a phone booth on campus, I called the first three. They each refused to see me or even to give me basic information over the phone. The fourth time, I mentioned Uncle Salvatore's name before I even said who I was and what I wanted to know. The funeral director, Spardini, agreed to give me a tour. I didn't bother calling the last two names on the list. One funeral home was about all I was willing to experience in my attempt to discover the final resting place, so to speak, of the body we'd seen at the morgue.

Spardini's parlor was on Danforth Avenue, a street of retail shops, small businesses and ethnic restaurants on the eastern edge of the city. Statues, urns, pillars and fountains guarded this portal to the world beyond.

"So you're Sal Portalese's nephew?" Spardini himself asked me when his shapely receptionist showed me into his office, which, behind the flashy casket showroom, looked like the office of a truck dispatcher. Invoices, funeral announcements, the gilded and beautifully tinted holy cards Italians use to commemorate a funeral, black-and-white photos and even a pinup or two graced the dingy walls of the little room. "The law school boy, am I right? Well, I can show you a thing or two that even a lawyer don't know about."

As if to make good his word in the least amount of time possible, Spardini led me directly to the basement. As we descended the creaky wooden steps, I remembered Uncle Salvatore's vague reference to extra bodies in the cellars of Italian funeral homes.

As if reading my mind, Spardini said, "I want you to understand right off that nothing underhanded goes on here. Every one of these here bereaved is accounted for. You got that?"

"Certainly, I—"

"We got lists listing lists. Records. Lots of records. We got a list even of every body that goes into or comes out of this country."

"Why would that be?" I asked, curious to see that list.

"Board of Health. You got some foreigner coming in here with a disease, we keep him out. Even if he's already dead."

"Could I have a look at the list?"

"Yeah, sure, later. Take a look at this first."

He flicked a switch on the wall of the stair landing and I found myself staring down at a double row of dormitory cots. Mercifully, only four of the cots were occupied. The naked, lifeless bodies of dead men and one woman looked so similar to the white plaster statues outside that I almost laughed.

Spardini made the sign of the cross and asked God to have mercy on his customers. "The embalmer came and went already, so I can't show you that. Sorry."

"That's okay," I choked out.

"The bereaved like to have funerals on Saturday. These ones died on time. Want a closer look?"

Remembering the raw-meat odor of the morgue, I held my breath and followed Spardini to the nearest cot. The woman who lay on it was about seventy years old. I noticed that her pubic hair was snow white. In reaction, I involuntarily sucked in a huge breath of air. It smelled not of flesh but of formaldehyde, like the dead frogs we'd cut up in high school.

"Seventy-six and not a mark on her," Spardini said with as much pride as if he'd created the woman rather than just laid her out.

"What did she die of?" I asked.

"These four," Spardini said, "they're all natural causes. We get way worse than this, let me tell you."

"Do you ever get any with bags over their heads?"

I was amazed I had the nerve to ask the question. Spardini gave me a thoughtful glance, as though there was hope for the law-school boy yet. "Glad to see you're interested," he said. "Yeah, we get 'em like that once in a while. Why do you want to know?"

"For school," I answered automatically. I hoped nobody was keeping track of the absurd information I was claiming to need for my legal education.

"We get 'em now and then. Suicides, I mean. They hang themselves, they drink a lot of wine and then jump off a bridge, they drive their car into a wall. Closed-casket cases, all of 'em. I don't gotta tell you we get a bit of a problem when the priest starts asking questions. But I get all mine into a Catholic cemetery. Guaranteed."

"I'll remember that, Mr. Spardini," I said, not knowing whether to laugh or cry.

"But nothing shady," he emphasized. "Don't get me wrong."

"Have you ever had to work on a murder victim?" I asked, feigning nonchalance.

Spardini neglected to respond. He glanced over the four corpses as if to make sure none had moved, then shook his head in one of those meaningless gestures I was used to in my elders, walked back toward the stairs and turned off the light. "Come on," he said. "I'll show you that list you wanted to see."

Back in his office, he dug through an in-box jammed with papers and finally found what he was looking for, a mimeographed document consisting of a couple of legal-size pages. "This here gets signed by the coroner and the chairman of the Board of Health. We get it every two weeks. The first page is bodies coming into the country. The second page is bodies going out."

Pure curiosity, not an expectation of learning anything, was my motive for reading the list, so I wasn't surprised to see no familiar name on the first page.

"Them lists is proof that nothing shady goes on here," Spardini reiterated.

As he spoke, I idly flipped to the second page of the list. My eye fell on the name at once: Everett Allan Adams, Gleason's father. He was listed as leaving the country accompanied by his spouse and by the cadaver of his deceased son. I reckoned back the days. The date beside the names was the same date Gleason had told me that his parents had gone to Switzerland.

"I wouldn't put a lot of faith in these lists, Mr. Spardini," I said. "I see a mistake on this one."

"What? What mistake?" He yanked the list out of my hand.

"I know this family," I said, pointing. "They didn't take a body out of the country. Just the opposite. They went to Switzerland to pick up a body. They're on the wrong page. The date's probably right, though," I added reassuringly.

Spardini studied the list. Then, in disgust, he threw it back on top of the pile of papers in his in-box. "Damn Board of Health," he said. "You can't trust 'em. In fact, you can't trust a person living on this earth. That's why I like working with dead people."

ON SATURDAY MORNING, a week after I'd visited the market with my mother, it was Michele's turn to take her. Which meant another week had gone by without my yet having met Billy Johnson. I was beginning to be afraid that Michele, for reasons known only to him, was now trying to keep Billy and me apart with the same enthusiasm he had originally shown at putting us together. That notion was dispelled, however, when, as he left the house, my brother gave me Billy's address. He even offered to come with me, but knowing that should I present this to Tuppin, the judge would require client confidentiality, I told Michele I would have to go on my own. I also had to accomplish an extremely important mission before I descended into the neighborhood in which Billy lived. Gleason had summoned me to Whitney Square, and I was going.

I needed to know for sure that Gleason had given back the rings to the proper authorities. His behavior had become incomprehensible by now. After I had seen him in Kavin's office, he had insisted he needed to work on the "murder" for his project, but he'd stopped showing up for class, never went to the library, was never seen on campus.

Thin sun spilled across the square as I walked up from Bloor Street and made my way to Gleason's door, which was answered by the same maid I'd seen before, a pretty blonde with a nice figure and a little smile of recognition.

Distracted by her, I at first missed the sound of voices coming from the parlor where Gleason's brother's portrait hung. The maid disappeared, presumably to get my host, but after several minutes had passed and no one had come for me, I headed toward the voices.

I did not immediately recognize the man who was seated so close to Gleason that his short brown hair almost touched the longer blond locks of my friend. The two men seemed to be in earnest conversation, each sitting on the edge of a spindly-legged chair. I cleared my throat to announce my presence. The brown-haired man glanced up in alarm. It was then that I realized with surprise who he was: Dr. Slater, the pathologist we'd met at the morgue, the man who'd disappeared along with the missing body.

Without his lab coat, he looked younger, thinner, and more like a fellow law student than a scientist. Like Gleason, he was rather formally dressed—cream-colored slacks and a dark blazer. I felt embarrassed to be wearing blue jeans and a University of Toronto sweatshirt, but not as embarrassed as I'd feel dressed in a suit when meeting Billy Johnson.

"Portal. Good. You remembered." Gleason jumped up and shook my hand. I was surprised by the gesture, confused by his welcoming politeness. Was he trying to impress the pathologist by this display of manners or was he just nervous for some reason? "You remember Dr. John Slater . . ."

The pathologist rose and extended his hand. In front of me flashed an image of what that hand had touched. I hesitated for a fleeting second before I shook it. I thought the pathologist noticed that tiny delay. Or perhaps I only imagined the pained expression that crossed his face.

"Sit down, sit down," Gleason told us both, grabbing another spindly chair for me, then sitting himself. "Portal, John has a lot to tell us. I'll let him give you the gist of it."

Showing little of the professional detachment with which he'd spoken in the lab, the pathologist began his story, keeping his eyes glued to the portrait on the wall of one of Gleason's ancestors. Absent the toneless inflection of scientific reporting, his voice was soft, his words whispery and rushed. I found myself leaning closer to hear him. "That poor creature you saw the other night," he began, "was only the second or third instance of suspected auto-asphyxiation I've seen in the five years I've worked on Lombard Street."

I remembered the grisly photos in the book I'd kept from the eyes of my father. "Auto-asphyxiation?"

"I believe so," Dr. Slater answered. "The victims of auto-asphyxiation sometimes cover the head, perhaps believing that it assists the asphyxiation. In reality, what it does mainly is hide the shame of suicide." He glanced at Gleason, who looked away. "Assisted by drugs and/or alcohol," Dr. Slater continued, "the suicide pulls a previously rigged-up rope until a state of semiconsciousness is achieved. Sometimes the victim passes out, which causes relaxation of the hand. In a case like that, the would-be suicide comes to. I think many more people attempt this act of self-destruction than actually achieve it because coming that close to death might well convince a person that life is worth living after all."

He paused as if expecting comments or questions. I waited for Gleason to utter some smart remark, but he was uncharacteristically silent. So I asked the first question that came to mind. "Are you saying that the woman whose body we saw at the morgue continued past the awakening and actually proceeded to strangle herself?"

I assumed that Dr. Slater, like us, had only seen the body for a few minutes, but had by now certainly come to his own conclusions on the matter. So I was surprised that it took him so long to answer my question. He removed his eyes from the portrait, studied his hands, the rug, the curve of Gleason's back as my friend sat with his elbow on his knee and his chin in his hand. "I suppose," the pathologist finally said, "that a person might have the strength of will, and of hand, to actually strangle himself to death. More commonly, in my opinion, when the victim becomes semiconscious, the head bends forward with the chin on the chest, effectively cutting off the air passages. Such a constriction also happens to a person who nods to sleep in a chair. But unless dulled by drink, drugs or in some cases illness, the sleeper experiences a "startle" effect when the air passage is threatened and reflexively raises his head to clear the obstruction and resume breathing. You've undoubtedly experienced this yourself if you've dropped off to sleep, then found yourself jerking awake with an abrupt, involuntary lifting of your chin."

I recognized what he was describing, but for me his explanation left more questions than it answered. "So was this woman a suicide or not?" I asked.

Dr. Slater shook his head slowly. "I have no opinion," he said. "I was not allowed to examine the body."

"Why?" I persisted. I expected Gleason to be, if anything, even more interested in this than I was. After all, he was the one proposing to build his project around it. But he just sat there, as if his mind were elsewhere. Presumably he'd already heard the story, but still . . .

"The chief coroner was reluctant to let me do an autopsy in front of you and Mr. Adams," Dr. Slater responded. "Obviously a death that looks as dramatic as this one is capable of attracting a good deal of public curiosity, regardless of how mundane the actual details might be—not that I, we, consider the demise of any citizen to be mundane," he added nobly.

Gleason looked up then and smiled. If there was mockery in that smile, I didn't see it.

"Dr. Rosen had had a hard day," Slater went on. "He'd already had to deal with the press that afternoon concerning the battle he's engaged in with the attorney general. Dr. Rosen demanded to know why you were in the building. For a man who sees his job as serving an informed public, his attitude was surprising. I told him that you were law students working on a project. He suggested, strongly, that I give you both a short tour of an empty lab and then get you out of the building as quickly as possible." The pathologist paused as though to make sure his facts were correct. I admired his carefulness. By Gleason's continuing silence, I judged that he admired it, too. "I told Dr. Rosen that shunting you out would make it look like we were hiding something. Finally he agreed that I could show you an autopsy already in progress in a lab adjoining the one in which the suicide was awaiting examination. But when I got downstairs, I found that the autopsy in the approved lab had already been concluded."

"So you took us into the forbidden lab," Gleason interjected dramatically, giving the story a horror-movie slant. I frowned at him.

Surprisingly, however, Dr. Slater smiled. "Yes. The forbidden lab."

"And now you've come to tell us you're in trouble because of what you showed us?" I offered.

Slater studied me for a moment. "No," he finally said. "No, I'm not in trouble." He hesitated. "In fact," he continued, "I think this all might be easier if I *were* in trouble. Then I could defend myself and a lot of questions could be answered. Instead, what happened is that the body disappeared from my view as completely as it did from yours. I was called upstairs on "a routine matter," asked to fill out a number of forms to record your visit. Chief Coroner Rosen said these were necessary in case the family of the deceased asked about outsiders viewing the body of their loved one. I thought this was extremely unusual. We work in the morgue, not a funeral parlor. And I'd never seen these forms before. They seemed to just ask for the same information over and over again in different ways and took a long time to complete. When I finished and got back downstairs, you had left. So had the deceased! When I went back up to Dr. Rosen's office, he was gone, too. I didn't know what to do. I sat out my shift. There were no more drop-offs that night. Nothing to work on. I thought about it all the next day, but when I went back to work late that afternoon, everybody acted as though nothing unusual had happened the night before. I saw no alternative but to act in the same manner myself."

"Has this ever happened before?" I asked. "I mean, has a body ever disappeared?"

Dr. Slater appeared to give the matter some thought. "In all the time I've worked at the morgue," he said, "I've never seen a questionable occurrence. Of course, most of the autopsies we perform are on the cadavers of people who died in questionable circumstances. Such deaths are, after all, our mandate. But never have I seen our protocols and procedures ignored as they were in this case."

"How ignored, precisely?" I inquired.

As if not wanting to restate the obvious, Dr. Slater hesitated before he answered. "I've never been relieved of my duties prior to the completion of the autopsy, never even had an assignment altered without my prior knowledge and written consent. Dr. Rosen prides himself on the respect he has for his colleagues. His record-keeping is extensive and meticulous. He keeps track of even the most minute details of procedures at the morgue."

"What about outside the morgue?"

Dr. Slater looked confused by my question. "I beg your pardon?"

"Are you personally aware of the unexplained absence of any living person in the last little while?" This was a long shot, so I was not surprised when Dr. Slater took his time answering. I *was* surprised when Gleason gave a start as though he'd been slapped.

Dr. Slater finally said, "Apparently there was a young prosecutor who disappeared, a man by the name of Neil Dennison. I have heard that nobody's seen him since he was found in a compromising position in a public place." He gave a small grimace that I found unpleasant.

I did not miss the look of alarm that crossed Gleason's face at these words. He shot Slater a glance, to which the pathologist responded with a discreet nod. I had the uneasy feeling that these two had some prior arrangement between them, some secret knowledge.

"Dr. Slater," I said, "since you've been kind enough to spend time with a couple of law students, not only at the morgue, but here this afternoon, I guess you must think there's some lesson in this for us. So what do you make of this case?"

I watched his face as he pondered the question. Unlike Gleason's, his demeanor could not have been calmer.

"As I stated, Mr. Portal, without a thorough examination of the body, anything I say is only speculation. I am not in a position to come to a conclusion. But if I *were* in a position to do so, I might conclude that the bag over the head was hiding something that someone didn't want me to see."

"Such as?" I persisted.

"Such as proof that the deceased was not the victim of suicide but perhaps the victim of a killer who knows how to make homicide look like suicide."

"Is that possible?" I asked in alarm.

But apparently, Dr. Slater had told us all he was willing to tell. He made hasty apologies and said he had to leave. His provocative statement seemed to echo in the room after he was gone. *Homicide made to look like suicide!*

"How did you get him here?" I asked Gleason.

"Easy," Gleason answered. "You remember that guard who tried to keep us out the night we went to the morgue?"

"Yes," I answered, beginning to feel uneasy again.

"Well, I went back to the morgue while you were babysitting Kavin the other day, and I gave the guy a little something to find Slater and talk him into a short visit to Whitney Square."

I was again so furious with Gleason for his obstinacy that I neglected to ask myself why Slater would agree to visit Whitney Square at the request of a guard. Or whether Slater was the sort of man to accept a bribe indirectly. "You bribed an official?" I challenged my friend. "You really are out of your mind."

Now Gleason gave me a look of hurt feelings. But it was fake. He'd heard my objections before. And I, remembering the look that had passed between the two men, could have sworn that Slater and Adams were no strangers. But why would Gleason lie? And in a way that made him look like a worse scoundrel than he really was—if such a thing were possible. I decided to give up on him.

"Bastard," I said coolly. "You're going to screw things up for both of us."

"Screw what up? Your next date with Sheldrake Tuppin? You're a self-righteous prig, Portal."

I decided not to examine that remark. "A member of the legal profession is obliged to go to the police if homicide is suspected," I declared.

"Oh yeah? Well, you're not even a member of the legal profession. And you know why? Because you're a boring brown-nose. You're worse than boring . . . you have the imagination of a plumber! And always will have. Plus which you're a coward."

We were both enraged, but this was no place for a fight. If I broke even one of the costly objects, it would wreck my law career. I'd have to pay for the damage instead of my courses. I stifled my rage and made for the door.

But Gleason intercepted me, reaching to a gleaming side table for a finely wrought box made of twisted silver studded with blue enamel medallions. He grabbed my arm and pushed the box at me. Inside were the two strange rings.

"You want to tell the police, you sissy britches? There, give them those. Tell them everything. Confession is good for the soul. Tell them your mommy told you that."

But at last I had shut out the sound of his silly ravings. I was distracted by something about the rings I'd noticed but not thought through. I stared at them as they lay in the box. I thought about all the rings I'd seen in the pawnbroker's shop. I even thought about my mother's wedding ring. It was iron. She'd sent her gold one to Italy to help Mussolini before he became a dictator.

The two rings were exactly the same size. Whoever heard of a set of wedding rings that didn't consist of a small one for the bride and a larger one for the groom?

Chapter 10

On the thirtieth of March, 1965, Viet Cong terrorists
bombed the American Embassy in Saigon, killing 13 employees and injuring 180. The next day, the word
"firestorm" was born. The day after, Dean Rusk told seventeen neutral countries that he wasn't interested in talking about peace in Vietnam. At the same time, Dr. Martin
Luther King was calling for a boycott of the entire state of
Alabama to protest the killing of a civil rights worker, and
Virgil "Gus" Grissom and John Young were back home after the first American two-man spaceflight. On the radio,
the Supremes were singing "Stop! In the Name of Love."

In a world like that, a lawyer who couldn't find a way to
make his life useful didn't deserve to practice.

I left Gleason's house and I left the rings with him. Seeing those unusual objects, staring at their identical size
and shape, I feared an unknown that was brand new to me
then, though it became familiar as the years rolled by. It
was that feeling of encountering something or someone
on the wrong side of the normal, the ordinary, the good.

Standing on that threshold as a young person, you're sure you stand on the right side. I told Gleason that he'd better inform Professor Kavin I would have nothing to do with his project.

There were no railroad tracks separating Rosedale, Gleason's part of town, from the rest of the city, but there might as well have been. I walked south and away from Whitney Square through the tree-shaded streets, and soon I found myself on an old wood-slat bridge that crossed Rosedale ravine before leading abruptly into a rather dilapidated neighborhood.

I dug in my jacket pocket for the scrap of paper on which Michele had written the street address of Billy Johnson's rooming house. As I walked south on Bleecker Street, each house looked worse than the one before: unpainted wooden porches sagging, windows broken and missing, bricks chipped, chimneys collapsing. I knew a lot about the maintenance of houses because of my father's profession as a *brickiere*. One thing for sure, a house neglected is a house destroyed. But these houses, as Michele had told me, were being neglected on purpose. Intent on building high-rise apartments, a major real estate development company had acquired pretty much the whole district, an area of several square blocks in the northeastern section of the downtown core. The developer had used classic techniques of blockbusting. First, while the neighborhood was still whole and apparently stable, the company had paid top prices for a few single-family dwellings whose surprised owners were thrilled to get so much for houses they hadn't even thought of selling. Into these homes, the developer had placed employees pretending to be the new owners but really acting as agents dedicated to destroying the values of the adjoining properties in any way possible, usually by the ordinary way of infuriating neighbors: dirt, noise and neglect. When those neighbors had had enough, the developers moved in with more offers of purchase, still higher than expected, but only marginally. Eventually the whole neighborhood fell like a row of dominoes until no one was left on streets like Bleecker except a few pathetic tenants of owners afraid to evict them without due cause, owners waiting for disgust alone to drive them out.

Spring is always a dirty time in a country of snow. The melting drifts free all the debris frozen in place since the autumn and leave deposits of refuse instead. Bleecker Street was no exception. I had to wade through ankle-deep litter to get to the path to Billy Johnson's door. However, once I got to that path, I saw it was swept clean. In fact, a slender young woman was standing on the rickety bottom step of the porch with a broom in her hand.

In those days, I could not yet tell the difference between Algonquin and Sioux, knew no distinction between Ojibway and Oneida. Even Michele had yet to read *The Book of the Hopi* six times and often forgot to use terms like "original people." He, like me, would have called a girl like the girl before me an "Indian."

"Hi," she said, shyly glancing up at me, her eyes black beneath the thick, straight fringe of her hair. "You lookin' for Billy?"

Surprised, I held out my hand for her to shake and replied, "As a matter of fact, I am." She ignored the hand and after a few moments, I awkwardly withdrew it. "He lives here?"

"Yeah," she said, "but he don't get home from work for half an hour. You a friend of his?"

"I'm Ellis Portal," I explained. "Michele Portalese's brother." I felt a slight embarrassment at the discrepancy, which she couldn't help but notice. She drew her perfect eyebrows into a frown that did not reach the soft curve of her lips. Her skin was as dark as a *termitana*'s, but golden instead of olive.

"You mean Mike?" she asked. "You're Mike's brother? Something else!"

She went back to her sweeping and, uncertain what to do next, I just stood and watched her. I couldn't see her figure because of the large parka she wore and I thought about how hot she must be. In this neighborhood, the concept of owning a winter coat and a spring coat would have been unfamiliar. The distinction here was between a coat and no coat.

As she worked, the weak early-spring sun caught her thick, shining hair, fell along the smooth, high-boned planes of her face and seemed to settle on her slim hands wrapped tightly around the handle of the broom. On one of those hands was the same strange configuration of markings I had seen on Billy's face. I wished I could ask what those marks were, but I lacked the words that would be polite in such an inquiry. I found myself tongue-tied in her presence. She was as foreign to me as my Italian ancestry was to the Anglos. But she seemed unaware of my scrutiny, which made me bold enough to study her longer. I took her to be a teenager, perhaps sixteen or seventeen. She reached up to push the rich fall of hair away from her eyes and I realized how beautiful she was, the way one realizes the beauty of a bird when it tilts its outspread wings toward the sun and the light turns them iridescent.

"What's your name?" I asked.

"Kee Kee."

"That doesn't sound Indian," I said with a smile.

She didn't smile back. "It's short for my Indian name."

I waited for her to tell me her Indian name, but she didn't. "You can wait inside if you want," she said. "Billy and me, we live on the first floor. Just go in." She gestured to the front door, which I now noticed was slightly ajar. I nodded, walked past her up the rickety steps and into the dim hallway of the house.

The front room was dark, a heavy curtain on the front window blocking the daylight. From one corner, a low lamp cast soft light over the furnishings of the pleasantly cluttered room. It was the sort of room Michele loved. Bookcases made of bricks and boards lined all four walls. Three easy chairs, each covered with a colorful throw, invited me to make myself comfortable. Above the bookcases, unframed pictures were tacked to the wall. I had not seen such pictures before: stylized animals in bright, clear colors and bold black-and-white renderings of what looked like the city, but painted in a style that was simultaneously primitive and polished.

I stepped closer to the wall.

"Like them? I did them myself."

I turned at the sound of the slightly familiar voice. Silhouetted in the doorway, Billy Johnson's posture had the same bold lines as his paintings. He looked smaller than when I'd seen him in the light of the stage, but better-looking in every other way. In fact, an unexpected bolt of envy shot through me—the envy a soft, pudgy man feels at the sight of someone slim and clearly strong. The envy a man feels when face-to-face with the fortunate lover of beautiful Kee Kee. Like her, he had long black hair, but his was fine, almost wispy. It had the surprising effect of making him seem intensely masculine, of setting off the powerful structure of his face.

"Yes. I like them very much. I see you're an artist as well as a poet."

"Not a poet, really," he said as he moved into the room. He gestured toward the chairs. I took one and he took another. Awkward silence fell between us as each, apparently, waited for the other to begin.

"I'm Mike's brother," I began clumsily, the unfamiliar nickname feeling odd on my tongue.

"Mike's a great guy," Billy Johnson said. He put out his hand. "I'm proud to shake the hand of the brother of a man like Mike."

We shook. I noticed marks like those on Kee Kee's hand but fainter. When I glanced up at his face, the marks were faint there, too.

"You want a beer?" he asked me.

"No, thanks. I just dropped by for a brief chat about your matter." I feared I sounded clumsy, like a boy pretending to be at work.

As if he meant to reassure me, Billy leaned forward, smiled again, raised his hand in a gesture of welcome. "Hey, man," he said, "you came here to do me a favor. Mike said you'd come and you did. That counts with me. I appreciate it."

"I'm happy to help," I said, relaxing a little. "Maybe we should start at the beginning. Tell me about the circumstances of your birth."

Billy sat back and gave the simple question more thought than it appeared to warrant. When he finally answered, I got the feeling he'd decided I was worthy to hear the personal details of his origins. "Like I wrote down on that paper for Mike, my mother and father were what they call 'Swampy Cree,' from the muskeg country eight or nine hundred miles north of here, just south of James Bay," he began. "I was my mother's first baby, so when my father found out she was expecting, he wanted her to go south to have me, because the birth would be in the middle of winter and he didn't want her up there in the cold."

I thought about Kee Kee. I could see how a man would be concerned.

"My father, he had friends here in Toronto, so my mother came down. My father hadn't seen these friends in a long time. They turned out to be drunks and bums. My mother had a sister who married outside of our nation. With no other place else to go, my mother got on the bus to Buffalo. Her sister took her out to the Tuscarora reservation. That's where I was born."

"How long ago?" I asked, as if it made a difference. It didn't if Billy was over eighteen.

"February 12, 1946," Billy answered. "I'm nineteen."

I nodded. "Certainly old enough to be required to register for the United States Selective Service."

"I did that," Billy said matter-of-factly.

"Why? Why would you register for the draft?"

Billy's eyes held mine. I was taken aback by his determined expression, one that made him look like a mature man. I was only twenty-three myself, but I considered anyone under twenty to be a child, except for my brother, whom I considered an old man. Such assurance as Billy's in a youth of nineteen astounded me. "I think I'm a U.S. citizen," he said. "Registering is the law and I obeyed it. Mike says it's the white man's law and the day will come when Indians stand up for themselves." He laughed. "Custer's last stand."

"I thought you were a resister, Billy. What changed your mind about the draft?" I asked.

"I *am* a resister," he said, raising his voice slightly but chillingly. "And I haven't changed my mind about the imperialist invasion of a sovereign country by aggressive outsiders."

"What?"

He leaned closer. "The Americans are bombing ammunition dumps a hundred miles from Hanoi. The VC have already got within thirty miles of Saigon. You know what that means?"

Actually I had no idea. Michele was always talking about Hanoi and Saigon, but I really didn't understand which was which. Nonetheless, I listened as Billy Johnson went on in a restrained, yet passionate, voice. "The Russians are afraid the United States is going to attack them. And the Viet Cong say they can bring hundreds of millions of Asians into Vietnam to fight the capitalist aggressors if they have to. What this means is full-scale war. A year ago, the United States was talking about fact-finding missions. Now they're bombing Hanoi. If I'm not a citizen, I want no part of this. But if I am . . ."

I could see why Michele admired Billy. What I couldn't see was why the two of them were so convinced that anything I might do would change matters.

"I can't help you on any political issues," I said. "But I can check out the status of your citizenship." I reached into my jeans pocket and pulled out the piece of paper on which Michele had written Billy's address. On the back I'd jotted a few notes, reminders of what I'd read in the U.S. federal statutes.

"What's that?" Billy asked.

"I did some preliminary research based on what my

brother told me about your case," I answered. "There are ambiguities in the law that might pertain to your circumstances. Specifically, there's a suggestion that in a conflict between tribal law and American federal law, tribal rights might prevail."

Billy Johnson laughed. At least I took the low rumble emanating from his throat to be laughter.

"What?" I asked.

He shook his head, his dark hair catching the dim light of the room and holding it the way water holds the moon. I was afraid I'd used words he couldn't understand. Like all first-year law students, I was in love with the sound of law, the cadence of statute and case, the arcane vocabulary, the long, flowing sweep of legal argument. "You're not as plain a talker as your brother," he said, "but you're a dreamer if you think Indian law could ever be more powerful than American law."

Now I shook my head. "That's not what I mean, exactly." I was finally beginning to get interested in the complexities of the case. Being faced with a real person, an actual client—if only a practice client—brought my case to life. It sharpened my thinking, too. "But it also occurs to me," I said to Billy, "that should I determine that you have a choice between American and Canadian citizenship, you can renounce the American citizenship and—"

Billy looked shocked. "No," he said calmly, "no renunciation. A man accepts the legacy of his birth or he is not a man."

As he spoke the soft light of the lamp flickered and went out.

"That's it," Billy said.

I thought he meant our interview was over, but I was mistaken. In the light that filtered through the heavy window curtain I saw Kee Kee slip in and sit on the arm of Billy's chair. She was like an angel hovering in the shadows.

"The stove ain't gonna work to cook supper," she said.

"You better light a few candles and build a fire in the fireplace for cooking," Billy said. "Looks like this is definitely it."

"What's happening?" I asked in alarm.

"The landlord's trying to get rid of us," he answered. "We've been out of heat for a month. Now he just cut off the electricity."

"That's appalling!" I gasped. "No one should be deprived of basic necessities for the sake of raising real estate values."

Billy and Kee Kee both laughed at my consternation. "You can really tell he's Mike's brother, can't you?" Kee Kee said.

"We're Indians," Billy Johnson added. "We can build a fire. Maybe we'll catch one of the rodents in the basement and roast him. Want to stay for supper?"

Awkwardly, I laughed now, too, realizing Billy was teasing me to put me at ease. But I only remained at ease for the moment in which it took me to put two and two together. I already knew the answer to my question when I said to Kee Kee, "What are those marks on your hand?"

"Rat bites," she said, as if the answer wasn't outrageous in the least.

FOR THE NEXT two weeks I avoided Gleason Adams. I kept an eye out for him at school, and if I saw him in the distance, I went the other way. My visit to Bleecker Street had fired me up, and I wanted to keep Gleason and his project at a safe distance. Immediately after class each day, I ran to the law library and searched volume after volume of law reports looking for cases to guide me in my analysis of Billy's situation. Soon I would have a brief to present to Sheldrake Tuppin. I would have to ask Kavin to give it to the great man, but I was sure I could talk the professor into doing it.

If any thoughts came to me about the mystery at the morgue, about Slater or Rosen or Garrey, the A-G, I pushed them away. I convinced myself that I was far better off working on my own project instead of having Gleason drag me down with his disreputable one.

But I did wonder how he was doing and whether he was indeed still working on the case of the woman in the morgue. I thought about the two rings, about the pawn-broker's astonishing estimation of their worth. I thought about how Gleason had called me boring, a plumber refusing to take chances. I remembered what Gleason had said about the man who'd gone missing from the prosecutor's office. The one found in a compromising position. I even discreetly asked a few of my fellow students if they'd known Neil Dennison, but got no answer that was helpful.

One night, exhausted from my studies but not yet ready to go home and deal with my family, I decided to walk up to a diner on busy Bloor Street. Behind Flavelle House ran a treed path that led up out of the campus. At the top, it wound between the classical perfection of the Royal Ontario Museum and the gothic bulk of McMaster Hall, which had been a Bible college but was now a music school from which issued the mingled sounds of cello wailings and soprano trillings. For reasons unknown to me, this pleasant path was called Philosophers' Walk. In daylight it provided a winding, shady thoroughfare ideal for several minutes' contemplation sheltered from the boisterous background noise of the city. At night it was not in one's best interests to use it alone.

On this particular evening, I felt a sense of relief when a fellow law student who was going to the subway station on Bloor offered to join me. We passed a few lamps that cast small pools of yellow light on the uneven surface of the walkway. Just before we reached the museum, the path veered a bit to avoid a small clump of bushes. "That's where Neil Dennison was found on his knees," my companion mentioned casually. "You know that as a prosecutor he was drummed out."

"I heard he disappeared," I said, trying to elicit information without seeming too eager or ignorant.

"Yeah," my companion said knowingly. "Here tonight, gone tomorrow morning. Just as if he never existed." He shook his head. "It's a shame, really. He was a bright guy. But I heard that nobody over at the A-G's office even mentions his name these days."

"Do you think he could have been murdered?" I asked.

My companion was silent for a moment. Then he laughed as if I'd made a joke and he'd suddenly got it. "Yeah," he said, "murdered by his father who wasted all that money on his legal education."

I despaired of learning more until my companion volunteered, "It's 147 to 149 inclusive, and 150, sub two, para b. You play, you die." He laughed again, waved, turned right onto Bloor Street and disappeared.

I skipped the coffee and went straight home. I thought I knew what the numbers referred to. I brushed past Michele, telling him, "Later!" when he said, "Let's talk." I rushed to our room and the shelf where I kept my books, including the Criminal Code of Canada. Section 147,

"Buggery or bestiality." Section 148, "Indecent assault on male." Section 149, "Acts of gross indecency." Section 150, subsection 2, paragraph b ". . . publicly exhibits a disgusting object . . ."

Interesting, even disturbing, but clearly had nothing to do with me, with Gleason, or with either of the matters we had considered for our project.

Which would by no means explain why the next night, I again strayed onto Philosophers' Walk, and the night after that, which was the first night on which I thought to leave the path itself, and consequently, the first in which I saw the odd denizens hidden behind bushes just beginning to bud and slinking along the sides of buildings almost invisible in the evening's dusky light.

To be honest, I saw no one on his knees. I saw no person assault another, but I did hear an argument that was so heated it could only be profoundly personal. I certainly witnessed no bestiality or the public exhibition of a disgusting object, but then, I would have been hard-pressed to recognize my mother in the semidarkness. I did hear groans and giggles and the nervous laughter of those simultaneously amused, aroused and ashamed. I was, it seems now, very much a naive boy at twenty-three who, despite all the dire warnings of nuns and priests, was only vaguely aware of the sounds of masculine mischief. For, in the shadows beyond the quaint lamp-lit twists and turns of Philosophers' Walk, the voices I heard belonged only to males. Embarrassed, I hurried back to the path and up into the street.

Without being able to say why, I felt a connection between the walk and the conversation we'd had with Dr. Slater. So the next night I went back again to the secluded spot. This time, I clearly heard the voice of Gleason Adams.

I pulled back into the shadows, straining to catch what he was saying and to whom. I was close to the west wall of the stately museum. A damp cold seemed to rise from the ground, embracing my ankles. I shivered soundlessly.

Or so I thought. I could hear my own nervous breathing. As insects suddenly seem to go quiet at certain moments in the night, the habitués of Philosophers' Walk fell perfectly silent. I held my breath and listened intently for a few moments, but when I realized I would hear nothing, I moved on.

As my foot hit the first step of the stairs leading up to Bloor, I felt someone lay a hand on my shoulder from behind.

Terrified, I sprinted up the steps, but the man behind me was slimmer and swifter. He reached the top of the stairs before me and stood blocking me, the brightness of Bloor Street silhouetting him, a sinister blackness against the light.

I drew a breath to shout, but before the sound left my mouth, my pursuer laughed. "Boo, old lady," he said. "Scared you, didn't I? You spend too much time in the library. You ought to be researching out here where the action is."

"Adams, you fool!" I couldn't believe the relief I felt. And the anger. "You idiot. Get out of my way!" I shoved him. He swayed as if about to topple down the stone steps.

But the danger of falling only made him laugh harder. "On your way home after a long day's brown-nosing?" he asked. "If so, may I advise that you're headed in the wrong direction. Unless Eye-tal town has moved recently."

Obviously my avoidance of Gleason had not affected his attitude toward me. He was as mocking and contemptuous as usual. At least he seemed to be at first, but as he accompanied me along Bloor, like somebody else's puppy who is determined to follow you home, I began to realize that he seemed jittery and defensive. "I guess you wonder what I was doing down there, right?" he said when we reached the diner. I didn't answer, hoping he would correctly read my silence as a hint that I wanted to enjoy a coffee by myself.

"Look, Portal," he said, holding open the door and gesturing in a way that made it clear he intended to come in, too. "I know you're mad at me, but you should listen to what I've got to say. You can't keep crossing the street when you see me. You're going to run out of streets."

"Don't be an ass, " I countered weakly.

"Come on, Portal, you can't deny you're avoiding me— and our project, too. Time's running out."

I scanned the brightly lit room with its long counter and chrome-rimmed padded stools. The less time I spent here, the sooner I could get rid of Gleason. Nonetheless, I selected an empty booth near the front window and slid into it. Gleason settled in opposite me. There would be no getting rid of him now.

"Look, Adams," I said, realizing I was treading all-too-familiar ground and wondering how I could possibly get Gleason Adams to give up pursuing me. "I don't know what you were looking for on Philosophers' Walk and I don't care. Inasmuch as I was down there myself, I'm not at liberty to question you. But I think I've made my position perfectly clear. I can't obstruct justice by withholding evidence and I can't talk privately to officials who should be talking to the police, not talking to us."

"Forget Slater," Gleason said offhandedly, "he's cool. Trust me."

"Gleason," I said, "this is the last time I'm going to explain this to you. I am not—"

"Yeah, yeah, I know," he interrupted. "You're not going to jeopardize your big law career by bending a few stupid rules. Listen, Portal, I'll forgive you for being chicken, and a righteous one at that. And you're going to forgive me when you see what I've got."

"Oh, great," I said sarcastically, remembering I had said all this before many times, "now you've got something else. Something besides Slater and the rings. Gleason, can't you leave me alone? I don't want to hear about it."

"Portal, just listen to me one more time. I've been doing some checking around. You're not the only person who knows how to do research. I've got a lead. I've got someone who saw our rings being worn, someone who knows firsthand who the wearers were."

"Don't call them *our* rings," I said in disgust.

But not enough disgust.

"You're interested, Portal. I know you are. I can tell. You've always been interested but you're too much of a coward to say so."

I shook my head.

"Come with me," he persisted. "It doesn't have to be tonight. We can go anytime. But I want you to come with me." There was a touching note of desperation in his tone. Gleason was good at such effects.

"Why?" I asked, not wanting him to need me, because I feared his need would draw me further into the danger I could so strongly feel in his words, his posture, his zeal, but, like an unpopular boy who feels he is finally getting in on the action, intrigued still.

"Because you make it legit."

"What?" I sat back sharply.

"Don't be so suspicious. All I mean is that to have my law school partner along will make these people feel more at ease about telling us what they know."

"I'm *not* your partner! I've told you that a hundred times! I *do not want* to speak to anyone whose interview comes as a result of a bribe or any other questionable behavior. Can't you get that fact through your head? But," I said, aware of my weakness, "if you can convince me that you're putting this together in a legitimate proposal to hand in to Professor Kavin—without resorting to anything illegal or underhanded—I'll help you with the proposal itself, including interviews. Providing you don't pull any fast ones, Adams."

He smiled as if he had won a great victory. "Anything you say, Portal. Anything! Come with me on Friday to meet my people. That way we can get started doing the job on your terms. Is that good enough?"

His puppy-dog eagerness was appealing, so appealing that I agreed to talk to "his people," completely forgetting that Friday night was Good Friday and my mother's big debut as the Virgin in the Passion play.

Chapter 11

The next afternoon after classes, I told Gleason about Billy Johnson. Gleason exhibited a great deal of interest in the complexities of the case and said he'd like to learn more, but the interest was feigned and we both knew it. I also told him that he should consider trying to get an interview with Chief Coroner Levi Rosen.

"Why would I want to do that, Portal?" he asked.

"Because it would legitimize your interest." And my own, in case anyone, Kavin for instance, or even Tuppin, found out I was working with Gleason. "Don't forget it was Rosen who let us into the morgue that night."

"Yeah, and Rosen who kicked us out."

"We don't know that."

"Meet with Rosen? No way!" Gleason shook his head, ending the discussion.

That Thursday I arrived home hoping to have dinner before I met Gleason downtown at the same Bloor Street diner where we'd had coffee. We planned to walk down to

St. Nicholas Street and catch Billy reading poems at the coffeehouse.

But nothing went according to plan that evening.

Arriving home, I noticed a black, late-model Cadillac parked in front of the house. I saw from the license plate that the car did not belong to Uncle Salvatore. That observation exhausted my ability to figure out to whom the car *did* belong.

As I stood studying the vehicle, the front door of our house opened and a middle-aged man I didn't think I'd ever seen before stepped out, adjusting the collar of his black coat and pulling on black leather gloves as he made his way to the curb, rounded the car and let himself in. I thought he smiled at me as he pulled away and I got the uneasy feeling that I had somehow been the reason for his visit. Was his smile a threat?

I tried to think of any reason Uncle Salvatore might be displeased with me, just in case the man was his minion. Perhaps my uncle knew that I'd visited his friend at the funeral home, but that would have pleased him, since he himself had given me Spardini's name. I had, of course, been perfectly respectful to the undertaker, and Uncle Salvatore liked it when I expressed interest in the business activities of his associates.

There was, I realized, a slight possibility that Uncle Salvatore knew about my visit to Billy Johnson or even, I shuddered to think, about my amateurish and awkward detective work in the wilds of Philosophers' Walk!

I decided I was being foolish and made up my mind just to go inside and ask the identity of the man in the black car.

I nearly forgot all about that, though, when I walked through the empty kitchen and into the middle room to find a scene that resembled an explosion in a clothing factory.

Some endeavors look absurd when done in a hurry and sewing is surely one of them. Surrounded by fragments of garments like those worn in the early first-century colonies of the Roman Empire, my mother and my sister were sewing as fast as they could. Arletta's hands moved so quickly I could hardly see her fingers except for a blur where some gold-looking woven braid was being attached to pieces of old bedsheet.

"What are you doing?" I asked.

"Togas," they both said at once, as though they had to talk as fast as they were sewing.

"We have to get all this done tonight," my mother said, raising her eyes from her needlework to glance around the room. Draped over each of the six dining-room chairs were two robelike garments in shades of blue, brown and deep red. It took me only a minute to calculate that these must be the robes of the Apostles. Even I, who knew nothing about the crafts of women, could see that the rough edges had yet to be hemmed. On the buffet were stacked several more togas. They were folded neatly and their edges showed the glint of gold. I wondered how long Arletta and my mother had been at it to produce that pile of finished work. On the table itself were more togas and robes, tangled in disarray as if someone had tossed them there in a hurry, no, in a *panic.*

"How come you two are both sewing now?" I asked. "Isn't tomorrow the Passion Play?"

My mother always did everything so far in advance that I sometimes wondered how she remembered what a given bit of work was *for.* It worried me to see her obviously caught in such stressful last-minute preparations. I was afraid she'd make herself sick. Beads of sweat dotted her forehead. Her usually perfectly arranged gray hair had slipped out of the bun she habitually wore and strands of it lay along her neck. I noticed with alarm that she'd unfastened two buttons of her dress. I blushed to see the edge of her slip peeking out over the top of the third button.

"The play *is* tomorrow," Arletta breathed. "So we got a crisis here, and if we have to work all night, we will."

My mother, without looking up again, nodded determinedly.

"How did you end up in this crisis?" I asked, now trying hard not to smile. The two of them were as intense as a couple of Roman gladiators, if the violence with which they stabbed their needles into the innocent white cloth was any indication.

"Mrs. Minelli was supposed to sew all the Apostles and all the centurions," my mother explained, keeping her head bowed. "She took the cloth in February. Nobody thought about it, but maybe we should of, because this was Mrs. Minelli's first year of working on the pageant. What we didn't know was that her husband forbid her from sewing."

"What?" I asked. "What could be wrong with sewing?"

"Nothing if it's for your own family," my mother explained. "But Minelli knew that some women do piecework for factories at home. He knew that sometimes the women make a lot of money and buy makeup and perfume and even movie tickets and magazines. He said he makes the money in his house and he decides who spends it and what they buy. So when he saw Mrs. Minelli sewing, he took all the cloth and rolled it up in a big ball and threw it out the back window into the alley."

"And Mrs. Minelli had to sneak out of bed after midnight and go down and get it," Arletta said, picking up the story and telling it with a great deal more disgust than was evident in my mother's tone.

"Yeah," my mother said, "and she hid the costumes in the basement until Minelli went to work. Then she brought them to the church. That was only today. Mrs. Minelli is forbidden to come to the play, and me and Arletta, we got to sew all this by tomorrow morning. The play is at noon."

"Can I help?" I offered, stunned.

Both females burst out laughing as if the idea of my sewing was too funny to contemplate, which, when I thought about the matter, it was.

"Michele says garment workers are among the most abused employees in the whole city," Arletta commented. "He says Toronto is full of Italian women working like slaves sewing clothes for rich people to wear and not even getting enough money to buy a new dress for themselves at Easter or Christmas."

That sounded like something Michele would say.

"How come you're home so early, Gelo?" my mother asked.

"Early?" I answered. "It's after six o'clock!"

Her eyes shot up from her work and sought the ornate clock, an anniversary gift from Uncle Salvatore, that sat on the buffet among the togas.

"Oh, no!" she cried. "I forgot to cook supper!"

She looked about to burst into tears. Surely it was the first time in her married life that she'd neglected this duty. Her face was pale, her features bereft, as if she'd spoiled her flawless record and could never now erase the blot on her householder's reputation.

"I wouldn't worry if I were you, Ma," I said. "If it mattered at all, Pa would have been in here complaining by now."

"He got mad and left when he found out we were going to help Mrs. Minelli disobey her husband," Arletta said.

I felt a stab of anger at this piece of news. I didn't know what infuriated me more, the Italian men who thought they had the right to control their women or the women who put up with it.

"I'm going to DeCamio's to get pizza for us," I said. "And when I come back, I would really be happy if the two of you took a break from the sewing and sat down with me and Michele and ate. Will you do that?"

My mother nodded as if to say, *When your husband isn't home, you obey your son.* Not much of a victory over the old ways, but at least we did enjoy the meal. It wasn't until we'd finished that I remembered the black car and the ominous stranger.

"Oh, I forgot!" my mother exclaimed, jumping up from the table. "That was Uncle Salvatore's travel agent. He brought the plane tickets for Monday—for New York City!"

Michele, Arletta and I crowded around my mother, who displayed the exotic items as though they were rubies, which, to us, they were. I hadn't dared to think much about this trip, in case Uncle Salvatore hadn't been serious about sending us. But now the trip was a fact and Michele and I had a mere three days to get ready.

"As soon as the pageant is over tomorrow," my mother promised, "I'll help you both pack."

We groaned collectively at the thought of our mother doing yet more work, but she pointed out that it would only be a little extra washing and ironing. When Michele mentioned that we'd have to get to the bank to change some Canadian money to American, my mother smiled and gave us a second envelope the travel agent had delivered. It was stuffed with traveler's checks in U.S. funds.

I waited until all this excitement subsided before making a move to sneak off to meet Gleason and Billy at the coffeehouse. I should have been concerned about taking a vacation at such a critical juncture in my schoolwork, but a week's interruption was not going to do my project serious harm, as the libraries at the university would be closed for Easter week anyway. I had hoped to have my proposal ready before Easter, but Professor Kavin seemed to be allowing me more time to work up the Johnson matter. And Kavin wouldn't be on my back during the holiday. Being Jewish, he didn't celebrate Easter, but he'd still take time off and so would Magistrate Tuppin, as the courts would also shut down.

In the end, I was unable to leave the house alone. Not only did Michele tail after me, insisting that Billy was his "client" as much as mine, but so did Arletta. She said that if I really cared so much about the rights of women, I'd make it up to her for being excluded from the New York trip by taking her to the coffeehouse. She said there was no school on Good Friday and promised my mother she would get up at five to finish the sewing if she could go with us. Michele assured my mother that no alcohol was served at the coffeehouse.

Many years later, when I was an established lawyer soon to be elevated to the bench, I was never seen without my entourage: juniors, students, clerks, secretaries, sometimes even my barber or my tailor if I was really busy and couldn't see them at their premises. In those days I never thought about my humble beginnings except to be ashamed of them. But now it amuses and touches me to think of my retinue that night: my faithful retainers Michele, Arletta and Gleason, who seemed unusually quiet, almost sullen, as we made our way to St. Nicholas Street and up the narrow staircase of the coffeehouse.

The place was jammed. Someone had placed a red-and-white-checkered cloth and a candle on each table. In the flickering light, I scanned the room in the vain hope of catching a glimpse of Billy. He'd told me he was there every Thursday and I'd taken him at his word, but finding him was not going to be easy.

The situation was made worse by the behavior of Arletta, who attached herself to Gleason like a barnacle and kept staring at him with the big moon-eyes she'd previously reserved for George Harrison. To top matters off, Michele ran into one of his buddies and the two of them got into some sort of an argument about whether Dr. King's boycott of Alabama was hurting his cause more than helping it. They were so loud that the emcee had to ask them to keep it down.

When we finally got a seat, we were crammed together with three couples at a table near the back. In the frequent breaks between sets performed by earnest folksingers, Gleason asked me more than once what we were doing there. He seemed alternately bored and nervously attentive to the shifting crowd, which eventually coughed up both Billy and Kee Kee.

I didn't know which of the two was the more beautiful. I had no notion of the traditional dress of the Cree and I harbored a suspicion that no one else in that packed room did either. But even if their dress was more Hollywood than Indian, Billy and Kee Kee were smashing. She wore a white dress fringed on every edge so that it moved like water at her slightest motion. A swirling design of beads in white, silver, crystal and turquoise radiated from the neck of the dress across her shoulders and down over the curves of her small breasts. Her long, thick, perfectly straight jet-black hair caught the low light of the room and shot back glimmers of silver and deep blue. I saw Arletta, who spent a great deal of time ironing her hair, stare openmouthed at the slick curtain that covered Kee Kee's beautiful head and obscured the features of her face, which always seemed turned away from the viewer.

As for Billy, it was hard to imagine anyone more handsome. Woven into his fine, long black hair was a slim strip of white leather from which dangled two sleek feathers, one white, one gray, bound together by a narrow string of blue and crystal beads. Billy wore blue jeans like the rest of us, but his fringed white shirt was similar to Kee Kee's dress and bore the same intricate beading. Later I learned they had made these clothes themselves.

We had only a few moments for introductions because both Billy and Kee Kee were immediately called to the stage. They were announced as special guests from "up north." Kee Kee read first, a simple, touchingly naive poem about spring. Her voice was so soft and low that, sitting at the back as we were, we missed half of what she said. Had she not been so lovely, it might have been irritating to listen to her, clearly struggling with her shyness in order to make her point, which I took to be her profound love for the person who made every day a spring day, to wit: Billy Johnson.

Hard as it was to tear my eyes from Kee Kee, I did so that I could see what effect she was having on my companions. Gleason was studying the couple on stage as if transported to a land inhabited by beings even more beautiful than he. Arletta was staring at Gleason with a disappointed look on her face. Michele was gazing off into space as if his body were in the coffeehouse and his mind on the barricades with Dr. King. Suddenly I was filled with the overwhelming conviction that I was wasting my time, if not my life. I listened to Billy's poems, which were tiresomely political. I decided there was little to be gained by hanging around here and was about to whisper to Gleason that I was leaving, when the emcee popped into the spotlight and called yet another break, promising that Billy would be "back in five."

Before Billy reached our table, Gleason was on his feet with his hand outstretched. The crowd was so noisy I couldn't hear what passed between Billy and Gleason as they clasped hands and moved away together toward the coffee bar.

Kee Kee sat down beside me but said nothing. Michele and Arletta were nowhere to be seen. The allotted five minutes of the break stretched to ten and during the whole time, Kee Kee and I sat without speaking.

Finally, just as the lights dimmed, an animated Gleason took the chair Michele had vacated on the other side of me. "I see what you mean, Portal," Gleason said. "We can help Billy. We can do this tribal law versus American law thing. We can get Billy to come with us when we present the case to the faculty. We can have him testify on his own behalf—as if it were an immigration-type proceeding. We can . . ."

I frowned at Gleason. What was he up to now? First he had acted sullen and bored. Then suddenly he bubbled with enthusiasm. I feared he was still toying with me, still condescending, making fun of me, that he had ulterior motives to behave so agreeably. But when the lights dimmed and Billy returned to the stage, Gleason's attention was even more intense than it had been before. He sat spellbound as Billy read poem after poem of his own, then announced he would conclude by reading a poem written by someone else, a poem that was a favorite of his and Kee Kee's. He held it up and read:

> *If you love me, leave me a kiss in the white cup of morning.*
> *If you love me, leave me*
> *As the river leaves rock, flowing free*
> *But remembering the shape of stone.*
> *If you love me, leave me*
> *As spring snow leaves the wood:*
> *White pulsation, fading to crystal, to mist, to absence.*
> *If you love me,*
> *Leave me by dying.*

I could not see Gleason's eyes in the darkness of the room, but I knew, nonetheless, that he was looking at me, that a message was passing between us, an urgent agreement to get Billy to tell us at once whose words those were.

But by the time the houselights came up again and the crowd thinned enough to walk through, both Billy and Kee Kee were gone.

THERE WAS DARKNESS at noon the day Christ died. I once saw a picture captioned, "A rare nighttime painting of the death on the cross." It wasn't night then and it wasn't night now as we assembled in Mount Carmel Church, anxious to see the result of my mother's hard work, but a gloomy dimness seemed to suffuse the sanctuary.

Michele, Arletta and I occupied one long wooden pew that smelled of furniture polish. We were among the first, and though we had been trained our whole lives not to talk in church, Arletta seemed unable to keep silent or to keep still, either.

"How old is he, Gelo?" she whispered. "Just tell me how old he is."

"As old as I am. Which means he's too old for you. So whatever you have in mind, forget it."

"Is he seeing anybody?"

"How should I know?" I thought about the many girls who'd been as interested in Gleason as my sister appeared to be. He certainly could not be said to be "seeing" any of them, though he led an active social life escorting the debutantes of Rosedale to the innumerable balls and cotillions, proms and teas that crowded their calendars.

"If he isn't, then maybe I have a chance?" Arletta giggled excitedly and I sincerely hoped she was kidding. She had as much of a chance of dating someone in Gleason's social league as she had of dating George Harrison!

"Where is he, anyway?" She wiggled and squirmed and looked over her shoulder. "He said last night he was coming. So how come he's not here?"

That was a good question. The church began to fill, mostly with women bearing votive candles that they'd carried through the neighboring streets. Gleason was nowhere to be seen among the worshippers, devout Italians dressed all in black for this solemn service on the holiest day of the year. Had he forgotten? I heard the organist strike a mournful opening chord and doleful music filled the church.

Behind us, the old church's main door, which was unlocked only for special occasions, opened with an ominous, rusty-sounding moan. All heads turned, anticipating the first marcher in the Passion Play procession, traditionally the parish pastor dressed as Pontius Pilate.

I felt an irrational rush of fear. What if, late as usual, Gleason came bounding through that door, his careless arrival delaying, disrupting, the majesty of the ceremony? My eyes swept the packed church, scanned the hundreds of devout, expectant parishioners, some of whom had stood praying outside the church since before dawn.

The great door creaked again.

Turning, I saw Father Rocco in the Pontius Pilate costume that Arletta had completed at six-thirty that morning. I saw a legion of Roman centurions, or what passed for a legion and what passed for centurions in the Toronto, Canada, of MCMLXV *Anno Domini*. I saw twelve Apostles, the one in seedy black obviously meant to be the traitorous Judas Iscariot. I saw a really pretty Mary Magdalene and several other good-looking weeping women. Bringing up the rear was my mother, whose feigned agony nearly broke my heart. Finally I saw Stefano DeMario of Bishop Bianco High School, a senior student who had won the 1965 "Why I Want to Be Jesus" essay competition.

Without intending to, I silently offered a prayer that God would somehow allow me to protect the innocent people of the world, people like these who humbly offered devotion in their naive way without ever giving thought to the evils that lay so near the doors of their church.

I lifted my head and saw out of the corner of my eye that Gleason had arrived, was in fact sitting beside Arletta. I glanced at her face. She seemed subdued. I glanced at him. At first I could see nothing unusual in his appearance. I quickly realized that he must have come to the front door of the church, seen the procession and walked around to the side entrance, then slipped into our pew.

Who among us had not done the same if we found ourselves late for church? It could not be this that had troubled my sister.

My attention was drawn away as my mother passed our pew. Deeply immersed in her starring role in the pageant, she couldn't be expected to see us, but she did. Her glance shifted from the sorrowful Stefano and settled on us. The pride in her eyes was unmistakable. To have been chosen to be Mary and to have three strong children in church to watch!

But who was this fourth young person? Her glance fell on Gleason. I saw the sorrow return to her lovely features. Naturally I assumed she was returning to her role-playing.

I looked back at Gleason. I saw his gaze had met my mother's. And I saw, too, something strange about his eyes. They looked dark, smudged. I couldn't understand what I was seeing, but his face in contrast seemed unnaturally bright, as if altered by the light of the church. The more glances I surreptitiously sent his way, the stronger became the feeling that he was in some way strangely changed from the previous night. He wore one of his usual fine silk suits, but the shirt beneath the jacket wasn't white. Could it be purple? Pink?

And then I saw that he was wearing one of the rings he'd stolen from the morgue. He was wearing it on the third finger of his left hand—the wedding-ring finger! No wonder Arletta was sad.

Before the altar, the centurions were jostling to get into proper alignment on the steps that led up to the communion rail. Pontius Pilate, the narrator of the piece, began to read from the text taken from the Gospel, and all the actors, including my mother, nervously kept their eyes glued to the pastor, waiting for their cues.

I became engrossed in the pageant but was aware that as it proceeded, Arletta seemed to move closer and closer to me, which meant she was moving farther and farther from Gleason.

Michele, who of course would have refused to come to church at all had he not been warned that his absence would "ruin everything" for my mother, hoarsely whispered to me, "What's gotten into Arletta?"

I shook my head, not willing to answer because we had reached the holiest moment of the day and the play, the moment in which the Lord calls upon his Father, then gives up his spirit.

Nonetheless, I couldn't help glancing toward Arletta and Gleason. She looked truly uncomfortable now and I could see why. Gleason was staring at the good-looking high school senior Stefano DeMario. Down the unnaturally rosy cheeks of my friend, two glistening tears coursed.

Other people were crying in the church, but they were old Italian women, not boyish WASP charmers from Rosedale.

I remembered something I'd not thought much about before. I remembered that Gleason had told me he'd called our house three times and spoken to my father. My father had not given me those messages. My father clearly had not wanted me to talk to Gleason Adams.

Suddenly I realized he didn't want me to have anything to do with Gleason at all.

Chapter 12

Before I was born, before my mother was born, the Glionna family ran Toronto's Little Italy from their hotel on the northwest corner of Chestnut and Edward Streets. If B. Sheldrake Tuppin looked out his window in 1965, he would still have been able to see the building next door to where Glionna's hotel had once stood—only a few blocks from Old City Hall. He would also have known, wise old goat that he was, what was going on in there. True, the Glionnas were probably fugitives from the New York City police, via New Haven, Connecticut. True, they exercised undue, if not despotic, control over a community in which they were hoteliers, bankers, employment agents and models of civic involvement. True, they had been accused of virtually enslaving street children and forcing them to work as musicians. True, they themselves had begun their dynasty as mendicant child musicians in Laurenzana, far to the south in Italy. But the Glionnas always knew the difference between those who were respectable and those who were not. Had they seen what I saw the afternoon I entered the building next door to the site once occupied by the hotel, the Glionnas would have, to quote my mother, "turned around a lot of times in their grave."

The bar, if that's what it was, called itself the Continental. In 1965 that name invoked images of European sophistication. Such notions were quickly dispelled the moment Gleason and I pulled up in his Jaguar. The first floor of the multistory building seemed coated in grime, as if dirt from the street had washed up against it and stuck, the way seaweed clings to the shore. Since it was four in the afternoon, I didn't expect much of a crowd in the bar, as I reluctantly followed Gleason through a double door whose windows had been replaced by warped sheets of gray, weathered plywood.

The smell of the place hit me before my eyes adjusted to the gloom. It was a complex and layered odor, not as entirely unpleasant as I would have anticipated from the look of the outside of the building. I smelled the yeasty fragrance of fresh beer and beneath that, the hint of beers past, some spilled, some no doubt regurgitated. I smelled cigarettes and the stale reek of years of smoke captured by dirty carpets, by curtains, by walls and floors. I smelled something I could not quite recognize: musty, sweet, slightly foreign, hauntingly familiar.

"What are we doing here?" I asked Gleason.

Before he could answer, two remarkable beings materialized out of the semidarkness. After a moment I could see them quite clearly: two women nearly as tall as Gleason. One was a brunette with a pixie haircut that set off her dark, liquid eyes. Her lips were a red pout. Her skin seemed pearlescent against the blackness of her blouse with its long tight sleeves and its neckline so low I could easily see the shadow between her breasts. The other was blond, even more pearlescent and pouty. She wore a short skirt split on the side almost to her waist. As I watched in astonishment, she rubbed a lean white leg against the front of Gleason's silk trousers. "Are you here for some entertainment?" she murmured at him.

He stepped sharply away from her, almost knocking the brunette into my arms. I stood still, frozen to the spot. The brunette reached up and stroked my cheek. Her hand was dry and cool. Involuntarily, I turned my face into her touch.

But the blonde was agitated. "Forget these two," she said to the brunette. Then she turned toward Gleason, pretending to study his face and his physique. "You're barking up the wrong tree in here, baby," she said in a mocking tone.

"I'm not barking at all, *baby*," Gleason replied angrily.

Despite the charms of the brunette, I was beginning to feel vulnerable. Instinctively I patted my pocket to make sure my wallet was still there. As the women receded into the shadows, Gleason seemed to regain his usual careless good humor. "Are you scared, little Ellis?" he asked.

"No," I protested.

Gleason laughed. "You act like a man who's never seen a hooker before."

There he was wrong. I remembered then, remember to this day, the first prostitute I ever saw. She had been standing in the doorway of a store on Times Square. I was nine and visiting the uncle I was soon to visit again. She was the most beautiful woman I had ever seen. Slender, black, with a tower of curly jet hair and a little white suit made of some fluffy material, like an angel's dress. On that early trip to New York, I had seen so many amazing things. I thought she was just one more. A wonderful lady. I'd stared at her until I felt the jerking motion of my father's hand and was pulled away.

"Adams, is this another one of your stupid . . ." I didn't finish my sentence. A burly waiter, or given his bulk, maybe a bouncer, stepped between Gleason and me. In his hand he held a filthy rag. He reached down to a nearby table, picked up a loaded ashtray, dumped the contents on the floor, swiped the table with the rag and moved on.

"No wonder the ladies go down to the bus station to use the can," Gleason said, shaking his head. "Look, Portal," he added, pointing toward a door that opened on a room with better lighting beyond, "we're here on the advice of someone whose name I'm not at liberty to divulge, but I can say that this party is aware of several women wearing rings like the ones we found. I've been told this is a likely place for those people to frequent. All we have to do is ask the right questions and we can learn the identity of the deceased. If we describe her to enough people here, sooner or later, her name is bound to come up."

His words sounded like legalese and his tone was mocking. As usual when I was with Gleason and his enigmatic obsessions, I felt I was verging dangerously on the edge of rage. "Gleason," I protested, "this is a law project, remember, not some idiotic wild goose chase like the ones Perry Mason sends Paul Drake on."

"Paul Drake. Right on!" was all Gleason had to say in reply. Frustrated but curious, I shuffled along behind as he cut through this second room. It had only a few tables and they seemed to be occupied by the sort of people who'd seen even fewer hookers than I had. I took them to be voyeurs, tourists from the suburbs who had come downtown for the afternoon to take in a little wicked big-city subculture. Catholic boy though I was, I held them in far more contempt than the hookers, who at least were trying to earn a living.

Gleason, too, seemed to have no use for this set of people. The bar or club, or whatever this place was, appeared to be a series of rooms laid out like a shotgun house. We passed through another door and once again I found myself plunged into semidarkness.

But this room was crowded. Shadowed couples lounged against a long bar behind which a small-eyed, black-chinned character doled out a steady stream of cocktails. At tables around the room's perimeter, pairs of people sat in intimate arcs, their heads nearly touching, their shoulders curved forward toward each other like parentheses. I found it truly remarkable that so grubby and ugly a place could harbor such apparently tender lovers.

In the center of the room, a single couple revolved to the strains of the theme from *Goldfinger*. The song came to an end. Started over again from the beginning. The couple seemed unaware of the interruption.

Gleason scanned the crowd as though looking for someone in particular. I couldn't imagine disturbing any of the lovebirds, but fortunately that wasn't necessary. A pretty woman caught sight of Gleason, rose and sashayed over to us on stiletto heels. She wore a perfectly respectable spring dress with a full skirt and a fitted bodice that emphasized her tiny waist. Her hair was neatly coiffed in a style Arletta called a French twist. Her makeup was discreet and flawlessly applied. She would have surely caught the approving glances of the Italian matrons at Sunday Mass, especially since she was clearly from Gleason's class and not mine.

"Sweetie," she said, putting her well-manicured hand on Gleason's arm, "if you're playing with the ladies tonight, you shouldn't have come all the way back."

"You're the only lady I play with," Gleason said as he kissed this elegant creature on the cheek she held out to receive the touch of his lips.

In that moment I recognized her. At Christmas the Upper Canada law fellowship had put on a dance for the first-year law students. I myself had escorted Maria Delrobia, a neighborhood girl who was beautiful but not smart enough for the law school crowd. It had been an awkward, tongue-tied evening. Except for the witty repartee between Gleason and his date—this lovely slim-waisted Rosedale deb. What was she doing in a dump like this?

"This is Ellis," Gleason said, and I extended my hand, which the woman shook with the perfunctory politeness I'd often experienced from Gleason's pals. "He and I are working on a little case for school."

"Marvellous!" She laughed. "And you want me to help. How?"

"Come here," Gleason said, and moved toward the bar, which was better lit than the rest of the room. She followed him and I followed her.

Gleason held out his left hand. When the woman saw the ring, she feigned shocked disappointment. "Sweetie," she said, "I'm devastated! Married? Who's the lucky witch?"

The two of them burst out laughing, their shoulders touching in the camaraderie of two people sharing an absurd joke. I wondered what was so funny about the possibility of Gleason marrying without informing an old flame. But then he *wasn't* married, was he?

"I found this ring the other day," Gleason said. "Now I need to find out who it belongs to."

The woman took Gleason's hand in her own. She studied the ring, turned Gleason's hand palm up. The light from the row of bulbs above them fell on the shimmering blondness of their hair, the smooth, youthful planes of their faces, on the circle of danger and doubt that held Gleason in its gold and silver embrace. "Sweetie," she said, "there are lots of ladies wearing rings like this now. I'm surprised you haven't seen it before. They're your kind of ladies."

Gleason smiled mysteriously and shrugged, his usual gesture when someone called him to account for some small failure he could not explain.

She went on, "The ladies I'm talking about are down at Letros in the Nile Room, not up here in, uh, Rosedale." She glanced in teasing contempt toward the corners of the squalid room where the shadowed couples continued their silent conversations.

"Are you sure about that?" Gleason asked. His voice lacked its perpetual know-it-all arrogance. Perhaps he was more bothered by her criticism than was usual for him, he who habitually found criticism of himself so ridiculous as to be amusing.

The woman smiled softly. "Don't be nervous, sweetie," she said. "Nobody's going to hit you. Not here and not at Letros, either." She thought about that for a minute. "Unless, of course, you ask them to," she added. When Gleason didn't respond, she went on, "Anyway, Letros is where they're doing this thing with the rings. You steal your father's wedding ring and the other person steals their father's ring. Mostly the rings are made of yellow gold, but sometimes one is white gold, like this one." She pointed at

Gleason's hand. "It's really cool when they're different-colored metal. Anyway, you get a with-it jeweler to cut them and put them back together the new way. The jeweler engraves the rings with whatever secret words you want, half and half. You have to get him to make sure the words cross the place where the rings are joined. That's what seals it. Let's see what this one says."

She was a close enough friend of Gleason's that he didn't protest when she slipped the ring off his finger and squinted at the inscription.

"Oh, yes," she said when she'd managed to make it out.

"You *know* that poem?" I asked in surprise.

For the first time the woman's eyes actually met mine. "Who doesn't?" she said coldly.

"It's by, uh, what's that guy's name again?" Gleason tried to fudge.

"Sebastien d'Anjou-Nouveau," the woman responded. "The poor guy was some seventeenth-century Quebec monk who got caught on his knees . . ."

As if the whole room had been listening to our conversation, there were twitters of laughter from every direction.

"You're sure?" Gleason persisted. "You're sure about people at Letros wearing rings like this?"

"Sweetie," the woman said, "you really ought to get out more." She turned away from the bar and toward the dimly lit room. "Girls," she summoned, "come look at this." As though she were in command of some odd, distaff army, a bevy of women stood up and moved toward us. As they stepped into the light, I was shocked to realize how many of them I recognized. There was the striking redhead who'd accompanied Gleason to the annual Law Day luncheon, the sweet brunette he'd brought to the

Barristers' Banquet, and even a petite, waiflike creature he'd told me was his cousin.

These beauties pressed close to study the ring, and all agreed with what their friend had told Gleason. Behind them in dark jackets and shirts and vests, their partners hovered as though forming a circle of defense on the outer ring of the gaggle.

My head began to swim. The sweet, perfumy scent I'd noticed before became overwhelming, and I grew dizzy as I realized that I knew what it was. The smell of Arletta's bedroom and my mother's clothes closet and the interior of Aunt Fay's champagne-colored Cadillac. The smell of the geisha, the harem, the sorority. The fragrance of the exclusive and intimate world of women among women. I reeled. Suddenly I understood that, except for Gleason, me and the waiter who'd emptied the ashtray on the floor, every person in the place was female.

"WE'RE EARLY, BUT that'll be an advantage in the Nile Room at Letros," Gleason said as we made our way through the downtown streets. "The place won't be packed yet."

I sat silently, I suppose one could say furiously, as he spun around corners and frightened pedestrians with his impatient driving. I had no idea what or where this Letros was, but I was certain it would still be there if we were five or ten minutes later in our arrival on its doorstep.

In the end, I don't think the whole trip down Yonge Street to King took ten minutes. We screeched to a stop across the street from the King Edward Hotel. You couldn't get more respectable than the King Eddie. Still can't. I breathed a sigh of relief when Gleason hopped out of the car, even though he signaled for me to come along as though I were his trained dog.

But we didn't cross the street. Instead of entering the hotel, where two liveried doormen in Beefeater hats awaited the fortunate guests, Gleason took a step toward another, nearer door. It was unmarked, as far as I could see, but here, too, a gatekeeper of sorts guarded the premises, a stocky man in a well-cut blue suit. The moment his eye fell on Gleason, he raised his hand and smoothed his hair. Several rings glinted on his fingers. He smiled at Gleason with a rapaciousness I clearly understood.

"Oh no, you don't," I gasped. "I'm not going in there. You can just forget it. I'm—"

Gleason turned on me so fast I almost crashed into him. "What is the matter with you now, Portal, you stupid sissy? We're doing detective work." I stood still, unwilling to cross the threshold but uncertain what else to do. Instinctively I felt the eagerness of the doorman to make a scene. He was already snickering contemptuously at my hesitation. Even the doormen over at the King Eddie were casting glances our way.

"Look, Portal," Gleason said, "I know you're not used to this sort of thing, but—"

"What sort of thing?" I interrupted, as if I didn't know. The doorman chortled and rolled his eyes. "You butt out!" I shot at him. I saw a swift look cross his features, the cowering look of a man who'd been bullied a good part of his life. Then his features hardened as if he remembered he didn't have to put up with bullying anymore. I was suddenly afraid he was going to hit me. "I'll wait for you here," I told Gleason. "I'll keep an eye on your car. You go in and do what you have to do." I shot another look at the doorman. He was stifling laughter.

I have spent time in the private company of famous men. I have spent time sleeping outside in winter with nothing for a blanket but the snow. I have spent time in which it was being decided which jail I would be sent to, which mental hospital, which woman's bedroom, but I have never spent a more tense half hour than the one that April night standing outside the door of Letros.

I was stared at, winked at, evaluated and sometimes— though by no means each time—dismissed as unworthy of further consideration by the exclusively male clientele. I became confused. Should I be flattered when they found me attractive and insulted when they didn't, or vice versa? Should I drop my eyes when other eyes sought mine or should I stare defiantly back? Or would that be construed as an invitation? I was alternately impatiently furious and bravely reconciled to the necessity of waiting for Gleason to return. Of course, I could have just walked away, but I didn't want to acknowledge defeat. Or would it have been a victory?

When Gleason finally did come out, he seemed like a changed man. His usually fluid, graceful movements were jerky and abrupt. His hands seemed to shake as he lit a cigarette from the stub of the one he was already smoking, then cast the stub to the sidewalk and ground it beneath his heel.

He didn't command me as usual to get in the car, just unlocked the passenger door, stomped over to the driver's side, yanked open the door and thrust himself behind the wheel. I was afraid to speak to him and didn't even try un- til he'd done a tight U-turn that left all three doormen gaping at us as we tore away along King Street. "What did you find out in there?" I finally asked.

He concentrated on the traffic headed north on Yonge Street as if too absorbed in his driving to answer any questions.

I tried again as we turned onto College Street and drove west toward Clinton. "Did you find out who the rings belong to?"

Still no answer. There was something so shaken, so shattered about Gleason's demeanor that I began to feel an emotion toward him that I didn't remember feeling for him before: pity.

Which is why, when he finally got to my house, stopped and waited for me to open the door to get out, I tried one last time to patiently inquire about what he'd found out in Letros. "Adams," I said calmly, "we've been friends. And now we're starting to hate each other. Maybe friendship is more important than these stupid law projects. If you learned something in there that's going to damage your project, believe me, you don't have to worry." I hesitated, thought, then plowed ahead. "We can work together. We can share the Billy Johnson project and go with it as a joint submission."

It wasn't until later that the utter folly of this idea hit me. If Sheldrake Tuppin was reluctant to take on one intern, why would he consider two? But it didn't matter. I didn't think Gleason even heard me.

"Ellis," he said, his voice flat, "they're closing ranks against me."

"What? What are you talking about? Who are 'they'? The men in the bar?"

"Yes. They knew all about the rings."

"They know you stole the rings?" I asked in alarm.

"Not exactly," he answered haltingly. "They believed me when I said I found one ring. I didn't say anything about there being two. But they said somebody must have stolen two rings and then lost one, because everybody knew the dead person had been wearing two rings secretly since the breakup."

"A breakup? That doesn't cut it. The dead woman broke up with her boyfriend but still kept their rings pinned to her underwear? That's pathetic!"

Gleason looked as if he were going to cry, as he had earlier that day in church. How could he care so much about this caper? Again I thought about how a few of the brightest and the best, a certain number of every first-year law class, suffered nervous breakdowns, often in the last few weeks of second term. Is that where Gleason was headed? Over a pair of rings and a murder? I felt sorry for the deceased, but really, this was just a practice law school case. If it was even that.

"Gleason," I said softly, "those guys in there, maybe they were putting you on. Did they tell you how they knew all this? Did they tell you who this woman was? If they knew so much about her, did you ask them to prove it by giving you something that can be checked out? Like, for instance, her name?" I laughed, beginning to feel that maybe somebody had finally pulled a trick on the trickster.

I reached out and put my hand on his sleeve in an awkward gesture of comfort. I felt I was being magnanimous, ignoring his constant epithets for the good of our friendship. But, as I expected, he ignored my touch. "Gleason," I practically begged, "please tell me why this is so important to you."

"Practically everyone knew the dead person, Ellis," he answered. "Practically everyone saw the rings on both partners. Everyone knew they broke up. Nobody had heard anything of the deceased since several days before the body turned up at the morgue. Nobody had seen the other partner for the same period of time."

"You mean both the woman and the man have disappeared?"

He raised his bent head and looked me straight in the eye. Despite his emotional turmoil, he couldn't hide his usual opinion of me, which was that I might be smart but I was a child compared to him and his more worldly take on life. "Portal," he said, "you really don't get this, do you?"

THE CLINTON STREET KITCHEN door was locked and my hand trembled as I fumbled with the key. When I finally managed to turn it, the door flew out of my hand, sprang back and banged hard against the wooden salt box that had sat by the door all winter and was now waiting for Michele or me to take it to the basement.

I waited for an outcry against this racket, but no sound came, no voice of sibling or parent. I sniffed the air like a hound. Even though I was too disturbed to eat, I longed for the reassuring fishy comfort of a saved Good Friday supper, the rich smoky fragrance of coffee thickening in a carafe on the back burner. But I smelled nothing. Glad everybody was out and hoping for a few moments' privacy in my room, I walked through the kitchen, but didn't quite make it to the door into the dining room.

"Where do you think you're going now?"

I jumped at the voice and turned. Sitting at the table in rigid and stony stillness was my father. I'd walked right past him.

"I'm going upstairs," I answered. "To study."

He stood up. He was almost sixty and the years of construction work had taken their toll on his knees. Sometimes his legs seemed bowed, but now they looked perfectly straight. His arms were locked at his sides, his fingers clenched into fists. My father's anger was not the firecracker that exploded in me when I was angry. His anger was the slow burn, the smoldering ember, the fire thought extinguished until it rose again hot enough to ignite everything in its path.

"Why," he said with clenched-teeth control, "did you bring that boy to your mother's holy play?"

"What?"

"I asked you a simple question, Angelo, and I expect an answer."

"Where is everybody, anyway?" I said nonchalantly, as if his question would disappear if I ignored it.

He took a small step forward. The sound of his foot shuffling against the kitchen linoleum brought to mind the image of the chains of the prisoners shuffling beneath the courtroom of B. Sheldrake Tuppin. The image made me step back, away from my father.

"I told that boy not to call here," my father said. "I told him you're a Catholic. You don't do what boys like him do."

"Pa," I said as calmly as I could, "I think you ought to mind your own business."

"Don't you dare talk to me like that!" He slammed his meaty hand, his workman's callused fist, hard on the kitchen table. China rattled. A little cup jumped out of its tiny saucer, rolled to the edge of the table and crashed to the floor, spewing a red-brown liquid the color of dried blood.

"Leave me alone, Pa. I'm tired. Church is God's house. Anybody can go there. As for Gleason, he's my partner at school. We're working on something together. We have to—"

"You use school as an excuse to run around with a boy like that?" He shook his head as if he was unable to comprehend my ignorance. "What would your uncle think if he knew where you go and what you do instead of going to the library and the classes he spends so much money on? Why does a lawyer need to go see somebody like Spardini? Or to the morgue? Or those other places you go?"

"How do *you* know where I go and what I do?" I screamed at him. "And who do you think you *are*, accusing me? I go where I have to go and I do what I have to do. If that's a problem for you," I railed, "I'll go live someplace else. Then you won't have to worry about who my friends are."

"You do that, you ungrateful—"

"And you can tell your snitches to lay off, too," I threw at him.

He turned his face away as if the unfamiliar word was a special kind of insult to him.

"Yeah, Pa. Snitch. Dirty little stool pigeon. Who told you where I was? Who have you got watching me? I'm a man. I'm not your little boy anymore. I'm not anyone's little boy."

"I don't know what you mean," he said, a little calmer. "Nobody's watching you. But I am warning you, you stick to school. You stop sneaking around in that boy's fancy car and bringing him to church for everybody to see. You're a man, all right, Angelo. You better remember that and start acting like one."

My fury, that quickly boiling stew of perceived injustice, was now as intense against my father as it often was against Gleason. Not even conversation with Michele when he finally came home and told me that it was my mother who had told my father that I was, as she put it, "helping that sad boy, Gleason" could stem it. Or study, for which I could not concentrate. Not sleep, which adamantly refused to come.

In the middle of the night I silently descended the stairs, went to the closet in the foyer by the front door, found my father's bottle of sweet Italian wine and drank until it and the night were gone.

THE NEXT DAY I was so sick I could do nothing to get ready for New York except say yes and no to clothes my mother was selecting for my suitcase. Late in the afternoon I picked up the phone to call Gleason, but all that I had seen and heard the night before reeled out in my mind like an X-rated movie. I put down the phone.

I HAVE NOT HAD many mystical experiences in my life, but I thought I was having one at Easter Mass the next day. The crucified Christ looked at me from the wall at the side of the altar and said clearly, "Put your hands in my wounds."

The voice terrified me utterly. I decided I had to give up my friendship with Gleason. I decided I had to come clean about the stolen evidence, the secret meeting with the pathologist at Gleason's house.

I could think of only one reason Gleason would be so obsessed about that woman's death, one reason he would bribe the pathologist, one reason he would steal evidence. I had to go to the police. And right now, too, because the next day I'd be on a plane headed for New York City.

It was not easy to get to the police on Easter Sunday. I had to listen to the entire lengthy Mass, eat the huge breakfast, help my relatives stage the Easter egg hunt for the extended family's dozens of small children, eat the huge dinner and then wait until the entire household had nodded off for a late-afternoon nap before I could get away without my absence again being noted and commented upon.

I also had to choose a police station outside our neighborhood, since all the local officers knew the families on the street by name. When I finally found myself before an officer at police headquarters on Jarvis Street, who agreed to listen to me, I was suddenly sorry I'd wasted my time and my energy. Not only was he sly, contemptuous and unhelpful, but for some unaccountable reason, telling him what I knew, or was convinced I knew, suddenly seemed like too big, too overwhelming a betrayal of Gleason, and I could hardly force myself to give the details necessary to form the basis for an investigation, let alone a case.

As I struggled, the officer grew increasingly impatient. A phone rang in the next room. "I gotta do everything around here today," he complained, and left me alone.

I drew in a deep breath and stood to stretch muscles cramped with anxiety. When I went to sit back down, I noticed the officer had left open on his desk a file he'd pulled at the very beginning of our interview. I glanced down at it and could see this file seemed to be a thorough dossier on the murdered woman. I read a description of the body, just as Gleason and I had seen it. There was an autopsy report, but all I could catch on that were the handwritten words in the space labeled "Conclusion." The words were "to come."

I dared not move any papers, though I could not see the name on the report or on the file tab. But on one of the papers, I could see that the space labeled "address" was filled in. I craned my neck to see what was written there. If the form referred to the deceased, I would have expected the address to be some street in a disreputable part of town.

It wasn't. The address in the file was one of the best addresses in town, Whitney Square.

I WALKED HOME, despite the distance, despite the unseasonably cold mid-April day. The sun, if it shone at all, seemed incapable of delivering any warmth.

What had Gleason Adams done? I took my mind back one more time to what we had seen and heard at the morgue. Everything hinged on the moment I'd stood on the threshold of autopsy lab C, the moment Gleason had hesitated and I had given him a little push to get him to enter that room. What had been on his face in that instant? Guilt? The guilt of a man who'd been caught?

I remembered the shifting shadows in the little parlor at the foot of the stairs leading up to Levi Rosen's office, the figures in the dim light at the end of the corridor. Had there been an air of conspiracy in that fetid place?

And what was I to make of Gleason's suspicious behavior since? True, he had the excuse of family difficulties, but could that explain his erratic appearances and disappearances at school? His peculiar emotional displays?

And what could possibly explain our strange pilgrimage to the places we had visited on Good Friday, the holiest day of the year?

I had not seen anything connected to Gleason but his address on that police form. Yet it had led me to the inescapable conclusion that the police were interested in him. Did they know he was secreting evidence in a homicide investigation? Well, *I* knew, and the time to do something about it had come.

I decided to give up on any story I wanted to tell and started home. Halfway there, exhausted, I stopped and sat for a few minutes in a park. Though it was cold, the grass was green and daffodils in full bloom nodded in the cool air. I wondered how they survived, considering that temperatures still dipped below freezing at night. Sometimes, I reflected, things that appeared to be delicate were, in reality, stronger than supposed.

How strong was Gleason Adams? More to the point, how strong was I? If I suspected the police were after my friend, was it my moral duty to warn him? My legal duty to turn him in?

As I sat there, the weight of my decision to become a lawyer felt crushing. Was it always going to be like this, facing conflicting courses of action, knowing that to obtain justice for one person meant the ruination of another? Knowing that in the same world in which innocent families ate Easter dinner in homes surrounded by budding daffodils, other families hid the murderous deed of one of their members? For, it suddenly occurred to me, Gleason's rich father had the connections, the resources, to do whatever was necessary to protect his son from the consequences of any behavior he might wish to engage in.

I wished I could talk to someone, but who? Not Gleason himself, surely. Not Kavin. I couldn't admit to the professor that I'd failed to alert the authorities about the stolen evidence. Not Michele or my father or Uncle Salvatore. What about Sheldrake Tuppin? I pictured myself approaching the great man, laying out with precision all that I knew. I could tell him how I'd followed the trail of the rings to the pawnshop on Church and the questionable haunts of the city's underbelly. I could explain how I'd searched for, yet failed to find the autopsy report . . .

No. No. I couldn't talk to Tuppin. Impossible in every way.

Then it occurred to me to find Chief Coroner Rosen. I was not so far from the neighborhood in which he lived, a section of the city that rivaled Rosedale and Whitney Square in elegance, but which, unlike Gleason's neighborhood, housed the families of highly successful Jews. It was not Easter Sunday to them. I would be interrupting nothing special by showing up at Rosen's house.

The idiocy of this idea did not fully strike me until I'd managed to find the address and was standing on Rosen's veranda. Through his front window, I could see him and his family sitting down to dinner. I also saw that a maid had noticed me and was coming toward the door. I turned and fled, ashamed to find myself in such a distraught state.

I walked for another hour and was almost home before I realized what I had to do.

The café at the corner of Clinton and College was crowded with men who had escaped from family Easter festivities. I glanced over the throng and, relieved to see that my father was not among them, I sat down at a small table near the window, ordered a double espresso and, borrowing a piece of paper and an envelope from the barrista, began to write.

I put it all down. Everything I had seen. Everything I had heard. Where I'd been and when. What I had concluded and why. When I finished, I put my name and address at the bottom. On the way back home, just up the street, I dropped the letter in the mailbox.

By the time it reached Levi Rosen, I would be in New York City, six hundred miles away.

Chapter 13

The entire 1964–65 Flushing Meadow New York City World's Fair was insufficient to take my mind off the troubles I'd left behind in Toronto. It was crowded, hot, costly and gimmicky, handily summed up by the fake word that for years to come would instantly call it to the mind of anyone who had been there: Futurama. The fair, like so many other predictors of things to come, had been right about some things—that someday every home would have a computer—and dead wrong about others—that men would live in leisure and harmony with other men. The fair had nothing to do with my future, but other things I saw on the trip to New York City changed that future forever.

"Have some more. Don't be shy. There's plenty more where these came from." Uncle Tony, aka Zi Antonio, my mother's "little American brother," speared an extra T-bone steak, held it up and glanced around the picnic table. "No takers?" He shook his head in amazement, as if each one of us hadn't already consumed a whole steak still sizzling from the barbecue set up on the rear patio of his ranch house in Massapequa Park, Long Island. I was a city boy, unused to the lack of sidewalks and amazed by the house lots that seemed to cover a Toronto block. Michele and I were treated like honored quests. Uncle Tony worked for the City of New York as a sanitation supervisor. Around here, in New York State, in much of New England, there were dozens of municipalities, but there was only one city and that was Manhattan Island. This uncle called himself "your average Joe Blow," but his house had nearly as much space inside as Uncle Salvatore's and considerably more outside. On this spring evening, far warmer than spring in Toronto, we could hear the cheery loud voices of my uncle's fellow Americans as they entertained in their yards on the other side of Uncle Tony's tall fence.

"Seems like you boys are doing just great up there in Canada. If you can't live in America," he commented, "Canada's sure the next best thing!" I saw Michele wince, but Uncle Tony didn't notice. "Law school. Social work," he went on. "Wow! I bet my big sis is darn proud of you guys!"

Michele smiled. He was a hit with our two cousins, gorgeous girls who'd been fat little toddlers when I'd last seen them fourteen years before. Catholics don't marry cousins, but the two teenagers were flirting with my brother openly. Michele was encouraging them without intending to, simply by being his serious, socially committed self.

"You slept on the *sidewalk* in front of the American Consulate?" one cousin gushed. "Far out!"

"You *picketed* against the Vietnam War? Neat-o!" the other enthused. "Did you get busted?"

My uncle, like most American workers in those times, was right-wing in his politics. I engaged him in conversation to steer his attention away from Michele and the girls. My aunt Linda, our hostess, was in the kitchen preparing some extravaganza she said was French. She pronounced it "Krapes Suzette" and said the recipe came "straight from Paris."

"So, Angelo, are you busy up there right now? As a law student, I mean," Uncle Tony asked.

"I'm at a place in my studies where I have to decide on a field of concentration," I answered.

He listened with polite attention as I explained about seeking the internship. "You do things different in Canada," he said. "My kids got summer jobs lined up already, that's for sure."

When he asked me what projects I was working on exactly, I had to bite my tongue. I didn't think he wanted to hear about Billy Johnson, the prospective draft dodger, or Gleason Adams, either. So I gave Uncle Tony some speech about helping the underprivileged. I saw one of the little cousins glance my way and offer me a pretty smile. "People who just need a little help to get on the road to a better life," I added for good measure.

"I got just the place to show you tomorrow," Uncle Tony said enthusiastically. "What time do they get up in the morning in Canada?" he asked.

I laughed. "Any time that's necessary."

"Good. You get Aunt Linda to wake you up when she wakes me up tomorrow. That'll be six-thirty. Then I'll show you something not everybody gets to see."

"IT's WHAT YOU would call a yacht in Canada," Uncle Tony said. Then he laughed and playfully punched my shoulder. "Just kidding, son. Climb in. It's clean as a whistle. Hosed it down twice just for us. Trust me."

From the deck of the garbage scow anchored off the Battery, the southern tip of Manhattan, a man in a dark green uniform printed with "NYC Sanitation" reached his hand out to me. I grabbed it and teetered for a precarious moment, one foot in the city and the other suspended over the Hudson River. The boat shifted and I tripped onto the deck, followed by Uncle Tony who hopped aboard effortlessly, as if he did it every day. "Which I *do* do every day," he explained.

As the thirty-foot-long boat pulled away from the shore, I felt exhilaration of an immensity I had never felt in Toronto. My sense of the complex geography of greater New York, with its five boroughs, its two rivers, its bridges and islands, East Side, West Side, up, down, Long Island, Jersey . . . was incomplete and confused, but I swore when I boarded that garbage scow, I could taste the salt of the Atlantic and feel the fresh ocean breezes as we sped away from Manhattan and westward toward and then past the Statue of Liberty.

With the wind in my face and the sun off the sparkling water dazzling my eyes, I savored the moment, not asking Uncle Tony where we were going. But when the boat took a sudden turn and I looked up, I was shocked at what met my gaze.

Occupying its own island and appearing to cover it totally, a palace like that of the Doge of Venice rose above us. Identical two-story wings flanked a central portion that was twice as tall. The building itself was pink, but every curved lintel, every massive arch, every corner and crevice and crook was outlined in stark white, which looked like Italian marble, carved and scrolled, curlicued and crenellated. At each of the four corners of the main section, a domed tower rose and at the apex of each dome, a spire as thin as a spear pierced the deep blue sky. The towers reminded me of the palaces of the sultanates in the books of my boyhood. In those imaginary lands, each tower faced a point of the compass and these did, too. One dome and one spire for each realm of the earth.

Stunned, I watched this vision approach. But the nearer we got, the more it appeared that this magnificent edifice was now a crumbling wreck. What must once have been brickwork worthy of the most skilled *muratore* was grimy and broken, chunks fallen away wherever we looked. A ragged, rusted barbed-wire fence enclosed the whole structure, but it was so bent and broken that any intruder foolish enough to venture across the river could merely step over it and gain easy entry. Dozens of arches soared above carefully crafted windows, each surrounded by white stone, but all the panes were smashed, the decorative wooden moldings rotted and chipped. Old wrought-iron light fixtures, dark green metal sconces, pitted by decades of raw wind and unrelenting sun, dangled from electrical wiring long since disconnected from any source of power. Here and there, a frayed rope or a tattered flag or a piece of cloth, captured and held by a random sharp object, waved in the breeze and made the building look as if it were gasping for breath.

"What is this?" I asked my uncle.

"This," he said, "is the gate to America. Ellis Island."

"Ellis?" I repeated, amazed.

"Yeah," my uncle said. "An English name. The guy that owned this island way back when was Samuel Ellis. He tried to get rid of it, but no takers. He died in 1794. A hundred years later, this place was built—or a place like it, which burned down. The second one—" he gestured toward the massive ruin before us "—opened for business around 1901 when everybody and his brother wanted to come to America. Especially Italians. More Italians came through here than anybody else, two and a half million in thirty years. By 1931, though, most people, including our family, were inspected before they even left Italy."

My American uncle seemed so much less Italian than the folks on Clinton Street in Toronto that I marveled at his bringing me to see this wreck where my ancestors first set foot in America. I looked around once more. The depressing stillness of a place that hasn't served any purpose for years seemed to have permanently settled over the island. My uncle's voice sounded hollow, strange, as if he were talking in church. I expected him to tell the boatman to turn back, that we would return to the mainland. Instead, he asked the man if he'd come back for us in half an hour.

Our feet crunched on gravel and broken glass as we took a short, wide path from the river to the main entrance. I glanced overhead, wary of falling bricks and disintegrating limestone, which I could now see formed the building's white trim, but Uncle Tony seemed oblivious to these dangers. If there had ever been a lock, it had long since rusted away. Uncle Tony pushed and a shrunken door, crooked in its frame of scaling wood and paneless windows, swung effortlessly inward, as if the ghosts of the sad old place welcomed him.

I stayed close behind as we navigated a dim corridor lit only where stray rays of sun found chinks in the wall. Rusted scraps of metal, shattered pottery, splintered furniture, yellowed papers, rags and rat droppings hindered our steps. A rank smell of mold, old plaster and dust mingled with the pervasive dampness from the river.

The narrow corridor seemed to go on forever and I was beginning to feel claustrophobic, when we came to an intersecting passage. As I turned the corner, my eye came level with a place on the wall where layers of plaster and paint had worn away. There, beneath the peeled plaster, I saw the type of florid handwriting I remembered seeing on papers belonging to my grandfather. I edged closer. I realized some of the writing was in English and that I could make it out. A few lines said: "1907. Antonio D'Amico. 12 years old come here from Limonzano, Italia to America. God bless my new home. I hope I stay."

Across nearly sixty years, the simple hope of this boy so moved me that I reached out to trace his words with my fingers, but my uncle's hand stayed mine, as though he were anxious to protect this testament from any harm. "It's really something," he commented. "The more the paint and plaster falls off, the more old sayings come out on the walls. It ain't New York without graffiti," he laughed. "I guess it never was." More seriously he added, "Looks like people who came here wanted to make their mark on America any way they could, right from the start."

"I guess so," I replied. We turned from the wall and walked on down the corridor, mercifully for only a short time. Ahead of us, a vast light-filled space suddenly opened to our view. We climbed up a long flight of stairs and stepped fully into the light.

To anyone, but especially to the son of a bricklayer, the three-hundred-foot-long room would be a marvel. Despite all the years of disuse, nothing had marred the stunning expanse of its vaulted ceiling two stories above us. Intricately intertwined rows of pale yellow tiles soared upward from pillars between massive semicircular windows. Sun spilled from these windows, filling the huge space with the welcoming gleam of morning. Though cracked and dirty, the concrete floor retained something of the smooth patina made by millions of immigrant feet.

"In this room," my uncle said, "the people sat on pipes lined up all across the floor while they waited to go through the procedures. Even though they'd just made a terrible trip across the ocean, they had to sit there until hundreds of people ahead of them went first. They had to be examined by doctors who put chalk marks on their backs if they were sick. They had to have their eyes popped open with a hook for inspection. They had to answer questions and talk to officials who sat on a big, high platform, like kings, looking down on them all. But nobody could do this stuff without the interpreters. They were government workers hired to help the immigrants. One of the best interpreters was Fiorello La Guardia, who one day got to be a mayor of New York. These interpreters, they knew all the right answers to the questions. They were patient. They were kind. Without them, the millions of people who waited in this room, including that boy who wrote on the wall, would not have been allowed to stay. Sometimes I think about what one person can do to help a whole lot of people. I think about those interpreters. And then I think about today's young men, like the boys willing to fight for their country halfway around the world . . ." He paused. His eyes swept the vast, empty hall. At first, the place seemed absolutely silent, then a sound like a whisper seemed to fill it. The breath of ghosts. The wind from the river. "You know, Angelo, if you're looking for what kind of lawyer to be— what kind of man, really—why don't you remember this place and what the interpreters did for the grandparents of people like us, poor *campaesani* looking for a better life."

"IT'S THE VILLAGE!" Michele nudged me with enthusiasm. "Not Gerrard Street or Yorkville, but the *real* thing. Greenwich Village!"

I stood with him on Bleecker Street, which I could only assume was, unlike the street Kee Kee and Billy lived on in Toronto, the *real* Bleecker Street. My brother could hardly stand still, he was so excited at the prospect of sitting in a real U.S. coffeehouse and poking around in real U.S. boutiques run by new immigrants from India, Mexico and other disadvantaged nations that Michele was eager to assist by purchasing their exotic wares.

I could hardly stand still, either. Everywhere I turned I saw a skirt shorter than the one I'd just been looking at. An up-and-coming mayoralty candidate named John Lindsay had recently described these as skirts that were short to allow girls to be able to run, which they'd have to if they wore one.

After several hours of coffee and entertainment that I found fairly indistinguishable from that which Michele enjoyed in Toronto, we met a young man who told Michele that he would take us to see something that no "politically aware" social worker should miss.

Of course I was dead set against our going off into the streets of New York with a total stranger. Visions of thugs who would beat and rob us flashed into my imagination. "Cool it, Gelo," Michele admonished when I managed to get him into the rest room to privately warn him away from clear danger. "The guy's only going to take us around the corner and down the block. Don't make such a big deal out of everything."

Reluctantly, I followed Michele and the long-haired Bohemian to whom we'd just foolishly entrusted our lives.

It was past midnight, but the street was alive with people and music. From one of the many little clubs came a coarse, whiny voice, accompanied periodically by a harmonica—"Bob Dylan," the sign by the club's door read. Thank God, I thought, I don't have to listen to *that* on a regular basis.

As we rounded the corner of Tenth Street and Greenwich, I heard a sound that wasn't music, though it had a weird and compelling rhythm all its own. It was the sound of hundreds of women and a few men shouting simultaneously in a raucous cacophony of English, Spanish and the particular accents of the American Negro.

"Come in here," our escort said, inviting us into a coffee shop directly across the street from the grim twelve-story building on the corner where all this noise seemed to be centered. No fortress was ever more forbidding, more apparently impenetrable. Yet, an unlikely army was assailing it from the sidewalk, appearing to believe they could fell it with purses, scarves, brown paper bags and white paper notes shaped like the jets Lyndon Johnson was increasingly sending to Vietnam.

"What *is* it?" Michele and I both asked.

"It's the Women's House of Detention," said our host, whose name was Boomer, I later learned. "It's remand only."

"What?" Michele asked.

"Pretrial custody," I answered. "You mean it's a gigantic holding cell for women awaiting trial?"

"Innocent until proven guilty," Boomer replied, his voice dripping with a peculiar irony that was becoming the tone of social outrage everywhere. "Freedom of speech!" political protestors would soon be ironically declaring when growing numbers across the continent would begin to be routinely scraped off the sidewalk by police. But if there were any police pigs in the crowd across the street, they certainly weren't visible to me.

Boomer led us to a table by a window. In those days restaurant windows still opened, and he cranked the one by our table to the width of about an inch. That was enough for the screaming across the street to be clearly audible. The homogeneous crowd began to separate into individuals whose small dramas now played themselves out before my astonished eyes.

I saw, for example, a grandmotherly woman with three small girls, each dressed as if for church. The four, arranged in decreasing order of height, stood holding hands. The two free hands, the left hand of the grandmother and the right hand of the smallest girl, who was little more than a toddler, pointed in the same direction, toward a window far above them, from which a pale figure frantically waved.

I saw girlfriends, sisters and mothers of the accused winding up like baseball pitchers to hurl some forbidden object toward the few windows that the prisoners had managed to open or break. And for every person who attempted to toss something *up*, there seemed to be another person in another quadrant of the melee who clawed the air in anticipation of something being thrown *down*, most often notes that, when they finally floated down to the sidewalk, were immediately pounced on.

There were nowhere near as many males in the crowd as females. The boyfriends, brothers or husbands, whatever they were, seemed to fall into two categories: the bereaved and the enraged. The former stared up at the fortress with big, sorrowful eyes, with hands over the places they thought their hearts were, with spoken promises that were no more audible to me across the street than to the women behind bars. As for the latter, the enraged lovers, they were perfectly audible, even from across the street. "You bitch!" one cried. "How could you do this to *me?*"

"This scene is so bad it makes me ashamed to be human," Boomer said. The popularity of such sweeping statements about the human condition had not yet reached Toronto that spring, but they seemed to be the latest trend in New York. "But guys like you, you're going to change all this."

I glanced once more across the street. A fistfight had broken out between two women vying for an enviable position near a street lamp. A person who managed to stand beneath one of the three light standards on that side of the building could be distinctly seen by her loved one inside the jail.

"Guys like us are going to change everything?" Michele repeated skeptically. "You mean *Canadians?*"

Both my brother and I burst out laughing, but Boomer didn't think it was funny.

"Canadians willing to take in men who refuse to be co-opted by the military-industrial complex. Social workers who refuse to assist in the replication of tool-died capitalists. Lawyers who are champions of the poor and not pawns of the rich . . ."

It was late at night. No, it was early in the morning. My eyelids began to grow heavy as if gradually weighed down by Boomer's rich rhetoric, the way a buoyant tarpaulin can be weighed down by a small number of strategically placed stones.

But I thought I forced my eyes to stay open. I thought I looked across the street again. I thought I saw a tall, thin woman in scuffed black pumps, a gray straight skirt, a slightly yellowed nylon blouse with a Peter Pan collar, a red cardigan. I thought I saw her raise her slim hand and let fly from her long, lean fingers a note, a white bird that soared up into the air's free current, then circled the Women's House of Detention like a patched and secret ring.

"Wake up, Angelo," I heard Michele say. "It's time to get back to Uncle Tony's."

I roused myself, but the dream lingered.

Who *was* that woman in the morgue? What had she known or done that Gleason Adams had, because of her, thrown his fate to the wind?

Chapter 14

"While you were with Antonio in New York, a man came from the government and brought you this."

Her face shining with hopeful pride, my mother handed me an envelope. On the front was my name typed in the crisp script of a topnotch electric typewriter. When I turned the envelope over, I saw, embossed on the flap, the elaborate coat of arms of the Province of Ontario. Beneath that was printed the address of the attorney general's office.

She watched intently as I tore open the envelope, my nervous fingers ripping the coat of arms in two.

"What does it say, Gelo?"

I studied the single sheet of letter-size paper. Centered at the top, that embossed coat of arms again. Beneath that on the left, the address of the attorney general and the address of the actual sender and my own address. Beneath that, a file number, then the date. The letter had been written four days earlier. At the bottom was the usual complementary close, then the signature, then the typed name, then the title of the sender, then the initials of the man who had dictated the letter, in capitals, and of the woman who had typed it, in lowercase.

"For heaven's sake, Gelo, tell me what it says!"

Despite all the formal information, the body of the letter consisted of a single sentence. "Please see me on Tuesday, April 27, 1965, at 2 p.m. at the morgue." The letter was signed by Levi Rosen.

"Gelo?"

"It's nothing, Ma. It's just a meeting I have to go to for school."

"Must be some big-shot meeting if they send a government man right to the house."

A WARM SWEETNESS softened the April air as I made my way east on Lombard Street. I was held up for a few minutes by a delivery truck blocking the sidewalk in front of Nu-Style Chesterfield. Two men wrestled with a long sofa upholstered in a pattern of green, orange and purple that reminded me of a snake writhing.

The truck finally pulled away and when it did, I saw that a few doors down, a man in a suit was standing at the top of the stairs to the morgue. As I got closer, I realized that the man was Rosen himself. I glanced at my watch. I was not late. Why was he so anxious to see me?

I tripped a little on the bottom step, which must have been the reason Rosen was smiling as he extended his hand when I finally reached him. His handshake was firm and warm, and with his other hand, he patted me on the shoulder and turned me toward the door, which opened without his having to touch it. On the other side, doorknob in hand, stood the guard Gleason and I had seen the night of our fateful visit. The man shot me a glance that told me he wasn't any happier to see me now than he'd been then.

Rosen said nothing as he preceded me up the curved stairs to his office. In the absence of small talk, I could hear myriad sounds around me. The morgue was buzzing. I heard the voices of men echoing in the corridor. I heard doors—and presumably drawers—being slammed shut. Faintly but clearly audible, the varying whine of an electric saw started up, cut into something soft, hit an obstruction, forced its way through.

"This way," Rosen said, but I already knew the way. Gleason and I had spent some minutes eavesdropping outside Rosen's door.

The office looked as though the chief coroner had taken one of the rooms of his Forest Hill home and transported it downtown. Smooth, pale blue, wall-to-wall carpet, a mahogany desk, a single glass-doored bookcase in which rows of legal and medical books were carefully arranged according to size. Rosen signaled toward one of two chairs in front of the desk. He took his own seat and as he did so, I caught a glimpse of a photograph on a mahogany credenza behind him. In the picture Rosen stood with a pleasant-looking woman and two teenage girls. The four of them were standing on Rosen's front porch, in precisely the same spot I'd stood on the day I was trespassing.

My letter, I saw with a sudden jab of fear, was sitting alone in the center of Rosen's desk. He picked it up.

"I understand you are a first-year law student," he said. He had a light voice, friendly. But he was a very powerful man and I felt I must weigh each word. Did he think my letter was the hysterical outpouring of a student who'd gone off the deep end?

"Yes, sir," I answered.

"And you came here as part of your first-year studies?"

Not exactly, of course, but I wasn't going to argue with him. "You could say that, sir."

Levi Rosen was not a man given to idle conversation. I knew that from what I'd read in newspaper articles about his feud with the A-G. It seemed that our idle chitchat was now through. He appeared to be studying my letter and I began to feel pure dread. If he took the letter seriously, would I be subject to police interrogation about my suspicions that Gleason was implicated in the murder of the woman whose body had disappeared? Worse, if Rosen didn't take the letter seriously, could he report me to the Faculty of Law and have me removed from the law program, the way that unfortunate young man had been removed from the prosecutor's office?

"You're quite a convincing writer," Rosen said, breaking into my thoughts.

"Sir?"

"You are observant and articulate, Mr. Portal. No doubt those qualities will serve you well in your legal studies."

"Thank you, sir." I was more grateful for this reassurance that he wasn't going to kick me out than for his appreciation of my literary skills.

"But I think you need to be reminded of a few things, and I feel it my duty to remind you, since you appear to be under the impression that some sort of irregularity has occurred in my department."

Such a steely edge emerged in Rosen's voice that his previous warmth and friendliness seemed something I had imagined.

"No, sir, I—"

"Don't interrupt me, young man. I called you here to listen to me, not to listen to you." He shook the letter. The paper was cheap and thin. It rattled. "You better learn— and fast—that a man of the law does not speculate. He does not question the decision of his betters with no cause except his own inept, uninformed opinions. And above all, Mr. Portal, a man of the law never—" he shook the letter again "—*never* creates a document, a record of accusations, he cannot substantiate."

"Sir, I—"

He stood. He was a short man, but then, so are a lot of bullies. "You and your friend were here because I okayed it," he reminded me. "But you came without an appointment. You showed up with no warning and you happened to come at a time of crisis." He gestured as if to indicate the whole building. "Crisis is our profession, that's true," he said. "But nonetheless, some sense of respect is necessary. Public trust works both ways. You trust the coroner to fairly determine the legal implications of a death. And I trust you, as a member of the public, not to interfere in the work you have mandated to us. I have the power—indeed, Mr. Portal, I have the moral obligation—to do my job in the way that I see fit. If I elect to have a deceased examined somewhere other than here, I order that body removed. That in itself means nothing. Do you understand?"

I was afraid to answer. Was he saying that the body of the woman had been removed merely because he had decided it should be? Fine. But why?

"Mr. Portal, I asked you a question."

"Yes, sir. Yes, I understand."

He sat down. For a moment, there was silence. Was he gathering steam for another onslaught?

Perhaps not. He was quiet, almost friendly again, when he resumed. "I understand your concern about your friend, Mr. Portal, but you must take my professional word for it that at all times, with the exception of war and riot, homicide is always, *always*, Mr. Portal, the least likely explanation for a questionable death. I suggest you sit down with your friend and straighten the business of this letter out with a good man-to-man talk. Do I make myself clear?"

"Yes, sir."

"Our interview is over, then," he said. "You may see yourself out."

I didn't need to be told twice. I nearly ran to the door. When I reached it, I turned to say goodbye. I saw Rosen open one of the drawers of his desk. My letter was still in his hand and I realized he was going to save it. On the way down the stairs, I wondered. If he was so concerned about my creating documents and so sure what I had told him was useless speculation, why didn't he just throw my letter away?

"You're late, Portal, which makes you only a little better than your friend, Gleason. He's absent. He hasn't made a tutorial in weeks. Where is he?"

"I don't know, Professor Kavin."

"Forget him for now. Come in, Portal. There's news."

"News?"

"Yes." I carefully removed a stack of papers and sat down while Kavin finalized the required preparations of his pipe.

"I've spoken to Tuppin about you, lad. There's hope."

"You mean Tuppin is going to take me on?" I should have been overjoyed with this information; instead I felt a stab of self-doubt. Rushing from Rosen's office to Kavin's,

I'd pretty much concluded that the gist of Rosen's warning was that I should mind my own business. But I needed time to think. All I could think right now was that Tuppin's interest in me could be cancelled by a single phone call from Rosen, despite all of Kavin's hard work.

"Patience, Portal!" Kavin smiled. "I'd say we've reached the point at which Tuppin is willing to take your proposition under advisement. Considering that you may, in fact, be as talented a protégé of mine as I once was of his."

"What?"

"I told him about your work with Billy Johnson. Tuppin wants more. He wants you to interview Johnson again. He wants as clear and complete a personal history on Johnson as you can put together. He wants to know Johnson's parents' lineage. He wants to know the exact time and location of Johnson's birth. He also wants you to find out what tribal treaty arrangements exist between the Tuscaroras and New York State. He also wants a similar workup on any treaties between the Muskeg Cree and the Province of Ontario." He pulled hard on his pipe. "Can you do this, Portal? You'll have to go out and talk to Johnson again."

"I don't think that would be a problem."

Only it was. Because when I got to Bleecker Street later the same day, there was a wrecking crew dismantling the house where I'd last seen Billy and Kee Kee.

I hoped against hope that Billy had told Michele where he was going and that Michele could pull himself away from Martin Luther King and Hanoi and Saigon long enough to help me find out where Billy had gone.

"I'M NOT SURE where Billy is, man. Like he and Kee Kee had to split. He appreciates that you tried to help, but

213

maybe you can't." Michele could be pretty vague for a man intent on saving the world.

"You got me into this, Michele," I told him, "and now my project depends on it. You've got to help me."

"Chill out, Angelo. I'll do what I can."

APRIL TURNED INTO May, the days turned warm, the black trees turned lacy green with new leaves. I was studying almost twenty hours a day now, researching the Johnson material, preparing for the final exams that moved ever closer. I tried to put Gleason Adams into a little compartment in my mind labeled "Other People's Problems, Not Mine," and I nearly succeeded. But when he missed yet another Kavin tutorial, I decided to look for him one more time. Call it curiosity, call it a hungry need for a friend, even one as dismissive of me as Gleason. I psyched myself up enough to get on the Rosedale bus and return to Whitney Square.

I remember that it was unseasonably hot that day, at least eighty degrees, but a strong wind blew, and from time to time, I had to brush the hair from my eyes. My studies had made me neglect my grooming. I was beginning to look as messy as Michele.

The grass of the square was that green that falls between the tentative chartreuse of April and the verdant lushness of June. Spiky crowns of dandelions dotted the park, but soon someone's gardener or one of the men who worked for the city would crop the errant flowers and mow the lawn into a smooth carpet beneath the oaks. Red and yellow tulips, the pink and white cups of our northern false magnolia, yellow daffodils, dark purple buds of what would soon be lilacs seemed to scent the air. Whitney

Square was paradise, but I felt that my friend was the snake lurking there. I didn't know what Gleason had done, but it was something illegal. There was no other explanation for his behavior. There wasn't much explanation for my behavior, either. Except that, try as I might, I couldn't file away the Adams matter as easily as Levi Rosen had filed my letter.

I took a deep breath of spring air, tugged on my rayon shirt and ran my fingers through my hair, which immediately sprang back again on my forehead. I wondered if Gleason's parents were home. It had been nearly two months since they'd gone to Switzerland to claim the body of their son. I dreaded having to ask them about the disappearance of their remaining son, but I had no choice. Nobody had seen Gleason in weeks. If he had truly disappeared, it could mean several things, chief among them being that he'd become a fugitive from the law. I wasn't going to suggest *that* to Gleason's parents. Then again, they weren't about to reveal such a thing to me, either, if they indeed knew where Gleason was.

Another foolish expedition of mine, I felt, as I pushed the ivory button beside the door and again heard the melodious chimes ring faintly from deep within the stately Rosedale home.

I waited. Across the square, a bluejay called raucously, its cry a shocking incongruity in the quiet confines of the park.

Still no one came. I turned, turned back, decided I should give it one more try and rang again. The instant my finger left the button, the door opened more forcefully than I expected. Startled, I jumped back. My foot caught on the flagstone step and I stumbled, grabbing the nearest object, which happened to be a juniper bush, in an attempt to right myself.

I heard soft, high-pitched laughter. I looked up to see the pretty little maid standing in the doorway. She wore her uniform, a cliché in black and white. "I like your hair," she giggled.

A person more familiar with the manners and morés of Rosedale than I was then would have taken her insolent casualness for the only thing it could mean: that her employers were absent and not expected to return anytime soon. I, however, did not realize this and, regaining my balance, politely asked, "May I see Mr. Adams, please?"

"You mean Gleason's father? Sure, you can see him. If you happen to be in Zurich."

"What?"

"Zurich. It's in Switzerland," she explained with exaggerated emphasis on each word. "Don't they teach you boys *anything* at the university?"

"What about Gleason, then?" I asked.

She didn't answer. "You look kind of, uh, hot," she said with a wide smile. "You want a Pepsi or a Coke?"

"Listen," I said, "I'm a little concerned about Gleason. He . . ."

She shrugged. "So he skips school once in a while. Big deal. You want a Coke or not?"

She was a cute little thing with dark hair wound into a few spit curls at the temple, a style I doubted she'd have gotten away with if her bosses were around. She had a nice figure, too, only a little disguised by her uniform. "Okay," I said, "a Coke would be cool."

"Come on in, then."

I expected to be seated alone in the parlor as I had been before, and have the maid return from the kitchen with the drink, but that's not what happened. Instead, she guided me straight past the parlor and through a long, narrow corridor that led directly to the back of the house.

We moved fast, but not too fast for me to make several observations, the main one being that the house was cold, the sort of cold that results from a building being closed up before the weather warms.

I noticed also that there was not a single light on in the whole, vast first floor. True, it was bright outside, but no window could light every corner of such big rooms. In addition, the window shades and drapes were all drawn shut. It was darker in Gleason's Whitney Square home than it had been in the deserted halls of Ellis Island.

As I passed, I noted that the portrait of Gleason's brother gazed out still from its appointed place, and it now seemed to me, as we neared the back of the house, that his spirit was standing guard here in some way, as if he were awaiting the return of those who had loved him and whose hopes for his promising life had been dashed.

"Here we are," the maid said. She gave a swinging door a good slap and it flew open to reveal an enormous sunny kitchen with sparkling new appliances, rows of casement windows opening onto a luxurious back garden, and a long white table with eight chairs around it set in front of the window, no doubt to give the household staff a good view of the garden while they ate. Nobody, however, sat at it now. This kitchen, like the rest of the house, had the feeling of domestic life indefinitely suspended.

"Is all the staff gone, too?" I asked as the maid set a Coke bottle and a crystal glass in front of me at the table. She plunked another bottle of Coke on the table for herself and sat cater-corner to me, her knees accidentally brushing mine. Either she'd hiked up her skirt in her employers' absence or the Adamses allowed their maid to adopt the short style that was making me feel very hopeful about the coming summer fashions.

"Yeah," she said, "they split." She shook her curly head. "It's really sad," she said, "about the Adamses' son—Gerard was his name; Gleason told me he used to call him Gerard of Gleason and Gerard . . . Anyway, Gerard got discovered dead in Switzerland a little while ago. I mean, they found his body. He was missing for a long time, lost while skiing or something like that. When they finally found him, Mr. and Mrs. Adams went to Europe to bury him and they said they didn't know when they could come back. Maybe even never. But I have to keep the house open just in case. Except it's not really open. I just—"

"But I thought they went to Switzerland so they could get the body and bring it back to Canada," I interrupted.

The girl's automatic response was, "No, I don't think so," but the minute she said it, she seemed to realize that maybe it wasn't a good idea to talk so openly about the family's business to a stranger, even if the stranger was Gleason's friend.

"Maybe," she said, "maybe they planned to do that. To come back with the body. I don't know. Anyway, they *didn't* come back. They stayed there and who knows, maybe they'll stay forever. Makes my job easy." She smiled and took a slug of Coke straight from the bottle.

"But what about Gleason?" I asked in confused alarm. "Where is he?"

"He couldn't care less about this place. He already moved out."

"He moved?" Now I felt that ancient fury begin to rise from the back of my brain and settle in my stomach. It was the old joke. I took a vacation and when I came back, my "friend" had moved without telling me. Once more, I was about to decide to give up my association with Gleason and his whole family forever, had not the conversation with the maid taken a completely unexpected turn.

"Gleason came with some other guys in a couple of cars and they took some pieces of his furniture, some books, all his clothes. He said he was moving to an apartment downtown and that he'd send his father the address. Then he went and I didn't see him since. That was about a week ago, maybe the day after Easter or the day before, I can't remember. To tell the truth, this whole family has acted weird for a long time, since just after I came here a year ago." She took another slug of Coke. "You see, there was this robbery."

"In this house?" I asked in surprise. Surely there were locks on every sparkling window and a burglar alarm hooked into the local police station.

"Yeah. Like in the middle of the night and everything. Except the police never caught the burglar or even figured out how he got in. And only a few things were stolen, too. Gleason's mother's room was messed up a little, but nothing was missing. Everything that got stolen was out of Gleason's father's room. And it was all jewelry. But the thing that really drove Mr. Adams off the deep end was that whoever the thief was, he stole something from right by Mr. Adams's face, from the table next to his pillow. Mr. Adams said the thief stole the piece of jewelry he cared most about in the whole world."

"What was it?" I asked. I hadn't realized I was holding my breath. I exhaled.

The cute little maid smiled sadly. "It was a really mean thing to steal," she said, shaking her head again. "That lousy burglar took something Mr. Adams wore every day for thirty-five years."

"His wedding ring," I said softly.

"Yeah," she repeated. "His wedding ring."

I WENT STRAIGHT from Whitney Square back to the Continental bar, back to the prossies, the other women, the *odor*. From the sublime to the ridiculous. It was two o'clock in the afternoon, and I figured the place would be pretty empty. By the time my eyes adjusted to the dark, I'd found the burly waiter/bouncer I'd encountered the last time. "I have to talk to you right away," I said, trying to sound tough and almost succeeding.

More used to peering into the semidarkness than I, he studied my face. A look of recognition crossed his features and I assumed that he remembered me.

He had the archetypical mug's face, the nose crooked from too many fights, the jaw hard and perpetually clenched, the eyes just deep enough to hide the fact that they were shifty. "I seen you in here before, didn't I?" Before I could answer, he added, "You're Sal Portalese's boy, ain't you? Not his son. One of his nephews."

The question startled me and I blurted, "Yes. Yes, I am."

A slow smile split the face of the man. "You better not let him catch you down here with the ladies—or with the fancy boys, either. Sal, he don't like those kinda people."

I thought about the society dolls I'd seen in the back room. "Look," I said, "I need to know if my friend has been in here again. The guy I came with a couple of weeks ago?"

The man smirked, opened his beefy lips as if to offer an opinion about something, but changed his mind. "I ain't seen that kid since the time I seen him with you, but that don't mean he ain't been around."

"Alone?" I asked.

"Who knows?" he answered. "How is Sal these days, anyway? You see much of him?"

I had the feeling that if I answered his question correctly, I had a chance of getting some answers to my own questions. "I'm on my way over there right now," I offered.

The man made a kind of growling noise, which I took to be laughter. "You're a big boy so you should know without my tellin' you that your little friend is a beard."

"A beard?"

"Yeah. A guy that escorts ladies who maybe would rather be with other ladies." He shrugged. "And if he needs a skirt for some fancy do, he's got a skirt. That's how it works."

"Did you ever see Gleason—my friend, I mean—in here with a woman? Maybe with a, uh, skirt?"

The thug looked at me like I was from another planet, which in a way I was.

"Sonny," he said, "I don't know what you're after, but whatever it is, you ain't gonna find it here. You wanna know about your pal, you go to Letros." He smiled widely. "Better stand with your back against the wall when you get there," he added.

I ignored his vulgar comment. "Just tell me if you ever saw Gleason with a woman, somebody he was with more than once—on a regular basis, that is." I could have added, "My uncle wants to know," but I wasn't about to lie again, especially about Uncle Salvatore.

"Nah, I ain't never seen that kid with a broad." He hesitated. "But," he said, "I heard he hangs out with some guy now and then."

"A guy? What does this guy look like?"

From somewhere on his person, the bouncer pulled out a twin to the filthy rag he'd had the other day and swiped the table between us in the same contemptuous way he had before. "He looks like a fag," he said. "What do you think he looks like?"

THE SAME SMARMY doorman I'd seen before stood outside Letros, and when he recognized me, he again had that tables-turned look of a man who was once bullied, now bully. "Hi, honey," he oozed. "All alone tonight? Maybe your pretty friend prefers somebody who's got enough nerve to actually come in."

He giggled lasciviously, obviously a person who could make a double entendre out of anything. I would have hit him, but I didn't want to get grease on my hand.

Reluctant as I was to enter the homosexual hangout, my drive to find Gleason grew stronger at every obstacle. The impulse that had sent me to the police on Easter Sunday, the determination that had made me seek out Levi Rosen— both were back in full force. It was now perfectly clear to me that Gleason had used me as a pawn. He had lured me to the morgue that night. He had lied about having an appointment. That had been a ploy to get me there, to use me to cover up that he was not at the morgue for a law school project. Gleason must have known in advance that the rings were on that woman's body. He had needed me to bolster his presence there, to further his sole objective, which I now saw more clearly than ever. Far from being a moment's careless impulse, a prank, taking those rings had been Gleason's sole purpose that night. He had taken them to save himself—at the expense of jeopardizing me. What better way to hide his deed than to present the case as a study to the Law

Faculty? Such a clever way to divert suspicion from himself was exactly the sort of thing Gleason would cook up. And he was arrogant enough to pull it off, too, dragging me down with him. I didn't know what Gleason had really done to that poor woman or why, but despite Rosen's anger and warning, I was not going to let this matter drop. I was not going to let Gleason Adams get away with murder. I was going to find him and hold him to account.

"Let me by," I said to the doorman, who stood squarely in my path, grinning. He refused to move; I felt an energizing jolt of dangerous anger. "Get the hell out of my way."

"You need a password, doll," he taunted. "I can't let just *anybody* in here."

"I'll give you a password," swinging at his smirking face and surprising myself. The good little Catholic boy?

But he was faster than I was. He grabbed my wrist, pulling it up between us, with such a hard grip I thought he would twist my hand off. His eyes were steely now and they held mine in the age-old challenge. Whoever dropped his gaze first, lost.

Or maybe not. Maybe the rules had changed. "People like you aren't in charge anymore," my enemy hissed. "You remember that, sister." He dropped my wrist, got out of my way.

Entering from the bright street, I had to stand still for a few moments for my eyes to adjust. I also had to calm down and slow down. My objective was clear. I had to find Gleason. Exactly what I would, or could, do with him when I did find him was far less clear. I forced myself to head further inside.

Maybe it was the early hour, but except for the fact that everyone in the bar was male, a not unusual situation for most bars in Toronto in 1965, I didn't see a thing in Letros I wouldn't have seen anywhere else. It had decent decor, reasonable bar service. I didn't even feel the need, as the bouncer had suggested, to keep my back to the wall.

By the time I was twenty-three, I had enough experience—I should say years of experience—of the geography and sociology of the bar. In this bar, as in every bar, at least one person was going to be there for the specific purpose of spilling his guts to some stranger for the price of a drink. And at least one person would be lonely enough or eager enough to probe the mundane secrets of the world that he would spring for that drink. The latter person today was me. The former was a guy in short sleeves and muscular biceps seated alone at the far end of the bar. I took a breath, walked over and asked if I could join him.

I was nervous, but only at first. I asked him if he came to this bar often and he said he did. He told me his first name. I told him mine. We talked about work. I was a contractor. He was an insurance salesman. Blah. Blah. Blah. It took another drink before he was willing to tell me all about the Letros regulars, whom I said I'd never met because I was from out of town. It took one more drink before I got him to identify Gleason Adams as an habitué of the place.

"He was here a week or so ago," my new friend began. "I'd seen him a couple of times before. He came in with this ring and asked around to see if anybody knew who it belonged to. I thought that was very strange."

"Why?" I asked.

"For two reasons. First, a number of men have rings like that. Even the inscription isn't unique. That poem by the monk, you know?"

"Yeah," I said. "Sure."

"The other reason I thought it was strange was the way he asked. He acted like he was just going through the motions. It seemed like a put-on. As if he were trying to impress somebody or trying to prove something."

I thought about that for a minute. "As though he was establishing some sort of alibi?" I asked.

The insurance man looked puzzled. "What do you mean?"

"Well, I answered, "not an alibi exactly. I mean, could he have been just pretending he didn't know whose ring it was?"

"Why would he want to do that?"

"I'm not sure." I recalled how distraught Gleason had been when he came out of Letros. "Did you see him when he left that day?" I asked.

The insurance man wrinkled his handsome brow. "I think maybe he got in an argument right before he left. Maybe somebody called his bluff."

"Called his bluff?"

"Yeah. I heard somebody tell him to grow up and face the facts. After that he got mad and stormed out."

If this was a clue to what was going on with Gleason, it wasn't much help. He got told to grow up and face the facts about once a day, on average.

I decided I'd got about as much information here as I was going to get. I thanked my new friend and got up to leave. As I turned to walk away, he put his hand on my thigh. "You have a phone number?" he asked.

I smiled to hide my nervousness and stuck my hand in my pocket to buy time to figure out how to get away gracefully. "I'm staying with a friend. I got his number here someplace." My fingers closed on a rumpled piece of paper. I pulled it out and studied it. "Here it is," I said. I reached for a cocktail napkin and carefully copied a number from the list onto it.

When I was a block away, my cowardly dishonesty hit me and I felt ashamed. But then, I thought, maybe the insurance salesman and Spardini the undertaker would dig each other. Stranger things had happened.

"HE'S IN A rooming house on Parliament Street. He doesn't drink at all, not a drop. And now he's got to live in a neighborhood full of drunks."

"Alcoholics, Michele. You yourself told me never to use the word *drunk*."

"Yeah, man. Right on."

We sat at the kitchen table with huge slabs of beef in front of us. For about a month after Easter, my mother worked hard to compensate for all the meatless Lenten meals recently served. I, however, was not the least bit hungry. I had hit a dead end with Gleason and now I was about to hit a dead end with Billy Johnson, too. I could feel it coming

"Can you give me the address, Michele?"

My brother cut a hunk off the steak on his plate, speared the piece with his fork, lifted it toward his face, but stopped before the food met his lips. He pulled the fork back and stared at it intensely. "I just thought of something, Gelo," he said.

I leaned toward him. "What? Something about Billy Johnson?"

Michele didn't seem to hear me. As if hypnotized, he just kept his eyes glued to that fork.

"Michele?"

"Gelo," he said, "I've just had an epiphany. Do you realize that animals are our brothers?"

"For God's sake, Michele! *I'm* your brother. And I've got a problem. If I don't interview Billy again, Tuppin's going to refuse me for sure. Then I end up with no summer placement. I would have to spend a whole extra year in the law program. It's the tenth of May. There's no time to lose."

"I'm going to be a vegetarian," was Michele's reply. "From this hour, I'm never going to eat an animal again."

"Michele, you weirdo! Nobody is vegetarian except Buddhist monks and *nonni* without teeth! Forget this latest dumb craze! Tell me how I can find Billy."

"Gelo," Michele said, finally putting down his fork, "I can ask Billy, but I don't think he wants to go any further on this draft-resistance bag."

"What?"

"He's grateful that you met him and were willing to help him, but he's starting to think he should just go."

"To Vietnam?" I asked in shock.

"Look, Gelo, you have to respect everybody's right to do their own thing, even if it's different from your own thing. Dig?"

"Yeah, Michele," I answered. "I dig, all right. I dig my grave with my own stupidity. I trusted you and I trusted Gleason Adams. Now I've got no chance of interning with Tuppin." *And no chance of bringing a killer to justice.* But I didn't tell the vegetarian that.

PREDICTABLY, UNCLE SALVATORE wanted a report about our trip to New York. Remarkably, he asked me out to lunch, and to the one place in town I would most happily have chosen had my preference been taken into consideration, which it most assuredly had not.

I had never been in Osgoode Hall before and the simple majesty of the place took my breath away. From the outside, the golden-hued stone building looked like an eighteenth-century English manor house. A wide drive of gray, hand-hewn paving stones separated the front of the building from a formal garden enclosed by a tall wrought-iron fence. Its intricately curved designs and cleverly engineered gates were originally intended to keep cows off the property of the Law Society of Upper Canada—or Yankees, depending on who told you the story. A light breeze blew pink petals from a row of flowering fruit trees. The petals drifted like rosy snow over banks of white tulips and purple hyacinths.

Inside were multicolored Byzantine-style mosaic floors, white marble balustrades, a double lobby two stories high topped by a square, stained-glass dome, portraits of chief justices throughout the decades of the administration of justice in the courts of Ontario, and also the only known portrait of Queen Victoria that showed her malformed left arm.

"There you are!" I heard the voice echo in the spacious lobby and spun around to see from which direction it came. When my eye caught him just inside the twenty-foot mahogany front door with its etched-glass windows, I noted that Uncle Salvatore seemed at home in this elegant old Ontario setting. Walking toward me, he didn't rush. He'd long ago told me that important men never hurry and had reminded me many times since. But there was a veiled urgency to his manner, as if he must not and would not keep some other important man waiting, a man, it could only be, who was even more important than he.

Naturally his attitude made me extremely nervous. Uncle Salvatore had a way of interfering in my life at just those moments I teetered on the verge of disaster. I offered a silent prayer that he wouldn't ask me about my law project, which, now that Billy was reluctant and Gleason fugitive, was not exactly about to win an award for academic excellence.

A court officer in official dress, including a knee-length black jacket with tails and white gloves, escorted us along a red-carpeted hallway and into a mirrored elevator that rose and deposited us immediately outside of a room that I had previously known only as a legend: the gilded Barristers' Dining Room.

"I thought only members of the bar could eat here," I whispered to my uncle.

He ignored the comment. "In a minute," he said, "you are going to meet a good friend of mine, a person who has reaped the full rewards of being a man of the law. I want you to pay attention, Angelo. I want you to listen to every word he says. You will lose if you don't."

Throughout my life, Uncle Salvatore had introduced me to my betters with just such a warning. In one ear. Out the other.

I nodded like a boy and followed as a uniformed waitress led us across the room. Hushed voices, the rustle of fine linen, the almost silent tread of feet on the smooth, royal blue carpet, the ring of crystal, the clink of silver against porcelain—these all seemed accompaniment to the melodious strains of a live trio softly playing in front of white silk curtains in a corner of the room.

I was so taken by the ambience that I failed to see our host until I was too close to adjust my facial expression and hide my shock when I realized who he was.

Magistrate B. Sheldrake Tuppin held court behind an array of crystal and silver that seemed to reflect back the sparkling vivacity of his smile. His eyes fell on Uncle Salvatore. "Sam!" he said, extending his hand across the white expanse of the best table in the house, set beneath a window draped in gold velvet with a sheer inner curtain open to reveal the garden below. "Such a pleasure, Sam. I'm so very glad you were free today."

"My nephew Ellis," Uncle Salvatore said.

I composed myself and stepped forward. In the book-lined confines of his chamber, the magistrate had seemed older somehow and certainly less dapper than he was today in a gray suit, subtly checked vest, and burgundy tie. Shockingly, he was not wearing a white shirt, but a very pale gray one with a razor-thin burgundy stripe. The effect was one of understated elegance and I made note of it for later imitation.

"Your nephew and I have had the pleasure of meeting before," Tuppin said. "Have a seat."

We both sat. And for the next two hours all I said was "thank you" and "no, thank you." Thank you to avocado stuffed with shrimp. No thank you to "a nice little chardonnay from France, which will someday be redundant because our vineyards in Ontario will produce one just as nice." Thank you the next time the chardonnay was offered and the next and the time after that. Thank you to steak tartare, which I did not realize would be raw and pretended to eat with the relish of an experienced gourmand. No thank you to salad or dessert or even coffee, because I thought I would be sick. Thank you, however, to a fifteen-year-old smoky, peaty, salty single-malt scotch with which I pretended to be unfamiliar so as not to arouse the curiosity of my uncle from whose liquor cabinet I had long been sneaking tastes of just such a drink.

Of course, there was a point to all this and through the haze in my head, I tried to figure out what it was. Celebration? Tuppin said nothing about the Billy Johnson proposal. He gave no indication that he was about to change his mind and take me on as an intern, after all, based on what he'd learned about my proposal from Kavin.

Perhaps, I thought, this display of what Michele called "conspicuous consumption" might be intended to encourage me to choose a branch of the calling that had a reasonable prospect of high financial return. Sheldrake Tuppin winked at Uncle Salvatore. "If the poor are left to help each other," the magistrate said, "they'll all perish. A man serves no one by keeping himself impoverished. A man who wants to serve others is wise to look to his own interests first. A successful man is far more able to help the unfortunate than an unsuccessful one."

Uncle Salvatore dipped his head ever so slightly as if in deference to the wisdom of the magistrate. It was a supplicant's gesture and cost me a moment of intense embarrassment. I think it embarrassed Tuppin, too. He looked away from my uncle without saying anything. If there was a lesson in this lunch for me, it was that even Uncle Salvatore could make a mistake.

Dessert was a sweet wine, nothing like the dusky Italian muscatel of my Sunday afternoons on Clinton Street. It was a clear, light, topaz-colored, costly sauterne. I couldn't resist holding it up to the light before I sipped. As I lowered the small crystal glass to my lips, I saw that Sheldrake Tuppin's eyes were on my face. He was smiling but there was no mirth in those eyes. "Young man," he said with uncharacteristic softness, "I understand you've had a bit of a dust-up with Levi Rosen."

"Sir?" I asked in alarm. How did Magistrate Tuppin know I'd been to the morgue?

"Well done, Mr. Ellis Portal. That upstart needs to be told now and again. My boss will be pleased."

"Your boss?"

Tuppin laughed. "Yes. Even I have a boss. His name is Garrey. Attorney General Garrey."

UNCLE SALVATORE WAS silent in the limo and so was I. It was no longer whiskey and wine that were confusing me. I struggled to figure out the implications of what Tuppin had said. Did he know I was searching for Gleason? Did he know I suspected my friend of murder? Could Tuppin also know that Rosen's fury had been aroused by my questioning the removal of a body from the morgue? And if Tuppin did know, did that mean my concern was in vain because the authorities were aware of that removal? *What if,* I thought in alarm, *the authorities were implicated in the disappearance of the body?* Had Rosen admitted as much? If that were true, then clearly there was a cover-up going on. I shook my head. I was beginning to feel I'd never solve this puzzle. Maybe I'd never see Gleason again. Did the thought make me happy or sad?

"Cheer up, son," Uncle Salvatore said, putting his hand on my shoulder as the car pulled up in front of our house. "You'll get what you want. Don't worry about it."

"PA TOOK A CALL FOR YOU," Michele said when I walked into the kitchen.

"A call? Who from? Where's Pa now?"

Michele shrugged. "Gelo," he said, "Billy Johnson wants to see you. He says today or forget it."

I had only a few minutes to wash my face, change into jeans and gather the copious notes I'd made on Billy Johnson's case. For all its interesting legal aspects, the case was tragic for Billy, at least as far as I could tell. I had decided I had the obligation to advise Billy to get a real lawyer. I saw only one way he could avoid going to Vietnam. I hated to think that telling him this and recording his reaction might be all I needed to complete my project.

I was surprised when Michele told me we were going to walk to Billy's new home. Not to his former dump on Parliament Street, but to a well-kept house not far from our own. "The anti-draft people are moving him around. They'll probably keep him here until he splits," Michele informed me. "They think he's going to change his mind and go underground. Then they'll go to the paper with the story. Billy will be a hero."

Billy and Kee Kee were staying on an upper floor in nicely furnished but, I noted, separate rooms. Nothing in the place seemed to be theirs, though. I wondered whether the wrecker's ball had smashed all the furniture I'd seen in their other home.

"Electricity went. Water went. And now we went," Kee Kee said. "We wanted to show them they couldn't get us out, but they were right and we were wrong." It was the longest speech I'd ever heard her make and at the end of it, she sank onto the floor beside Billy's chair and rested her head on his knee. He reached down and tenderly smoothed her hair. Seeing that gesture made my message a little easier to deliver.

"Billy," I began, "I've put a lot of hours into your case and I made a number of cogent discoveries about tribal law, Canadian immigration law and U.S. federal statutes. But the fact of the matter is I found no way to prove that you are exempt from any law binding on an American citizen. If you don't renounce, and I take you at your word that you refuse to, you have but one recourse left to avoid the draft. And you're going to have to act fast, because my research shows the law regarding the action I'm about to recommend is probably going to change soon, too. Then you will have no choice. You will be drafted."

Billy stroked Kee Kee's shining black hair again. "What do I have to do?" he asked.

"It's not so very bad," I said, smiling. "What you have to do is marry Kee Kee. And right away. Childless married men are still exempt from the draft, but they won't be exempt for long."

Now it was Billy Johnson who smiled. But it was a smile of defeat. "I can't, man," he said. "I can't marry Kee Kee."

I couldn't understand why. She was so sweet, so lovely. Suddenly a thought struck me. I glanced at Kee Kee. She raised her head. "Is Kee Kee your sister?" I asked. "Is that why you can't marry her?"

"Kee Kee is my sister the way you and Michele are my brothers, Ellis," he answered solemnly. "And someday—I guess when I come back from Vietnam—I will marry her. But I can't marry her now. Because now, she is only twelve years old."

I thought he was kidding. I thought he and Kee Kee were putting me on. And indeed Kee Kee did seem to find the situation humorous. With her face against Billy's knee, I heard her muffled laugh. She lifted her head and smiled, a perfectly innocent, angelic smile. The smile of a little girl who always trusts the grown-ups.

I worked almost all night—in the library until it closed, then at home until far past midnight. Before she went to bed, I talked Arletta into getting up at 5 a.m. to type the final version of my law project. She insisted on the outrageous fee of a dollar a page.

But it was worth it. By 8:30 a.m. the proposal was under Kavin's door, and by noon Sheldrake Tuppin had accepted it "for serious consideration." Kavin said that phrase almost always meant yes.

I felt triumphant. But not for long. When I got home from classes that evening, my mother told me Michele was too sick to eat. I couldn't imagine what might be wrong. I ran upstairs and found my brother not in his bed, but sitting on the edge of it, his head in his hands, his dark curls entwined in his fingers.

"What's wrong, Michele?" I asked, moving carefully toward him. He raised his face and I saw that he was crying. "What's wrong, man? What happened?"

"I just got a call from Kee Kee," Michele said. "He's in Buffalo. He's handing himself over. He's on his way, man. He's on his way to Nam."

I sat down beside Michele. "You can't take this personally," I said. "You did all you could. If you get emotionally involved like this, you'll burn out and never be able to help anybody. I know this is a bummer, but you'll get over it. Don't let feeling cloud your judgment. As I said, don't take it personally."

It was only a little while later that I learned I should have listened to my own advice.

Chapter 15

Disappointed for Billy Johnson but thrilled at Kavin's reception of my project, I hunkered down for the final onslaught of the year: studying for exams. Nobody mentioned Gleason Adams. Nobody seemed to notice he was not around. Like the man who had "disappeared" from the prosecutor's office, no trace of Adams seemed to remain.

If my conscience bothered me, I salved it with the memory of those cold eyes of Sheldrake Tuppin. Why should I ruin my chances of success to save a flaky snob like Gleason? I confined my thoughts to Gleason's legal transgressions. I didn't want to think about any other kind. I was no longer sure what role he had played at the morgue, because the incident itself no longer seemed to matter. I was more worried about my future than about Gleason's past. Besides, I was now in twenty-four-hour study mode.

On the evening of the day I completed my first exam, exhausted and deep in thought, I neglected to do something I'd been doing regularly recently: I neglected to avoid Philosophers' Walk after dark. Instead of going the long way up University Avenue and around the corner to Bloor Street, I absentmindedly cut through the familiar space between buildings.

It was another sweet May night, the air scented heavily now with lilacs bursting into bloom. Though it was nearly 9 p.m., it was not yet totally dark. Realizing my mistake, I hastened my steps along the shadowy, winding path so I could get off it as quickly as possible.

But I was not quick enough. I heard the determined tread of someone else on the path, someone walking behind me.

I walked faster. My pursuer, if that's what he was, quickened his pace.

My heart began to pound. Not from exertion, not in those days. The May evening seemed suddenly to turn as steamy as August and a thin film of perspiration coated my face, the back of my neck where my hair curled hotly, my trembling hands that I shoved in my pockets in order to appear nonchalant, my chest beneath the white shirt my mother had starched and ironed. Stones on the path skittered away from my rushing steps. I was running now, so fast I could feel wind brush my ear, wind scented with lilacs.

I kept my ear cocked, aware of the possibility of clandestine laughter from beyond the trees and the hushed declarations of promises ashamed of daylight, but I heard nothing. Perhaps it was too early in the evening for assignations.

Who was the man running after me? I didn't want to know. I only wanted to get away. And when he breathily called my name in a voice I almost recognized, I did not turn back, but instead, in a burst of speed, sprinted for the steps ahead, steps that led to Bloor Street and safety.

"For heaven's sake, Portal, slow down. Wait for me."

I dashed up the stairs, but at the top, I stopped and turned. Silhouetted against the bright lights of Bloor, I was actually far more vulnerable than I had been in the shadows below, but only if my pursuer intended to shoot me, which, of course, was not the harm I really feared.

"Wait," he cried again. Darting out of the shadows beneath the trees, he reached the bottom of the stairs. I stepped sharply back and the glow from the street fell on his face.

"Dr. Slater!"

"Portal," he said, huffing as he began to climb the stairs. "Don't run. I have to talk to you."

He was dressed as I was, in a suit, but rumpled and the worse for wear.

"What are you doing here?" I asked stupidly.

He struggled to catch his breath. "Gleason Adams told me I was likely to find you leaving Flavelle House at nine when your exam was done."

An exam Gleason himself had missed.

I stepped down and moved forcefully toward the pathologist. Now it was Slater who jumped back. "What do you mean Gleason told you?" I asked. "You know where he is, where he's been for the last two weeks while I've been going crazy looking for him?"

"Portal, there are some things you have to know."

I felt a flash of fear. Had Gleason been arrested? Or something worse? If Gleason was in danger, who was there to rescue him? Or was it already too late for rescue? Then another thought occurred to me. I remembered the books I'd read about suicide and murder. I remembered the classic potential presuicide symptoms: hyperactivity alternating with periods of unusual calm and morose quiet. Radical changes in behavior. A lack of interest in one's ordinary tasks and obligations.

"Dr. Slater," I said, "are you telling me that Gleason is . . ." The right words wouldn't come. How did one ask a pathologist whether someone was his . . . what? Patient? Client? Cadaver? "Is Gleason dead?" I forced myself to ask. "Is that what you're trying to tell me?"

"No. No, Portal, not that." He glanced around. "Let's go along on Bloor and somewhere we can talk. I won't need much time to explain what I've learned. You can decide what to do with the information."

I didn't like the sound of that, but we walked along Bloor Street with Dr. Slater remaining silent beside me until we were sitting side by side at the counter of the diner. I couldn't help but reflect that the last time I'd been there, I'd been trying to get rid of Gleason. Was it too late to get him back?

"I have to begin by telling you that Adams sent me to find you."

I was surprised that this man, who had met Gleason only two months before, now seemed close enough to be taken into his confidence, but the only question I asked was, "Does Gleason need my help? Is he in trouble?"

"Yes, I think you could call it that." Dr. Slater seemed to study the liquid in the cup in front of him. He didn't elaborate.

"What's wrong?" I pressed. "Where is he?"

The pathologist seemed to think about his answer for a painfully long time before he finally yielded his response. "Those irregularities the night you and Gleason came to the morgue," he began. "You must have thought about them often."

I flashed back to that March night. The scuffle at the door, the reluctance to admit us, the changes of light in the little parlor at the bottom of the stairs, the overheard argument with the chief coroner, the brief examination of the strange cadaver, the body's disappearance, the rings. "Yes," I said, "I have." What was this all about if it wasn't about those irregularities?

"The body did not come unescorted to the morgue," Dr. Slater said. "Many of the people we see—I mean, of course, the dead who come into our charge—are unattended. Often we have difficulty locating next of kin, friends, neighbors, even casual acquaintances. However, I have discovered that in this instance, the deceased came in a hearse that was sent at the request of Dr. Rosen. Though I was unaware of it at the time, I now know that in that hearse, accompanying the deceased, was a man named Neil Dennison."

Of course I remembered the name. The young ex-prosecutor, the lawyer who was called on the carpet for conduct unbecoming an officer of the court.

"Dennison, I believe I told you when I last saw you," the pathologist said, "is the man caught in a compromising situation in the vicinity of Philosophers' Walk."

"*He's* the next of kin of the dead woman whose body we saw?" I asked in confusion.

Slater shook his head. "No," he said, "which brings us to a second unusual occurrence that night. The body, I now know, did not disappear. It was taken away by the deceased's true next of kin, the parents. The odd thing is these people arrived at the morgue *with* the body."

"They were there, weren't they?" I asked. "Waiting in that little room, waiting while Gleason and I went into the examining room." I had to close my eyes for a moment to fight off the image of a mother, probably not unlike my mother, seeing her child as we had seen that corpse.

"While you and Adams were detained at the front door, we were doing what we could to maintain the dignity of all concerned: the hysterical mother, the grieving father, the deceased. But not," he added softly, "Neil Dennison. Apparently he disappeared into the rain of the night and was not seen again until . . ."

"Until what?" I asked in alarm. I remembered that the last time I'd seen Dr. Slater, that afternoon he'd come to Whitney Square, he'd not only mentioned Dennison, he'd mentioned murder. Was that what he was talking about now?

"Mr. Portal," Dr. Slater said with seeming difficulty, "I've come to ask you to go to Gleason Adams and help him deal with everything he knows about this sad case. I'm deeply sorry to be so mysterious, but I've compromised my situation considerably already and I don't want to do it anymore." He dug in the pocket of his rumpled trousers and pulled out a small slip of paper. He pressed it into my palm with the furtive urgency of a man passing a counterfeit bill. By the time I unfolded it and read it, Dr. Slater himself had disappeared into the night.

IT WAS NOTHING more than an address in a part of town I didn't know. It was nearing 10 p.m. I was exhausted from having written the exam and I faced hours of study before I'd be ready for another exam in the morning. The last thing I needed was another confrontation with Gleason, one in which he confessed that his carelessness had resulted in an action capable of ruining his life.

I went to the address anyway. The neighborhood, a little north of the central core, was not a bad one, not at all. It was the sort of neighborhood the destroyers of not-real Bleecker Street probably had in mind, a series of white, high-rise apartment towers set amid open green spaces vibrant with the increasing lushness of spring, not now visible to the eye, but fragrant in the night's light wind. Outside the tower that matched the address Dr. Slater had given me, a fountain gurgled and splashed. Well-dressed couples lounged beside late-model cars parked in the drive that circled in front of the building's impressive entrance, all glass and curved concrete.

Just inside the doors stood a console of black marble and atop it was a chart listing all the tenants' names and their apartment numbers. Gleason's name was not there, but Neil Dennison's was. At the sight of the name, I almost lost my nerve. No matter how disillusioned I might be about Gleason and his secret life, I still wanted nothing to mar my name, nothing to taint my chance to become more than the lawyerly drudge I was well on the way to being. Despite my current complications, my ambitions were pristine. I dreamed of the day I, too, could invite influential people to Osgoode Hall for lunch.

So I hesitated before I pressed the button beside Neil Dennison's name, as if the button itself could somehow contaminate me.

Which did not matter at all. Because when I did press the button, no one answered.

No one answered the next morning, either, when, at the end of a sleepless night, I'd borrowed the truck before my father went to work and driven to Dennison's building.

After I'd written the day's exam, my thoughts returned to Dr. Slater. I'd seen him at work, so I felt sure he was legitimate. Nonetheless, as I reconstructed what he told me and matched it against what I remembered about our trip to the morgue, I decided certain events there did not lend themselves to logic. Once more, my insane curiosity bumped against my cautious nature. I *had* to find out how a body could be reclaimed by relatives in the middle of an autopsy. And if Slater—and presumably Rosen, too—had known the next of kin were in the building, how could they allow that autopsy to begin in the first place?

I remembered, too, that when I'd visited the morgue alone that subsequent afternoon, I had not found any coroner's report on the body we'd seen.

I decided to visit the morgue again, but I phoned first and asked if Dr. Rosen was in. I had no intention of speaking with him. I still felt ill when I remembered how he had yelled at me. No, I phoned to see if he was out and the coast was clear. He was. It was.

The receptionist at the morgue, the same pretty girl who'd helped me before, recalled me, and she proved to be even friendlier than the first time. She seemed exceptionally chirpy and cheerful and, suspecting she might be happy to see me, a young man with a future, again, I decided to ask her out before I left her that day.

"I need more information about standard procedure here," I said when we'd completed smiling preliminaries.

"Sure," she said. "What do you want to know?"

I leaned on the counter, gazing down on her where she sat at her very tidy desk at the front of which, with its felt back toward me, stood a picture frame.

"If next of kin arrive here to pick up a body and the autopsy doesn't get completed, would there be a report filed the same as when the autopsy is complete?" I asked.

"Normally," she answered, "no body is ever released before an autopsy is complete." She seemed lost in thought for a moment. "Unless . . ."

She rose, approached the counter and nodded for me to step aside so that she could open the counter section that allowed her to exit. She crossed to the filing cabinet I'd checked the last time I was there. I watched as she went to the same drawer, pulled it open and flipped through files until she came to the document she was seeking.

"Sometimes," she said, "we're advised that a body has been re-venued after an autopsy has begun. Under those circumstances, we file a 'to-come' instead of a report, meaning the autopsy results will be forwarded from the new jurisdiction." She held up a typed white index card as though it were some sort of trophy. "This might be the case you were here about before," she said, handing me the card. "That body *was* re-venued, released on the sworn assurance of the next of kin that an autopsy would be performed as soon as the body reached its destination."

"You mean whoever picked up this body intended to take it out of Toronto?" I asked, studying the card. I recognized the address of the person who had brought in the body as that of Neil Dennison, the disgraced prosecutor, but I was not prepared for the address of the people who had taken the body away. Once again I found myself staring at Gleason's address on Whitney Square. Once more I was filled with the painful ambiguity of my feelings. Pity for the man who was my sometime friend warred with rage for someone who had manipulated me, with rage in the ascendant. Had he been involved in this corpse-moving from the start, even before that night in the morgue? Had he known on that night who the murdered woman was? And that his parents were involved? Clearly he knew now.

The girl took the card from my hand. As she did so, I noticed that on her left hand, a brand-new engagement ring sparkled. So much for her eagerness to go out with a young man with a future. This was not turning out to be my good-luck week.

She studied the card. "It's a code L-7," she said cryptically. Then, seeing my puzzlement, she explained, "They didn't just sign an affidavit to take the body out of the jurisdiction. They signed an affidavit to take it right out of the country."

I thanked the girl, disappointed that I would never get to know her better, but staggered that I'd been struck such a blow. The pieces of the puzzle of the body in the morgue were falling into place. I didn't need to see Spardini the undertaker again, fortunately, to be able to picture that "mistaken" entry on the Board of Health manifest. Gleason's parents had not returned to Canada with a body. They had *left* Canada with a body. Why? Because they were in a perfect position to cover for their son, Gleason Adams, a murderer. Not only were they powerful people who could influence the chief coroner to release the body of the victim, they also had the perfect cover: the excuse of having to bury the supposedly just-discovered body of the son who had died years before. Gleason had killed and his parents had saved him by covering it up. Perhaps his so-called friends had helped, too.

I needed time to think. I walked up Church Street past the shops of the pawnbrokers. Of course Gleason would steal those two rings on the body. Hadn't he already stolen his father's wedding ring to make the rings for himself and Neil Dennison? What had the two of them done to that poor, pathetic woman? And why? Was she blackmailing the two lovers?

The more I thought about it, the more I knew I really, totally despised Gleason Adams. Everything between us had been bogus from the start: he had used me in the "project" for Kavin, involved me in the theft of the rings as part of that project, dragged me to homosexual haunts like the Continental and Letros. What fun he must have had with his buddies inside Letros as he joked about the naive fool he'd left standing outside, the fellow who was lending him credibility.

I also felt profound contempt for his rich parents. Even if he had the resources, my father would never have aided and abetted a homicide in an effort to save my sorry hide.

I worked my theory over and over in my mind just the way I would someday work on my jury presentations as a criminal defense lawyer. I tried to construct a scenario that fit all the facts. I thought about the shabby clothing of the deceased, the absence of any jewelry except for the concealed rings. Obviously the woman had obtained the rings under questionable circumstances, then refused to return them to Gleason. Blackmail or not, the result from Gleason's point of view was the same. Having those rings fall into the wrong hands meant ruination.

Gleason could have read the same books I'd read. He could easily know as much about homicide that looked like suicide as I did. And he would have delighted in the double puzzle. A homicide that looks like a suicide that looks like a homicide. He could easily have strangled the woman with the cord, catching her unawares from behind. Then he could have rigged up the suicide ruse.

I walked more rapidly, hardly realizing that I was storming toward Yonge Street, toward the subway that could take me to Neil Dennison's apartment one last time.

246

Then, I thought, *Dennison discovers what Gleason has done. He's got nothing to lose since his career is already over, but he wants to protect his lover. Between them, they come up with a plan. First Gleason goes to Whitney Square and talks to his father. Then he comes to me and tells me we have an appointment at the morgue. Dennison brings in the body. It's brilliant. What killer would deliberately show up at the morgue just as the body of his victim is being brought in? In the meantime, old man Adams does whatever it takes. He pulls strings and gets the body out of there before anyone can examine it properly and ask the right questions. Slater,* I thought, *Slater, who is the only honest man in the whole scenario, wants to put right anything that, in his limited capacity, he can. He comes to me.*

I was truly boiling over now. Enraged for the sake of the unknown deceased. Enraged at having been duped. Enraged at the position Dr. Slater had been put in. But when I realized the thing that enraged me most, I was shocked enough to stop momentarily in my headlong rush to the subway. I was enraged that Justice, that mysterious mistress to whom I was about to pledge myself, had been prostituted by evil men. It was in her cause that I flew down the subway stairs and grabbed the northbound train to Neil Dennison's apartment.

If you love me, the blindfolded goddess whispered, *leave me by dying.*

Chapter 16

I found them as I had feared: in each other's arms.

I didn't bother trying to ring the apartment. I followed one of the tenants in the front door and found the apartment shown on Slater's note. I knocked but nobody answered. I tried the door. It wasn't locked.

The man who had to be Neil Dennison was naked. Limp, sick, emaciated, as though he hadn't eaten properly in months, he still projected the aura of a male model. Gleason, incongruously dressed in a white shirt open at the neck and the wrinkled trousers of one of his fine suits, sat on a couch with his arms around Neil and the man's head on his shoulder. This was one of those charged moments in which one notices every detail, and the detail I noticed first was that the cording on the well-made couch was exactly the same as the cord around the dead woman's neck.

When Gleason's eyes fell on me, his face filled with such relief that I simultaneously felt both my own power and a fearful sense of the responsibility that had suddenly been thrust upon me. I did not know it then, but I would come to experience that expression on the faces of clients a thousand times as the years went by, at first on the faces of the ordinary people of my parents' community when I began my practice, then, as I became defense counsel, on increasingly high-profile defendants. Most often, I would come to see that expression of hopeful gratitude on the face of a man sitting in custody. I feared, of course, that Gleason would soon be in jail. For now, he was smiling, a weak and thankful grin. I hesitated. What is more frightening than to be called upon to be a savior? What calling is more impossible to resist?

"Ellis," he said, "thank God. Thank God you're here."

Gingerly, I moved toward the couch. "What's wrong with him?" I asked, nodding at Neil.

With a tenderness I could never have imagined him possessing, Gleason slid Neil's body away from his own, stretched the thin legs out on the couch and, reaching down, picked up a blanket from the floor and carefully covered his friend.

I just stood there. I hardly knew where to begin. "Why did you send for me, Gleason? What can you possibly expect me to do to help you?"

"For now," he said, "I think I just need you to call an ambulance."

"Tell me what's wrong with him. They won't send an ambulance unless they know."

Gleason glanced at the man, who lay motionless on the couch, eyes closed. "He's sick because he stopped eating weeks ago. He took pills, too. I had to leave, just to get some juice, which is all he'll drink, and somehow he got to the pills. I thought they were all gone, but he must have had some hidden. I don't . . ." He stopped, as if he'd forgotten the question he'd set out to answer. I had to get him to focus, because I didn't need to call only the ambulance, I needed to call the police.

"Gleason," I said, putting my hand on his shoulder, "you have to listen to me. I know what you did and I can help you."

His desperate eyes searched my face. "What?" he said, seeming genuinely puzzled, "What do I have to listen to? What are you talking about?"

I gave his shoulder a gentle push and he sank into a nearby chair. I crouched down, the way you do when you speak to a child. "I know everything, Gleason. I know about the body at the morgue." He flinched but I continued. "Neil here brought in the body. I know your parents came and took that body away—out of the country."

Gleason nodded. He glanced over at Neil, who seemed to be peacefully asleep.

"Gleason," I said, drawing his attention back to me, "I have to turn you in."

"Turn me in?" he gasped. "You're going to tell Kavin about me? He'll have me removed from the program. They'll throw me out if they know. That's exactly what Attorney General Garrey's office did to Neil. Exactly."

He was clearly about to lose it. How else to explain that his first thought of the consequence of his murderous actions was being thrown out of law school? How could he imagine that a man who had perpetrated culpable homicide would ever be allowed to practice law?

Again, I learned in an instant something that no law school could ever teach. I learned that a lawyer absorbs the panic of his client, retains it, keeps devastating emotion from overflowing and damaging the necessary interchanges. Calmly I said to Gleason, "If Neil is your lover, what happened to him may affect your defense, but for now—"

"He isn't my lover!" Gleason declared vehemently, his face incredulous. "I thought you said you knew . . ."

"I know what you did and can speculate as to why you did it. We can work something out on a defense here, Gleason. We can—"

"He isn't my lover, you stupid fool!" He sprang up, sending me stumbling backward. It took me a minute to right myself and by the time I did, Gleason had already reached the telephone. Once more, I felt fury at this man who kept knocking me back on my heels, literally and figuratively. I grabbed the receiver, tore it out of his hand. Anything he said now, anything that was noted, even the observations of a complete stranger, of a telephone operator, for instance, could be used as evidence against him.

"Gleason, wait," I pleaded. "Before you talk to anybody, you have to agree not to admit that you killed that woman. Be rational. But you can tell me everything. I can help." Would he ever, in this world or the next, do the same for me?

He stood still, took a few deep breaths, for once seemed to be exposed, without his false cover of arrogance and superiority. Then, without looking at me, he said, "I didn't kill anybody. And the dead person wasn't a woman. It was my brother, Gerard." His voice faltered. "Gerard of Gleason and Gerard."

THE AMBULANCE CAME. If the attendants were shocked by anything they saw in the apartment, they didn't show it. Swiftly and efficiently, they bundled Neil into a blanket, strapped him to a stretcher and carted him away.

Gleason's Jaguar was in the parking garage in the underground. I took the keys and drove us down Yonge Street to St. Mike's hospital. At first, Gleason was quiet, but then he began to talk.

"Neil was Gerard's lover, not mine," Gleason said. "It was Gerard who was with Neil when he was caught on Philosophers' Walk. When Gerard found out that Neil was going to lose his job as assistant prosecutor as a result of the arrest, Gerard took both their rings and told Neil he'd found somebody else."

Gleason stopped talking and stared out the window as I drove. Out of the corner of my eye, I could see young women prancing down the sidewalk. I had to fight myself to keep watching the road instead of them. Skirts seemed to be getting shorter by the hour.

"It was a lie," Gleason resumed. "Poor Gerard, he never understood how things work. He really thought that if he broke up with Neil, Neil would get his job back. When that didn't happen, he . . ." Gleason's voice broke and he was silent again.

"He what?"

"He went to my father. It was the first time my father had seen Gerard since he'd disowned him four years earlier. My father told Gerard what he'd told him at that time. That he had only one son now. Me."

I glanced over at Gleason. His mouth was set in a grim line. I thought of all the times I'd wanted to wipe the smile off his face. "But Gerard came back," Gleason said, choking on the words.

"Dressed as a woman?" I was beginning to understand.

"Yes. He thought that if my father refused to listen to reason, he might respond to blackmail. So he came back to Whitney Square. Gerard didn't know that Neil was worried about him, was watching him. Neil followed Gerard to the house, and found Gerard and my father fighting. They were actually trading blows." Gleason let out an ironic little laugh. "I'm not sure how Gerard learned to fight in high heels. Perhaps he'd done it before."

"For God's sake, Gleason!"

"Neil and my mother, who was also there, tried to break up the fracas. They almost succeeded. But my father, in his fury at a son in high heels, took one last swing at Gerard, who ducked, tripped and fell, knocking against a table. That stupid vase you saw at the house fell and hit Gerard on the back of the head. It was enough to kill him."

I hoped I would make a better lawyer than a detective. "Gleason," I said, "how long did you know about Gerard? Did you know on the night we went to the morgue? Did you deceive me?"

"Ellis," he answered, "Gerard disappeared four years ago. I really believed my father when he gave me the tragic news about the skiing accident. There might even have actually been such an accident. Gerard did ski. He did like to ski in Switzerland. But he was a quiet, private person. We lived in a big house. I had my own problems. I just wasn't close to him."

"But you had to suspect something."

I could feel that old con again, feel Gleason's eyes on my face, preparing to give me some slippery quasi-facts. I didn't turn toward him. I could read him like a book. How safe is it to go further, he was thinking.

"In this life," he said with more than an echo of that old sanctimony, "you have to learn what to expect from other people and to protect yourself against them. Being charming, being flippant and careless—it's like a mask. People are always off-guard when you tease them, when you daz-zle them. They fail to notice things they might otherwise clearly see. But Gerard was shy. He didn't know how to hide what he was except by keeping to himself. I didn't even know, would never have guessed, what was going on with him until he told me one day when he was seventeen and I was twelve. My initiation into the love that dares not speak its name."

He paused as if to gather strength to go on. "But my fa-ther wouldn't abide the idea that he had a homosexual son. He was cruel to Gerard, putting him down, threaten-ing to have him institutionalized, calling him 'sissy.'" Glea-son paused and I liked to believe he was remembering how many times he had used the same epithet to me. "So Gerard left. I know now he went underground. I don't know what he did for money. I don't want to know. His name was never mentioned in our house again. I believed it when my parents said he was dead. I didn't see him for years—until the night we went to the morgue."

Ahead of us, the traffic stalled. It was Friday afternoon. The weekend rush hour was in full swing. I knew Gleason must be anxious to get to the hospital, but there was noth-ing I could do to speed up our trip. I knew, too, that the time had come for some answers.

"I've spent all these weeks trying to discover as much as I could about my brother," Gleason said. "Our family isn't like yours. We don't live on top of one another. For years I thought my brother was dead. Then, in that dreadful moment at the morgue when I recognized the broken Timex that Gerard always called his good luck charm, I re-alized he had died only that day, perhaps had even been murdered. Later, my parents told me they had been at the morgue making arrangements to go to Switzerland to pick up my brother's body. Lies, of course, but I had to know the truth, stay out of my father's way and satisfy Kavin, too. That's where you came in."

He smiled, half teasing, half sad. Then he went on. "Remember, you asked me what day I had made the appointment at the morgue. There was no appointment. I had gotten a call from a Dr. John Slater, who said he knew me from the clubs."

"Which means?"

"Oh God, don't be obtuse. He meant that he and I and my brother shared a bond. Anyway, in that phone call he said someone I knew was in trouble and he thought I should come in that evening. I thought that a bit strange, but when I called the morgue back, it turned out he was legit. It was at that point that I decided to ask you to come with me."

And I had been reluctant to help him with his project.

"It's taken me a long time to fit the pieces of the puzzle together. I had no idea about Neil Dennison. The rings were the only clues I had to a probable murder and lies all around. I took the package by instinct, but I'm glad I did. I think Slater wanted me to take them, and wanted to help us out on the case, but couldn't compromise himself professionally. He remembered what had happened to Neil. And before he could be really forthcoming, he was hauled away by Rosen at my father's behest. I can't tell you how hard we've worked to find Neil. He just disappeared after the death."

Gleason's erratic behavior suddenly began to make a lot of sense, but there were still some holes in his story. "If Neil got caught that night on Philosophers' Walk and subsequently lost his job, why didn't Gerard get called in, too?"

"Luck and fast reflexes, maybe. He had no job to lose, anyway."

He laughed and poked me in the ribs. "You're not afraid of fags, now, are you? That night in the Nile Room at Letros was the turning point. Every man there treated me as if I were the one who had caused Gerard's tragedy. Still, I learned enough to find Neil. I had to give him back his ring. The other one I'm keeping to shove down my father's throat."

It was a while before he spoke again. When he did, he was calmer and so was I.

He turned again to me, his eyes red. "Let me explain a few things to you, Ellis. Neil has become my friend because of his relationship with my brother, and after he recovers and has some counseling, I'm sure he can apply to be readmitted to the bar. Of course, he helped my father make Gerard's death look like suicide, but he also called Rosen and told the coroner everything. And Rosen was able to arrange a private autopsy with a ruling of accidental death. The coroner said the faked suicide was irrelevant, the act of a grieving and frightened family. So he authorized my parents to take Gerard's body out of the country and to bury him in a place where none of their Whitney Square friends will ever go."

"Why is Neil so devastated?"

"Neil loved Gerard and felt he had betrayed him." Gleason paused. "Honestly," he said, "this whole sad thing could have been avoided if those two had just talked. Instead Gerard is dead and Neil has nearly killed himself with guilt and mourning."

"What about you, Gleason?"

"I mourned the loss of Gerard a long time ago. But that's not what you mean, is it, Portal?"

"No."

"Look, all I've done is skip a few weeks of school in order to find Neil and get him some help. All I've done is mess up Kavin's stupid project assignment and miss a couple of useless exams. I figure you're going to get me out of trouble there."

"Me?"

"Sure." His voice was picking up, as if the horror was already behind him. "You probably aced those exams. You always ace exams. Besides that, you're Kavin's little darling, his favorite."

"Now what are you going to spring on me?"

"Portal, you've been my only friend in all this. Help me one last time. Go to Kavin for me. Explain all this in a way old Smokey can understand. Break it down for him. That's all you need to do. Then you can forget everything else."

We were both silent for a few moments. But forgetting was the last thing I was going to do. "Gleason," I said, "this whole affair happened because of a few lines in the Criminal Code. Do you realize that?" I thought about my brother, my beloved Michele with his Martin Luther King, Jr., and his Billy Johnson, his Negroes and his draft dodgers, his bed on the pavement of the street that runs in front of the American Consulate. "We can fight this."

"What? Fight what?"

"We can fight Sections 147–150, sub b, inclusive. We can take the position that what happened to Neil is contrary to his rights as an individual, as a citizen. If we start right now, we can take the case all the way to the Supreme Court if we have to. By then, we'll be admitted to the bar. Neil himself will be our client. No person should be discriminated against by the law because of personal choices he makes in his private life."

Gleason reached out and put his hand on my shoulder. It was the only time in our years of friendship that I ever remember him touching me. "Portal," he said softly, "forget about this. It's not your fight."

"Injustice against anybody is my fight," I responded passionately.

"No. You need the kind of clients that will get you where you belong. You're not Kavin's favorite and Tuppin's new little friend for nothing. You shouldn't be wasting your time with the Neil Dennisons and the Billy Johnsons of this world, Portal. You've got what it takes. You're headed for the top. You can look back down on me when you get there!"

I HANDED THE BAG with the cheese bun in it to Aunt Fay. She took it between her thumb and index finger as though it were a bomb and set it down on a reproduction Chippendale table.

"Sammy's real busy today, Angelo," she said. "He can't see you. He told me just to give you this. He said don't open it until you get home."

She handed me a long white envelope, sealed tight. I had no choice but to take it, thank her and leave.

When I got home, everybody was in the kitchen. All the groceries from the morning shopping were put away, but Arletta and my mother were still busy with food, chopping tomatoes and eggplant for *caponata*. My father sat in the corner reading the paper. Michele had his nose buried in a book, a cup of steaming coffee in front of him.

"What's that?" Arletta said, eyeing the envelope the second I walked in the door.

"It's a letter from Uncle Salvatore," I said.

"Open it," everybody but my father commanded.

It was Arletta who was the first to see what the envelope contained. She grabbed the contents and waved them over her head, whooping and hollering until my father told her to shut up.

"He did it!" She yelled anyway. "Uncle Sammy did it!"

She danced over to me and planted a kiss on my astonished face. "You're the best brother on the whole planet," she said. "Look at this! Four tickets to the Beatles concert. In the very front row!"

WITHIN A WEEK, Uncle Salvatore did see me. He told me his friend Sheldrake Tuppin needed a helper and I was it.

Within a month, Gleason Adams was declared exempt from his exams *ex post facto*. Given the excellence of his presentation on proposed civil liberty changes to the Criminal Code, the Law Faculty decided that his unexplained absence would not be held against him or noted on his academic record, since the absence was due to research. Snow job completed.

Within four years, Neil Dennison was fully reinstated in the prosecutor's office and the Criminal Code of Canada was amended to allow private acts between consenting adults.

Within five years Billy Johnson returned from Vietnam with a Purple Heart. Eventually he married Kee Kee. They had a daughter and lived happily for a short time before he died at the age of thirty-six, but that's a different story.

Within ten years, the House of Detention was razed to the ground, and later a community garden rose on the spot. The garden blooms there today.

Within thirty years Ronald Reagan asked Lee Iacocca to restore Ellis Island. He did. It became a national monument to the people who passed through it and to the fulfillment of their immigrant hopes.

I STILL HAVE, it seems, hopes of my own. When I tired of watching my son and his wife from my window, I sat down at the computer and drafted my response to the Fellowship of Barristers and Solicitors. Will I return to being a member of the bar? Of course I will.